Scarlet Roses
Book Two of the NOLA Shifter Series

Angel Nyx

Angel Nyx Publishing, LLC

This is a work of fiction. Names, characters, organizations, places, events, and incidences are either products of the author's imagination or used fictitiously.

Copyright 2017 by Angel Nyx. All rights reserved.

No part of this book may be reproduced, or stored in a retrieval system, or transmitted in any form or by any means, electronic, mechanical, photocopying, recording, or otherwise, without the express written permission of the publisher.

Published by Angel Nyx Publishing

Cover design by Najla Qamber Designs

For Maria...
Who would have thought downloading a free book would lead to such a wonderful friendship? Thank you for all your words of encouragement, your guidance, your advice, and most importantly, your friendship. You have been a huge support on this crazy journey and I am so grateful, and lucky, to know you. You rock, girl!

Foreword

The NOLA Shifters Series is set in the Louisiana Bayou. Many of the characters you will meet are Cajun. Their speech patterns reflect this. Too often, authors are leery of using a dialect that is specific to an area or to a group of people. I feel it would be an insult to anyone who is Cajun for me to make my characters Cajun while having them speak perfect English. I hope you enjoy this little glimpse into their world!

Author's Note

While each book is a stand alone, books one and two run congruent with each other. As a result, there are scenes that only loosely take place in the first book that are more in depth in this, the second book. The remainder of the series is not so closely intertwined.

Prologue

At the tender age of ten, Emelise learned a very hard, very painful life lesson. Never depend on a man to provide for you. Her mother had met Sean Scotsdale when Eme was four and they'd quickly moved in together. He became the father she wanted but didn't have. Emelise, as young as she was, believed he would be there forever. The day he packed his things and left was the worst day of her young life.

"I know it hurts, sweetie; it hurts me too, but we'll be okay. We're strong; we can get through this. We don't need a man to take care of us," Adelaide said as she rocked her daughter. Sean would be the second, and last, man she allowed into her life. From that day on she devoted herself solely to raising her daughter to be a strong, independent woman.

Fifteen years later that strength would be the only thing that would get Emelise through the worst event of her life.

Emelise looked at the clock and sighed. Her mother was still out. You'd think it would be the other way around—she would be the one out and her mother would be watching the time—but Adelaide had needed a night out with her friends and went out while her daughter was at work. It was late now though. The jazz club Emelise worked at had closed at one; it was almost three in the morning, and Eme had expected her mother to be home before now. The sound of a car pulling up outside reached her and she frowned. She knew what her mother's car sounded like and it wasn't the one that pulled up outside their home. Before she made it out of her bedroom, there was a knock at the front door and her frown deepened. When she opened the door and found a police officer standing on the other side, she grew concerned. "Can I help you, Officer?"

"Sorry to disturb you at such a late hour, Miss. Do you know an Adelaide Rousseau?"

"Yes, she's my mother. Oh gods, don't tell me she got herself arrested or something." The instant she said it she knew that couldn't be why the officer was there because if her mother was arrested she'd be getting a call to bail her out.

"I'm sorry, Miss Rousseau, but there has been an accident. Your mother is being transported to St. Joseph's Hospital and Medical Center's trauma center."

Emelise felt her entire world stop with those words. "Oh gods," she whispered. "What...what happened?"

"Another car crossed the median and hit her head-on. Do you have someone you can call to drive you to the hospital?"

She shook her head. "No. It's just me and my mother." She was shaking but she forced herself to stand tall, or as tall as her 5'4" would allow. "Thank you, Officer, for telling me. I need to go; I need to get to her."

"I'm very sorry to have to deliver such bad news. I'll give you a police escort to the hospital."

She nodded and went to grab her purse. She locked the door behind her and drove her car on autopilot because she didn't even remember the drive itself. She was glad the officer hadn't realized just how shaken up she was. She rushed into the ER and approached the desk. "My mother was brought in by ambulance, Adelaide Rousseau," she said and tried to not snap at the receptionist to hurry up while she looked her up on the computer.

"Miss, your mother is in surgery; someone will come get you when they can."

Emelise was staring at the doors leading into the back of the ER when she was finally approached. "Miss Rousseau?" She knew. When she looked up and saw the doctor's eyes, she knew what he was going to say. "She's gone, isn't she?" Tears fell as the doctor explained they'd done all they could but there was too much damage and they'd lost her on the operating table. Emelise barely heard him. There was paperwork she had to sign, and then a bag was handed to her. Inside it was her mother's purse, her phone, and what jewelry she'd been wearing at the time of the accident.

During the three weeks it took for Emelise to get all of her mother's affairs in order, go through things, and get rid of what she didn't need, pack what she wanted to keep, and get the house listed for sale, Emelise had made a decision. She'd wanted to open her own night club and her original plan was to do so right there in Phoenix. Now that she had other options, she knew where she wanted to be. It made little sense, this driving need to go to New Orleans when her mother was so sure she wouldn't be welcome there, but she couldn't ignore the way she felt. She had to go to New Orleans.

She'd scanned properties that were for sale, made some calls, got some photos of several potential spots that were in fairly high volume areas of the city, and made arrangements to meet with the realtor to look at the one that caught her eye the most. She knew from what the realtor said about it that the place was a bar, until the owner died several years ago and it had been sitting empty and untouched since then. It already had the bare bones of what she would need even if it did need a good cleaning and possibly a complete overhaul of the interior. It was the one. She was sure of it.

Emelise took one last look around the house she'd grown up in before she stepped out and closed the door behind her. She handed the keys over to the realtor, who would handle the sale for her, and took a deep breath of morning air. It wasn't too hot yet. By early afternoon the sun would be scorching the sidewalks, but she would be well on her way to New Orleans by then. Of course, she'd be driving right into more heat, this time coupled with humidity. She wasn't sure how much different that was going to be from the dry heat of the desert, but she'd adjust even if it took a while to get used to it.

She felt a little trepidation as she made her way to her car, but she chalked it up to being nervous about starting a new chapter in her life in a new city. She knew anything could happen, but at least she was going to a city where she knew at least one person. Her best friend, Lily, lived in New Orleans so she wasn't going to be completely alone.

It was strange, really. One would think that having grown up there in Phoenix, she would have a large group of friends, people she would really miss when she left, but she'd never been that close to any of the girls she'd gone to school with. Having to keep the fact she was a leopard shifter from them had made getting close to any of them a bit difficult. How could you be close and share secrets if you had to keep the biggest secret of all? There was only one person she was really going to miss, a fellow shifter and coworker at the club she'd worked at, but they would keep in touch.

She slid her sunglasses on as she slipped into her car, turned the radio up, and she was on her way. She was both excited and nervous about what the future might hold for her, but she sure as fuck was going to meet it head on. She was no shrinking violet, she wasn't a wallflower, she wasn't going to let a little uncertainty stand in her way or change her mind. She would chase her dreams and, by Goddess, she would succeed because failure wasn't an option.

Emelise drove out of Phoenix with a light heart. Yes, she missed her mother—she would always miss her—but letting her grief bog her down wouldn't do her any good. She would live her life and keep her mother's memory alive. She knew her mother wouldn't want her to wallow in misery day after day just because she was no longer here. "Look out, New Orleans, here I come," she said as she left the town of her birth behind her.

It was a little over twenty-one hours to New Orleans from Phoenix, but because she did a little sightseeing along the way, it took Emelise twice as long to get there. Her first view of the city was as the sun was setting. The red, gold, and orange sunset, reflected off the waters of Lake Pontchartrain, as she neared New Orleans, was breathtaking, and even at a distance the city seemed to be filled with life. She'd been exhausted from the drive, but now that she was there, titillation thrilled through her, and once she checked into the hotel she'd booked ahead of her arrival, she found herself wandering the streets.

While she wandered, she thought about all she had to do, starting the following day. She needed to meet with the realtor to look at the old bar and sign the paperwork, because, really, she'd already made her decision without seeing it physically, to start looking for an apartment, catch up with her best friend, oh, and then there was the whole 'being in the Black Water Pard's territory uninvited'. On the bright side, she was a leopard, and her mother had been a part of the pard before she'd taken off, so getting the Alpha to let her stay probably wouldn't be too difficult. On the downside, she had no idea who the Alpha was or how to contact him, but she was hoping Lily did. She was a wolf in their territory; she had to have met the Alpha at least once, right?

Chapter One
Emelise

"It's perfect." Emelise turned to the realtor. "I know, it's going to need a lot of work—I can see that already—but it's still perfect. It has the bare bones essentials for a club; it's even got a raised platform for the stage. I might be petite, but I'm not one of those dainty little things who is afraid to get her hands dirty," she added at the look the man gave her.

"Are you sure about this, Miss Rousseau? I have a couple more properties that are in better condition."

"Were they bars?" She waited for his response, which came in the form of a shaking of his head and a quick 'No ma'am'.

"No? Then yes, I'm sure. It would cost more to completely change everything than it will to upgrade this one and get it cleaned up."

"Well then, if you're sure, as you requested, I brought the paperwork with me. We can get it signed and the building is all yours."

Eme felt like she was signing her life away, but once everything was signed and the keys were in her hand, she couldn't help but squeal with delight. It was hers! She was one step closer to her ultimate dream. Okay, her second ultimate dream. Like every other shifter, she also dreamed of one day meeting 'The One', the one person who was her other half, the one shifter who would complete her. Not that she *needed* a man to be happy or complete—hell no—but it might be nice to fall asleep in a man's arms and know he'd be there *if* she needed him. "Bah, get over yourself, girl; you've got more important things to worry about than finding a man. Like meeting the local Alpha and rubbing it in your grandparents' faces that your mother did just fine without their help, and you're proof of that." She walked through the building and took mental stock of all she would have to do.

The entire second floor was set up in a way that, if she'd wanted to, she could turn the space into rooms and rent them out, but she was considering turning it into her own massive apartment. She'd think on that and make a decision later. For now she had calls to make. She had to get an electrician in to check the wiring and tell her what it would cost to get it up to code; she had the building inspector coming in half an hour to tell her the same thing—sure, the realtor had inspected the place prior to listing it but Eme wanted to cover all her bases. Then she had to compile a list of brewery delivery companies in the area and find a master woodworker to restore the woodwork to its original glory. So much to do, so little time to do it.

While she waited for the building inspector to arrive, she sat down with her laptop and began a search of the best places to get local brews as well as liquor. She was awaiting her liquor license; she'd applied for it prior to talking with the realtor face to face, and she hoped to have it in hand by the time she needed to start stocking the shelves. One of the benefits to having worked in a jazz club back in Phoenix was that she'd managed to network some contacts and already had a few musicians lined up to possibly be part of the entertainment for the club. She wanted to give local talent a chance as well because, let's face it, New Orleans was filled with musicians of every kind, but especially jazz. She would no doubt have a list of potentials by the time she opened the doors.

When the building inspector arrived, she followed him as he moved through the building, checking everything from the floor to the ceiling. As he made notes, she began to get nervous and chewed worriedly on her bottom lip.

"Well, Miss Rousseau, you seem to have lucked out. You'll have to get an electrician in here to rewire some of the outlets and replace the fuse box to update it to code, but overall, your inspection passed. I will have to come back before you open to check everything one final time, but as it stands, once you get the work done, you'll be good to go."

Emelise flashed him a grin. "Thank you so much. You're awesome," she said as she walked him to the door.

"Just doing my job, ma'am. Welcome to New Orleans and good luck with your venture," he said before he left.

Once he was gone, Emelise spun around with her arms spread wide. She had such visions for the club. The walls were bare brick, and she contemplated covering them with drywall and paint, but if she was honest with herself, she loved the rustic look of the brick. It needed a good cleaning and possibly some sections of mortar filled in, but the walls were still in really good shape, as far as she could tell. She added a mason to her list of people she needed to consult before she locked up and headed out. She really wanted to go sightseeing but that was going to have to wait. "Apartment hunting first; you can have fun later," she told herself.

By the time Emelise finally returned to the hotel to crash, her feet were killing her but her spirits were high. She'd looked at more apartments in one day than she'd ever expected to and she'd caught up with her best friend. Okay, so she was apprehensive about meeting with the Alpha of the Black Water Pard. She would have put it off for a few days, or weeks, or months, if she could have, but Lily wasn't giving her that chance. It would have been nice to meet with the leopard from a more stable position. Living out of a hotel room wasn't exactly ideal.

"Nothing you can do about that; you'll just have to stand up to him if he tries to order you around," she murmured before she turned the light off and let sleep claim her.

Emelise was awake before sunrise, and when she realized she wasn't going to fall back to sleep, she got up, showered, and left the hotel to get something to eat. She just grabbed a breakfast sandwich from a deli she passed by and headed over to what would become her club. She'd spent a little time the night before compiling a list of tradesmen to call while she started the tedious process of cleaning the interior of the old bar. With one hand, she used a broom to grab at cobwebs while she dialed a number on her cell with the other.

"Pinnacle Electric, this is Mandy; can I help you?"

The voice on the other end sounded about twelve years old but Emelise shrugged. "I certainly hope so. My name is Emelise Rousseau. I've just purchased a piece of property on Decatur, and the building inspector said that I needed to get an electrician in here to rewire some things."

"We can certainly help with that. Let me check the schedule to see who is available," the young woman said. She was silent for several minutes. "No one is available today but we can send someone out tomorrow at eight."

"That's perfect," Emelise assured her. She gave the girl the address and the number where she could be reached and hung up. "One down, . Let's hope I have the same success with a mason." She still hadn't decided on a master woodworker for the bar restoration yet, but she could focus on that once she made sure the place wasn't going to burn up or fall down around her.

"Good mornin' and thanks for calling Oak Moss Masonry. What can I do for you?"

"Good morning to you, too. Well, hopefully you can make sure this place I just bought isn't going to fall down around me," Emelise said to the man who'd answered the phone. "My name is Emelise Rousseau. I just bought an old bar on Decatur; I'd like to keep the original brickwork but I want to make sure it's in good condition."

"You bought the old Happy Fish Tavern? I was wonderin' who that was. I noticed it wasn't for sale anymore. I knew old Zeke; he was a good man and one hell of a bartender. Sure, I can come check it out tomorrow afternoon; I've got a small job first thing in the mornin'."

"Tomorrow afternoon is good. The electrician will be here in the morning so with any luck, they'll be done by the time you get here."

"I'll be there a little after noon then, Miss Rousseau. Name's Mike Barlow."

"I look forward to seeing you, Mr. Barlow," she replied and hung up. She squealed and then jumped at a knock on one of the windows. She made her way to the door and peeked out to find Lily standing there. "Girl, you can stare through that window 'til the cows come home and pigs learn to fly, and you won't see a damn thing through all the grime," she said with a laugh once she opened the door all the way. "Get in here."

Lily laughed and gave her a one-armed hug. "I brought coffee and croissants," she said and set the bag and drink carrier on top of the bar. "Wow, Eme, this place is huge, or at least it feels like it is. I guess once you have chairs and tables in here it won't seem so big, but dayum, we have got our work cut out for us!" She took a quick look around at all the cleaning that had to be done.

"Yeah, I know, but all the other properties would have needed a shit-ton of work to turn them into a club; this one has all the bare bone essentials I need, including a stage platform."

"I see your point. Well, let's get to work. Please tell me you brought gloves and garbage bags." The main area of the former bar was mostly dusty, but at some point in the past, vagrants had gotten inside and left garbage strewn all over the place, near the back of the building.

Eme snickered at the sad puppy-dog look on her friend's face. "I should be mean and tell you no, but there was no way I was touching some of the garbage in this place with my bare hands."

"Oh, thank Goddess. I don't have to make a mad dash for the nearest store then."

Emelise hummed as she worked on a section of the building. "Oh, I have both a mason and an electrician coming tomorrow. I decided to keep the brick walls because I think they give the place an older ambiance."

"I like the brick walls, too. They give the place character. So what color scheme are you going to go with for the décor?" Lily asked while she worked on removing the grime from the windows with window cleaner and cleaning rags.

"I'm thinking either teal and black with hints of gold or red, black, and gold."

"I should have known. Those are your favorite colors. Do you have a name yet?"

Emelise nodded. "Scarlet Flux."

"Oh, I like. You really should go with the reds then—maybe a dark scarlet or crimson with black and gold accents."

Emelise thought about it. "You know, you've got a point. With the name, the red scheme would work better. I'm going to have a mix of tables and booths in here because not everyone likes to sit at a table. Booths can give a more private feel if you're on a date."

"Good idea. Oh man, I am so looking forward to seeing this place when it's ready to open. I know it's going to be great."

"I hope so. This is what I've wanted for a long time; I hope it doesn't flop."

"It won't. Have faith."

They spent the rest of the day cleaning, before they parted ways to shower, so they could have dinner and head out into the swamp, so she could meet the Alpha of the Black Water Pard.

There are moments in a person's life that define the path their future will take. For Emelise, meeting the Alpha of the Black Water Pard was one of those moments. Not that she'd been unaware of that while she sat in that boat staring out at the swamp. She'd sat there imagining what it might look like in the daytime, with the sheen of light on the water, the pale green of the moss swaying as an idle breeze moved through the trees, and the sound of frogs and insects buzzing and humming. She was sure it was beautiful in the daytime even if it felt a little creepy at night. She was completely unaware of how much her life was going to change.

The moment Caine Bordeaux had touched her, Emelise knew she was lost. She wouldn't admit to it, especially not to him, but she was. She'd long since accepted that she wouldn't ever find her mate since there were no leopard shifters in Phoenix. She was okay with that. She'd learned a long time ago that men couldn't be depended on to be there for you when you needed them. The only father figure she'd ever had taught her that when he walked out on her and her mama when she was ten. She neither wanted nor needed a man in her life.

Her eyes had locked with his and she'd struggled to look away from their pale depths. She'd feared if she stared into them too long she would get lost and never be able to find her way back. By the time he leaned away from her, after growling that they would talk later, she was shaken. Heat had flushed her skin, dampness pooled between her thighs, and her leopard snarled to get out. When Caine led Declan away from them, her eyes traveled down his back. Fuck he had a nice ass. *Stop it, Eme, it doesn't matter how sexy he is, he'll just be like every other man out there—not around when you need him the most.*

Meeting her grandmother for the first time was another defining moment. She'd followed Eulalie into the small house a short distance from Mia's. Much like Mia's home, it was filled with older furniture that was well-cared for. There were photos scattered about, and the mantle over the fireplace was filled with a mixture of photographs and small trophies. She moved to them to get a look at them.

"Some of dose were your mama's," Eulalie said when she noticed her interest in the trophies. "Your mama played softball from da time she was able to pick up a bat. She loved to play. Her team in high school won a lot of division games; her junior year, before she left, dey even won a state championship. She could have gone to college on a full scholarship if tings had been different."

Emelise turned to look at her. "And I wouldn't exist, so forgive me if I don't feel like it's a bad thing that she got knocked up."

"Dat's not what I meant, child. I just meant dat is what could have happened."

Eme watched her. "Why did you disown her? You have all these photos of her, her trophies out; that doesn't seem like the kind of thing a person does when they disown their own child."

Eulalie motioned for her to take a seat. "Can I get you some sweet tea, cher?"

She wanted to scream at her to just get on with it but she forced her frustration down. "That would be great, thanks," she said before she perched on the edge of the sofa. The scent of jasmine reached her and she closed her eyes. That was her mama's favorite scent and just smelling it brought a pang of sorrow to her for a moment. She knew it would be a long time before the pain of losing her mother faded.

"Here we go." Eulalie placed a glass of sweet tea on the table in front of Emelise, then sat in a rocking chair with her own. "What do you know of what happened between your mama and us?"

Emelise sipped the tea a moment before she replied. "Mama told me that, when she realized she was pregnant, she only had two choices. She either had to run away, if she wanted to keep her baby, or let it be killed because the boy she'd given her virginity to was human. She told me that, after I was born, she called and her father answered the phone. She told him why she'd left, and he told her not to come back, she wasn't welcome here anymore. She wasn't even seventeen years old and her own parents turned their backs on her." Her anger rose and she had to force it down.

Eulalie nodded at her. "Dat did happen, yes. Her papa did tell her dat," she confessed. "Now, don't go gettin' mad 'til I explain. You met our Alpha, Caine; he's a good man, a good Alpha, but he wasn't always our Alpha. He challenged the old Alpha, Zachary Eitenne, some eight years ago, and defeated da old bastard. It was Zachary who wouldn't let your mama come home. Her papa, he knew if she came, old Zachary woulda ripped you outta your mama's arms and thrown you into da swamp to feed da gators. He only wanted pure-blood leopards in his Pard. It broke her papa's heart to tell her she wasn't welcome no more." Tears slipped down Eulalie's cheeks. "I tried to reach out to her a few years ago, after Caine took over and we found out where she was. Her papa was real sick; he wanted to tell her he was sorry; he wanted her to know he'd hated his self all dis time because he had to hurt her to keep you safe. I begged her not to hang up on me. She told me to never call her again, dat we were dead to her and to her daughter, and hung up. Her papa died a few weeks later."

As Eulalie explained what had happened, the real reason why her mother had run away, and why she'd been disowned by her own parents, the anger Emelise felt faded and was replaced with remorse. All this time. If her mother hadn't been so stubborn, she could have been repairing the relationship with her mother, and she would have had those last few weeks with her father before he'd died. "Oh gods," Eme whispered. "All this time, I've been so angry. I've wanted to come here and rub it in your faces that mama made it on her own without any help from her family, that she'd raised me to be strong and independent, just like her. I wanted to tell you how you really missed out on the amazing woman she turned out to be and feel smug about it, but now all I want to do is weep for all the lost time. Mama didn't have to go to her grave thinking her parents didn't love her. She didn't have to die believing she was leaving me completely alone." Her own cheeks were wet with tears and she wiped them away.

"You had a right to be angry, child. You believed you were abandoned by your blood. You had no way of knowing the reason behind her papa's hurtful words. Your mama, did she have a good life?"

"She did. I mean sure, things were tight sometimes, but Mama got a job at a diner almost as soon as she settled in Phoenix, which she did because her car broke down there. She was able to rent a little place for a while until she saved up money to buy a house for us. She got her diploma, she did finish that, because she said she'd never been a quitter before; she wasn't going to start just because she had a baby to take care of."

"That sounds like my Adelaide. She was always so determined to succeed." Eulalie smiled a little. "Did she find happiness? Did she ever get married?"

"No. She thought she was going to. His name was Sean. They were together for six years before he just up and left one day. He was the only papa I knew and Mama decided after he broke her heart she was done with men. They couldn't be counted on to be there and to stick by you so it's always best to only depend on yourself."

"There are good men out there, cher. Don't let your mama's bad experiences jade you about that. Your papere was at my side until the day he died."

Emelise snorted. "I'd call him the exception, not the rule," she replied. Yeah, she knew she was jaded but it had kept her heart safe so far.

Eulalie shook her head. "You're too young to be so jaded, child. I'd like to get to know you more." The air was suddenly filled with roars from the Pard and a big grin split her face. "Mia must have had her baby. Come, cher, let's go see. Will you come back to talk, let us get to know each other?"

Emelise nodded. "Yeah. I'd like that," she said, voice thick with emotion. She wasn't alone anymore. The feeling of elation at that thought was almost overwhelming.

Chapter Two
Emelise

Looking around the bar that held so much potential, Emelise thought about her first visit to the Pard, and her reaction to Caine when he'd convinced her to dance with him. Had it really only been two days since she'd met Caine? If she really let herself think about it, it almost felt like she'd always known him. She'd felt their connection on a physical level—it was like a jolt of electricity—and she'd known, in that moment, that dancing with him was so not a good idea. He was already making her body crave things she didn't want to be craving. Being close enough to him that their bodies were touching, breathing in his scent, would only make things harder for her. Still, she'd let him pull her close, despite her decision to keep him at a distance. Maybe it wouldn't be so bad to let him in. Maybe he would be the exception to the rule, as well. She blinked at her wayward thoughts. No way. No way in hell was she letting herself go there. She couldn't depend on a man to stand by her; she'd learned that when she was ten years old; no way was she going to let herself forget that.

A knock on the window closest to the door pulled her from her thoughts and she went to answer it.

"Good mornin'. Are you Emelise Rousseau?"

Eme looked up at the man standing outside the door. Sometimes she really hatred being vertically challenged. She wasn't short, damn it, she was vertically challenged! The shirt he wore bore the logo for Pinnacle Electric so she knew he was there to check out the wiring. "Good morning. Yes, I am. You must be the electrician. Come on in," she said and stepped back.

"Yes ma'am. I'm Alex Carlson," he said and offered his hand.

Emelise shook it before she stepped back. "Nice to meet you. I'll let you get to whatever you need to do. The building inspector said that some of the outlets needed to be rewired and it needed a new fuse panel box, but if you find anything else that needs to be done, you have free reign to do your job. The entire upstairs has electricity, as well, so you'll have to check that out too," she informed him.

"Will do, ma'am," Alex said and went to work.

Emelise tried to stay out of his way as she worked on getting the area of the bar, she'd started on the day before, completely cleaned up.

Alex Carlson did a thorough inspection of the wiring before he approached her. "The buildin' inspector was right—some of the outlets down here need to be rewired, and the entire upstairs needs a complete rewire or else it'll be a fire hazard. The panel box is an easy replacement; I already have one for it, but I'll have to do the wirin' first. I can get the downstairs done day after tomorrow; the upstairs will take about two days to complete. I'll bring in an assistant with me on both jobs, if that's alright with you, ma'am."

"That's fine. I'd rather it be done right than have it done half-assed and have a fire break out." They set a time for him to start and Emelise walked him out.

The original plan was for the mason to come that afternoon but he'd had to cancel due to a family emergency. Emelise rescheduled with him before she called it quits for the day and locked up behind her. It would be two days before he was able to go in to check the the walls for structural damage, which gave her plenty of time to go shopping in Baton Rouge with Lily and Shelli.

Caine

There are moments in life that define a person and who they will be. One of those moments, for Caine, came eight years ago when he challenged the Pard's old Alpha, Zachary Eitenne, for his position, and won. At the age of twenty-two, Caine became the youngest Alpha in the United States. It was a position he was hell bent on being the best at. His Pard deserved an Alpha that cared about them and their well-being. Within the first eight years, the Pard went from looking like they were smack dab in the middle of a third-world country to looking like any other suburb in the US. Sure, they still had some struggles—being in a southern state with a fairly high unemployment rate coupled with a low minimum wage didn't make for extreme wealth—but what community didn't? The important thing was, they were no longer living in squalor, and not a single member of the Pard went without their basic needs being met.

Another defining moment for Caine was the night he'd met his mate. Emelise Rousseau had taken his breath away the moment he'd seen her. He'd wanted to ignore everything else and focus on her, but duty came first. It wasn't until they were celebrating the birth of Gage and Mia's son that he'd gotten his chance to be close to her.

Caine couldn't help thinking back to the moment. Caine scanned the commons, the central area where the party was taking place, looking for Emelise. He found her standing next to Lily and made a beeline for her. Along the way he let his gaze trail over her. She was a tiny thing but she had curves his hands itched to trace. He moved in behind her and leaned down to growl in her ear. "Dance wit' me, cher."

Emelise turned around to face him but she made no move to take the hand that was held out to her.

"Dance wit' me," he said again, watching her face. He saw the struggle in her eyes. She wanted him too, but she was a proud woman; she wasn't going to give in so easily. He liked that. He liked that his woman had a backbone. As Alpha, he needed someone who could stand at his side, not someone who would cower in the face of adversity.

After a moment of hesitation her resolve seemed to crumble as she took the hand he held out to her. When she slipped her hand into his, Caine gave her a wicked smile and pulled her close. He kept hold on her hand and held it against his chest as his other arm snaked around her waist, pulling her flush against him. He heard her soft gasp and smirked. With her pressed against him, there was no way she couldn't know that he wanted her. His cock throbbed with need but he wouldn't rush things with his mate. No, he wanted her to crave him as much as he craved her, and he knew from the way she'd hesitated in taking his hand that she wasn't there. Yet. He held her close and lowered his head, burying his nose in her hair to breathe in her scent as they danced. Unfortunately, he didn't get to hold her as long as he wanted before Lily interrupted them and then she was gone, leaving her scent clinging to him.

The celebration of the birth of Gage and Mia's son lasted two days, which wasn't uncommon for the Pard since Caine became Alpha. As a result, Caine had two very late nights in a row. Despite the late hour in which he'd finally gone to bed, Caine was up with the sunrise. He'd earned the money he'd put into rebuilding the Pard, into one of financial strength and security, by being an investor, and as such, he had to be up first thing in the morning to make sure things stayed on course. His chosen profession made it easier to run the Pard because he didn't have to be gone every day. Later in the morning, he was at his desk in his study going over a recent acquisition when there was a knock on his front door. With a sigh he pushed away from his desk and went to answer it. "Mornin' Remy. I'm surprised to see you're up already." Technically it was late morning but he knew Remy, the leopard was most likely up all night.

"Yeah, well, some people don't know how to be quiet around here," Remy grumbled.

Caine chuckled. "Dat is very true. Come on in. Dere's coffee in da kitchen if you need a cup. What brings you by dis mornin'?"

Remy followed him inside and went straight for the coffee pot. "I got a text from Lily. Seems your mate bought herself a bar dat needs some heavy cleaning and Lily asked if da Pard could help wit' dat. I told her I'd send some of the boys over but I thought you'd want to know about it, too."

Caine cocked a brow. "Did she, now? I wonder what she's plannin' to do wit' it. A'course we'll help. Dat's what we do; we help each other out wit' tings dat need doin'." This would give him the chance to see her in the sunlight. He wanted to really see the color of her eyes.

"I'll let her know some of da Pard is coming over. I 'spect you don't want her to know you're gonna be dere, too, yeah?"

Caine laughed. "No, I don't want her to know. She might change her mind just because she's fightin' what's between us."

Remy smirked. "Dat's what I thought. I'll let you know when dey're ready to go," he said and drained his cup of coffee before he rinsed the cup out and left.

Caine went back to his study and quickly finished what he was doing so he would be ready to go when the others were. If his stubborn little mate thought she was going to get away from him this easily, she had another think coming to her.

Emelise

Temperatures in New Orleans, in late spring, weren't that bad. According to the weather man, it was hovering at around 77 degrees outside, but inside the bar it was a good bit warmer. Emelise attributed that to the fact she didn't have electricity to run fans to cool things down. As a result, within the first hour of cleanup, her clothes were already starting to stick to her. Strands of her hair had come loose from the braid she'd put it in and were clinging to her neck and face thanks to the sweat. Worse was the sweat pooling between her breasts. She was really beginning to rethink her decision to not wait until after the electrical work was done before she started really trying to get the place cleaned up.

Emelise was wiping sweat from her brow when her phone vibrated in her pocket. She took it out and glanced at the number. It wasn't familiar to her, but since it was a New Orleans number, she opened it to find a text from Remy.

Emelise, Lily told me about your little problem. Some of da Pard will be dere soon to help start da cleanup. Whatcha gonna do wit' da place once dat's done, cher?

Eme read it and shook her head. Only a Cajun would type the same way they spoke. *Haven't you ever heard the phrase 'Curiosity killed the cat'? Just kidding, I couldn't help myself. In answer to your question, I'm opening my own jazz and blues club, which is why I bought an old bar. It's on Decatur, used to be the Happy Fish Tavern. I'll be here all day so whenever they get here is fine.* She included the address in the text and hit send before she got back to work.

She had an hour, before Mike Barlow arrived, to check out the brickwork for any damage that needed to be repaired. She debated on continuing working but decided she needed a short break and went down the street for some coffee and a Danish.

Caine

When they pulled up outside the old bar, to discover Emelise wasn't there, Caine figured she'd gone to get something to eat and would be back. "Might as well relax 'til she's back," he told the others and they settled in the back of the truck. All five males were recently out of high school but they hadn't decided on what they wanted to do with their adult lives yet and this would keep them out of trouble. He leaned against the driver's side door and kept his gaze moving, taking in the area and any possible dangers that might be present. He would not let his mate be at risk; he didn't give a damn if she argued with him about it. Her safety was important to him.

They'd been there about ten minutes when he saw her sauntering up the sidewalk with a bottle of water in one hand and a small bag in the other. He took in the way her jeans hugged her curves and sat low on her hips and how her tank top gave little glimpses of her smooth stomach. At one point, he caught a glimpse of black ink and cocked his brow. His mate was tattooed? That little peek made him want to peel her shirt up slowly to reveal whatever it was she had etched into her skin.

Caine lifted his gaze to her face just in time to see the flash of heat in her eyes before she forced a look of nonchalance. Oh, he was definitely going to enjoy getting under her skin and getting her to let herself go in his arms. The way she moved, he wanted to drag her off somewhere and kiss her breathless just to feel her body flush against his. *Reign it in; she's not ready for dat.*

"What are you doing here?"

Caine smirked and let his gaze trail over her. "Come to check out da place my mate bought."

She rolled her eyes at him. "Yeah, right, and I'm the Queen of England. You're just here to give me a hard time."

"Oh, I'd like to give you someting dat's hard, cher, but it isn't time," he replied with a husky growl. He definitely wanted to give her something hard. And thick. And long. He wasn't a small man and he knew, given her petite size, it would be a very snug fit once he was inside her wet heat. The blush that heated her cheeks had made him hard and he'd had to bite back a groan. "If you're here, you might as well come on in."

Caine locked gazes with her and nodded. "Lead da way, cher."

Once inside, he watched her, even as he moved around the building. "Lily was right; dis place needs a major cleaning. But it looks solid, dat's good." He moved to the bar and ran a hand over it. "Have you found someone to restore dis? If not, I'll let Gage know he's needed. He's da best woodworker in New Orleans. He and Remy have dere own carpentry and architecture business," he told her when she gave him a quizzical look.

"No, I haven't. That was the next thing on my list. I've already gotten an electrician in to take care of the wiring that needs to be replaced, and I have a mason coming to check the brickwork in the walls to make sure it's structurally sound. That would be awesome if Gage could do the woodwork, once the other stuff is done."

"He'll be glad to help a member of his family."

Eme blinked at him. "You know about that?"

"A'course I know. Mia told me last night dat you two are cousins. Dat's a story I'd like to hear about sometime. Where did you get da idea to open a club of your own?"

"I've always loved blues and jazz, and as soon as I was old enough, I got a job at a club in Phoenix called The Inferno. I did a little singing from time to time, but mostly I tended bar and helped with the daily running of the club. I knew a month into working there that I wanted my own club one day."

"You are an impressive woman, Angel."

"Thanks, I try," she said with a wink.

He smirked at the wink and motioned to the pard members who'd come in. "Where do you want dem to start, cher?"

"Oh, yeah, right. I've got cleaning supplies behind the bar. They can start wherever they want, really." Within minutes they were spread out around the main area of the bar with gloves and cleaning supplies.

Caine pitched in with the cleaning for a bit before he wandered up the stairs. "Whatcha gonna do wit' da upstairs?" he asked when he came back down.

"I'm not sure yet. I was considering either turning it into a couple of small rooms to rent out or turning it into one big apartment for me to live in. Why?"

"You don't need to live up dere; you can have a house built on da compound."

Emelise shook her head. "Not happening, so don't even go there. Why were you asking about the upstairs?"

"Well, I was tinkin', you could have part of da ceiling between floors opened up so it looks down over da stage and ground floor, and it could be a VIP section of da club."

Eme blinked at him. "Holy fuck, why didn't I think of that? That's a great idea. I'm sure it can be done; I just have to get a contractor in here to look at it and give me an idea of what it will cost to do it."

Caine laughed. "I do love your exuberance, Angel. I'm sure you would have thought of it, given a little more time." He watched her for a moment, and the pride he saw on her face as she worked to clean a thick layer of grime from the top of the bar made him smile. He wanted her to have this. He could see how much she wanted to open her own club, and he wanted to make that happen for her.

"If you need any help financing da work to get dis place to where you want it to be, all you have to do is ask, Angel," he told her as a knock on the door drew her attention away from him.

Emelise

Every time Emelise thought she had her wayward thoughts and emotions under control, Caine said or did something else to throw her completely off. She hadn't even considered turning the upstairs part of the building into a VIP section, by opening up part of the ceiling, so that half of it overlooked the ground floor. When he called her Angel it sent warmth through her. Other than her mama calling her sweetheart sometimes, no one had ever really called her by an endearing pet name, and she realized she liked it. She liked him calling her Angel. *Fuck, I am in so much trouble.* How was she supposed to keep him at arm's length when he did things like that?

The knock at the door was a welcome interruption before she said or did something she might later regret. "Saved by the knock," she said under her breath and went to answer it. A dark-haired man, with broad shoulders and a solid build, stood there, tool belt slung low on his hips. "You must be Mr. Barlow?"

"Yes, ma'am. Mike Barlow, at your service," he said and offered his hand.

"Emelise Rousseau," she said with a smile and slipped her hand into his.

"Pleasure, Miss Rousseau." He held her hand a moment longer than was maybe necessary as his gaze moved over her briefly.

"Please, come in," she said and stepped back.

"Seems you've got quite the cleanup crew in here," Mike said once he followed her inside.

"Yeah, don't mind them. My best friend enlisted their help, since the place needs some heavy cleaning and some minor repairs, before I can start converting the space to the way I envision it." She motioned to the walls. "As I told you on the phone, I really like the exposed brickwork so I'm hoping it's sound enough to keep it."

"I'll do a thorough check and let you know if there's any structural damage," he told her and headed for the closest wall.

"Great, thanks so much," Eme replied.

Caine

Caine stood off to the side, just a little, so he could see whoever was at the door without them really noticing him watching them. He watched as the man's eyes trailed over Emelise's body, as if he had a right to look at her that way, and his leopard snarled in his head. She was his mate; the human had no business looking at her like he wanted to undress her. It took every ounce of willpower Caine had to not go over to him and smash his face in with his fist. Who the fuck did he think he was?

Caine kept his eyes on Emelise as she slipped her hand into the human's, and the way the man lingered, made him want to rip his throat out. He needed to get a grip on his sudden flash of jealousy. He was an Alpha; he had better control than this. As soon as the other man walked away, Caine's hand snaked out and curled around Emelise's arm before he pulled her toward a corner away from the others.

"What the hell?" Emelise gave him a startled look. "What in the fuck is wrong with you?"

"What's wrong wit' me, Angel, is I don't like to see my mate flirtin' wit' other men," Caine growled at her. "Dat little smile you gave him when you shook hands wit' him wasn't necessary."

"Oh, for fuck's sake, Caine, I wasn't flirting with him. I was being nice—something you clearly have no concept of. Besides, you don't *own* me, Caine Bordeaux, so you can drop the possessive, controlling bullshit right the fuck now."

Her anger should have pissed him off but instead it just made him want her that much more. Her temper was a turn-on because she had a backbone and wasn't afraid to stand up to him. He liked that. "Maybe not, but you're still my mate, like it or not, Angel, and I don't share what's mine," he growled before he crashed his mouth down on hers. He was already tired of treading lightly with her when all he wanted to do was get her naked and make her scream his name while she orgasmed around his cock.

Emelise

Emelise was spitting mad when Caine pulled the neanderthal, possessive, controlling shit as if she was his property. She wanted to hit him, or maybe dig her claws into him, to wipe the smirk off his face when she'd hissed at him and it did little to dissuade him of his attitude toward her. He was such an overbearing, arrogant jerk; who in the hell did he think he was? Just because his leopard was her leopard's mate didn't give him any right to try and control her.

Eme saw the flash of something in his eyes seconds before his mouth crashed down on hers. She should have jerked away, she should have hit him, she should have done anything other than what she actually did, but her traitorous body responded to him in a way she'd never responded to a kiss. Instead of pulling away from him, she molded her body against his, a soft gasp escaping, to be muffled by his lips at the feel of his erection pressing against her. Her fists gripped his shirt a moment before they let go and snaked up to wrap her arms around his neck. She gave herself over to the kiss and the heat it caused to course through her body.

Any chance of denying the connection between them, the intense attraction they shared, disappeared the moment she gave herself over to his kiss. Moisture pooled between her thighs, heat flushed her skin, and her brain went on meltdown. There were no thoughts in her head; there was no room for them while he held her against his body.

His hands were suddenly on her body and she lost all control of herself. Her own hands slipped beneath his shirt and, as her leg wrapped around his hip, tugging his erection closer to her, her nails raked down his back.

Caine

Caine was lost. That was all there was to it. He hadn't expected

Emelise to return his kiss with the same heat and passion, but the moment their lips touched, she responded to him with an intensity that was almost surprising. A growl escaped him and he pushed her against the wall as he deepened the kiss. Hunger tore through him when her arms wrapped around his neck to pull his mouth closer to hers.

One hand slid beneath her shirt and moved up to cup her breast as he devoured her mouth. He completely forgot they weren't alone. The only thing he could think about was how much he wanted to feel her skin and kiss every inch of her delectable body. He massaged her breast until her nipple stiffened then he pinched it lightly between his fingers.

When Emelise wrapped her leg around him, tugging him closer, he lifted her just enough for his cock to press against her core. As her hands slid beneath his shirt, he ground against her and was rewarded with the feel of her nails raking his skin. He moved to start working her shirt up to get it off just as someone cleared their throat.

Reality came crashing down and Caine froze where he was. He broke the kiss and lifted his gaze to hers only to find her not looking at him. She looked embarrassed and he couldn't blame her but it wasn't her fault. "Sorry, Angel," he murmured, voice ragged with need.

Emelise

Emelise was so caught up in the way his hands felt on her body and the need raging through her that she'd completely forgotten there were others in the room. Just when she was on the verge of begging him to just fuck her against the wall, someone cleared their throat. The sound broke through the haze of lust and drowned it faster than a dunk in the Arctic Ocean would have.

"Sorry, Angel."

She heard the raggedness of his voice but Eme wasn't sure she believed he was sorry. "Bullshit you are," she hissed. "We both know that was you trying to stake your claim like I'm some piece of property you have to mark as yours. Why don't you piss on me while you're at it?"

Caine's eyes narrowed at her. "I'm arrogant, cher, but I'm not a bastard," he growled and stepped back.

Emelise saw the flash of hurt in his eyes and instantly regretted what she'd said but she couldn't take it back. She sighed softly and closed her eyes. "I'm sorry, that wasn't fair to you." She took a moment to compose herself before she turned her attention to the man standing a short distance from them. "I apologize, Mr. Barlow." She knew her cheeks were red from embarrassment. It deepened at the way the mason stared at her for a moment.

Mike Barlow cleared his throat again before he responded. "Don't worry about it, Miss Rousseau. We all get caught up in things now and then. Some of the bricks will need to be replaced, there's some damage to the grout in a few places that needs to be repaired, but once that's done I'll put a protective coating over everything, and you'll be good to go."

"That's great. When can you do it?" She moved away from Caine to work out the schedule with him. She also made a mental note to talk to the electrician again since she was going to be converting the upstairs to a VIP section. Some of the wiring would have to be rerouted to accommodate it.

Caine

When Emelise accused him of kissing her that way just so he could 'mark' her as his, the words cut deep. Yes, he was a possessive man, he wouldn't deny that, but for her to dismiss their attraction, and their kiss, in such a way, was painful. He'd kissed her, not because he was staking a claim, but because she moved him so deeply he just couldn't help himself.

He watched as she moved away from him to work out a schedule for the mason to come in and do the work that was needed. Even though he hadn't intended for the kiss to get so out of hand, part of him was glad it did because the human would know she wasn't available now. In his mind it was worth pissing her off.

A quick glance at his watch made Caine groan. He had to get back to work. "Josiah, send word when y'all are ready to go back to da compound and I'll send someone to meet you at da docks. I need to get back; I've got work to do."

"Will do, Alpha. Don't worry, we'll keep an eye on tings," Josiah replied.

Caine nodded at him and moved to Emelise. "We'll talk, later, Angel, I've got to get back to work." He wanted to kiss her again, but he wasn't sure where that might lead so he settled for kissing her cheek before he left.

Emelise

Emelise watched him go before she huffed out a breath, smoothed the stray hairs that had come loose from her braid, and went back to work. By the time the sun started setting, she had the name and number of a building contractor who would come and check out the second story of the building to see if they could remodel it into a VIP section. On her way back to the hotel, she got something to eat and then, after a quick shower, she sat down and went through her finances to make sure she still had enough to cover everything. Sure, Caine offered to help, but she didn't want to be beholden to him for the financing of her club. It was her baby; she wanted to be the only one with a financial say in what happened with it.

Later that night, when Emelise and Lily got together to watch a movie and have a bitch fest, she confessed to her best friend about the kiss and the aftermath of it. "I was pretty unfair with him since I know he didn't really do it to mark me as his territory."

"Give him a few days and then talk to him, Eme. He'll understand you were just frazzled by everything."

Eme sighed. "I hope so." By the time she made it back to her hotel room she was worn out, but her dreams were less than peaceful. No, they were erotic and left her feeling antsy and needy the following day.

Chapter Three
Emelise

Two days after the very steamy kiss she shared with Caine, Emelise was at the Pard's compound visiting with her grandmother. She'd just gotten herself an apartment, and she would be heading to Phoenix the next day with Lily to get all of her things out of storage, but she'd promised her grandmother she would have dinner with her so there she was. She was going to try her damnedest to avoid Caine. She was still in an emotional upheaval over the kiss they'd shared and the embarrassment she'd felt upon realizing she'd forgotten they had an audience. "Hello, Mamere Eulalie," she said when her grandmother opened the door for her.

"Hello, child. I'm glad you came for dinner. I thought you'd like to meet more of your family," she told her because there were several people in the living room. "You've met Mia's mama, Eliza, but that's her papa, Efram, her sisters Sophie, Adele, and Constance, and her brothers Beau, Auguste, Dempsey, and Julius. Eliza and Efram were blessed with two sets of twins: Mia and Julius and Adele and Auguste."

Emelise was stunned. "I...had no idea I had such a big family. It was just me and mama for so long, this is...a little overwhelming."

"Don't sweat it, cher, we don't bite. Much," Julius joked. "Call me Jules. It's awesome to have you back in da family fold. When Mama filled us all in on ever'ting dat's happened, we were pretty shocked, too. It's not ever' day your long lost cousin finds her way home."

"I guess this is a bit of a shock to all of you, as well. You can call me Eme; that's what the people who matter to me call me."

Sophie, the youngest, approached her. "I made dis for you," she said and held up a beaded bracelet. Each of her siblings had one already.

Eme smiled down at her. "Aw, thank you. It's really pretty," she said and slid it on her wrist. "How old are you, Miss Sophie?"

"I just turned eight last week. Mama says I'm gettin' to be a big girl."

"Yes, you are. Well then, happy belated birthday. Soon enough you'll be driving your mama crazy wanting to stay up later and go out more," Eme replied with a wink.

Sophie giggled. "I like your earrings," she said, noticing the feathered earrings hanging from Emelise's ears.

"I made these myself. I found an injured hawk when I was living in Phoenix and nursed it back to health; it left a few feathers behind and I thought they'd make awesome earrings."

"Cool! It wasn't ascared of you?"

"It was at first, but it settled when it realized it was safe."

"Come on, Soph, it's time to eat," Eliza said to her daughter. "She gets excited easily," she told Emelise.

"I was the same way when I was her age. Of course, some might say I still am easily excited," she joked as she followed Eliza to the table. There was so much food laid out and before Emelise knew it, her plate was piled high.

"So, Eme, what are your plans now dat you're in New Orleans?" Beau asked.

"I purchased an old bar that's been sitting empty for a few years, and I'm converting it into a jazz and blues club."

"You definitely picked da right city for dat kind of club," Adele said with a soft laugh. "Da Big Easy is da home of blues and jazz."

"Oh, I know. I've already got some potential acts lined up, and when it gets a bit closer to opening, I'm going to try to find local talent to give them a chance to shine too."

"How are you financing dis endeavor?" It was Mia's papa, Efram, who spoke that time.

"Part of is money I've saved over the years because I've worked, by choice, since I was sixteen. The rest is from selling the house I grew up in back in Phoenix."

"Dat couldn't have been an easy decision. At least I know it wouldn't be for me if I was in that position."

Emelise looked at Eliza and shook her head. "It wasn't but my mama wouldn't have wanted me to hold onto it just to let it sit empty." She bit her lip a moment and turned to Eulalie. "Mama wanted to be cremated and then have her ashes scattered over her favorite area in the desert. I kept just a pinch; I've got them in a special box I had made, if you'd like them."

Eulalie gave her granddaughter a somewhat sad smile. "No, child, you keep your mama's ashes, what you have left of dem. She'd want you to keep dem."

"What was it like growing up in da desert?" Dempsey asked around a mouthful of food. He was twelve and like most boys, he couldn't shovel the food fast enough.

"Dempsey Efram Lafluer you know better den to talk wit' your mouth full!"

Dempsey swallowed what he had in his mouth and gave his mother a sheepish smile. "Sorry, Mama, sorry Mamere Eulalie."

Emelise was enjoying this look into the family she'd never known about. She wondered what it was like having so many siblings, so many people in one house. Her own childhood had been fairly lonely, and there were many times when she'd wished she had some siblings to play with. "It was really hot in the daytime, but colder at night, especially in the winter. It's not like the heat you have here, with all the moisture in the air. It's a dry heat that can cause you to get heatstroke really fast if you aren't careful because it will dry you out quicker than jerky over a fire," she said with a wink at him.

They all cracked up at that. "You're definitely one of us, cher," Beau said after a moment.

Auguste nodded in agreement with his older brother. "She is. Dat's someting Papere Buford used to say all da time."

"So that's where my mama got it from. I always wondered about that but she didn't like to talk about her past much." She was quiet a moment. "I know she loved you though," she said to her grandmother. "I remember a few times, when I was younger especially, I would hear her crying because she missed her mama and papa. She never regretted keeping me, but sometimes it was hard on her, especially during the holidays."

"If I could go back in time and change tings, I would, child. I would have driven to where she was when she hung up on me, but I was afraid. I was afraid she'd slam da door in my face and I'd lose my Buford before I got back. He was so sick and we didn't know how much longer we'd have together in dis life. So I stayed and I lost da chance to make tings right wit' her."

"Don't beat yourself up Mamere Eulalie," Eliza said gently. "I don't think Emelise told you dat just to upset you."

Eme shook her head. "No, that wasn't what I meant at all. I just wanted you to know she didn't really hate you. She was hurt and she wanted to protect herself, and me, so she pushed you away when you called. I know that had to be why she did it. Life had taught her that no one stayed true, she couldn't depend on anyone but herself, so she kept others at arm's length. She didn't even date, not after Sean Scotsdale, the only papa I ever knew, left us six years after he moved in with us. He broke her heart and she just decided that was what people did."

"That's so awful," Constance, the only one who hadn't spoken yet, said. "I can't even begin to imagine what it would be like to not have anyone else around. Having all dese brothers and sisters, it gets crazy sometimes, but I wouldn't change it for anyting."

"I was just thinking it must be something to have so many siblings. It got pretty lonely at times, being an only child. But Mama did her best, and I had a few friends. No one I could get really close to because they were human, but they were still friends."

"How did you and Lily become friends?" Eliza asked.

"Lily lived in Phoenix for a while, before she ended up here in New Orleans. I was at the diner, where Mama worked, when she came in, and we knew right away what the other was. She looked a little down at the time so I plopped down in the seat across from her with a strawberry shake and some curly fries, told her it was on the house, and introduced myself. We hit it off right away."

"Lily seems to have a way of endearin' herself to others," Eliza agreed. "She did the same when she came to meet wit' Caine. She wasn't afraid to stand in front of him wit' a bunch of leopards watchin' her warily, and by da time she left, her and Mia were already makin' plans to get together."

Eme laughed "Sounds like Lily. I think it's the Alpha female in her; it helps her to put others at ease." She glanced at the time and groaned. "I should be getting out of here. I've got an early day tomorrow, but I promise I'll be back to visit again soon."

"Why don't you just move to da compound?" Beau asked his cousin.

"Because I like my independence. Maybe if I'd grown up here I'd feel differently about it, but we can't change the past, right?"

"As long as you come to visit, child, it doesn't matter if you live here or not," Eulalie told her granddaughter.

"Thanks. It was so great meeting all of you, it really was. I look forward to getting to know my extended family more," Emelise said before she left to go find Remy. He was the one who had brought her there, and he'd told her to let him know when she was ready to leave.

Caine

Caine was trying to work, emphasis on the word trying. His mind kept wandering to his mate and he wondered what she was doing. He really needed to get this trouble with the jaguars settled so he could focus on getting her where she belonged: in his arms and in his bed. With a frustrated growl he closed down his laptop and went outside. Maybe a run would help.

He was halfway across the compound when his gaze fell on a very familiar form. "Evenin', Angel," he growled as he approached her from behind.

Emelise turned quickly at the voice. "Hello, Caine."

"What brings you into da bayou and were you really goin' to leave wit'out sayin' hello?" His gaze raked over her and his hands itched to pull her close so he could kiss her again.

"I was visiting with my grandmother and met the rest of Mia's family, her dad and siblings. And, yeah, that was the plan. I just really don't know what to do with you, Caine. You're arrogant as hell, dominant, frustrating, and, okay, I admit it, you're sexy as fuck. You make me a little crazy and I can't cope with that right now. I have way too damn much going on at the moment with working on the club and trying to get to know the family I thought didn't want me because my blood isn't pure. I just don't have the time to deal with you too."

"At least you're admittin' you're attracted—dat's a start." He reached out and brushed a wayward tendril of hair behind her ear. "Relax, cher, I'm not goin' to pin you up against a wall and ravish you, even if dat's exactly what I want to do. You're a challenge, Emelise Rousseau, and I love challenges. But mark my words, Angel, I will have you in my bed begging for my cock, and it will be soon." He saw Remy approaching and nodded. "See she gets back to New Orleans safe," he told his lieutenant before he walked away from them. If he didn't put distance between him and Emelise, he was going to make a liar out of himself by pushing her against the nearest wall and devouring her mouth. She was just so fucking sexy and the heat in her eyes drove him insane with need.

Emelise

Fucking hell! Is the universe really so against me tonight?

"Took you long enough," Emelise said with a glare when Remy finally joined her. She knew her cheeks were warm from Caine's parting words, and she was sure Remy knew whatever it was had also turned her on. That was the downside to being shifters: you could smell when someone was aroused. Damn the man for putting thoughts of them naked and sweaty together in her head.

"Sorry 'bout dat, cher. We've had some run-ins wit' da jaguars from over in Lafayette. One of our females was harassed earlier and I had to talk wit' her."

"Oh, shit, is she okay? That's definitely more important than taking me back to the city."

"She's shaken up a bit but dey didn't hurt her, far as I know. If dey did, she ain't talkin'."

Emelise shivered. "I hope she's okay." Lily had told her the Pard was having some trouble with the jaguar clan but she hadn't realized it was that bad. "Thanks for the ride back," she said once they'd reached the docks where she'd left her car. "Maybe I should invest in a boat of my own and learn the route so I don't have to bother anyone."

"It's not a bother, cher, but if you decide to do dat, let me know—I'll hook you up wit' a seller." He glanced at her. "I'd offer to teach you how to drive a boat and teach you da route but I tink dat's best left to your mate. My Alpha might get da wrong idea and I like my head attached to my body."

Emelise rolled her eyes. "Yeah, he's likely to go all neanderthal. Thanks again, Remy. Have a good night," she said and headed to her car. A quick shower before bed was just what she needed to relax the tension in her shoulders. She had a long couple of days ahead of her.

Chapter Four
Emelise

Phoenix, Arizona. It was the city she was born in, the city she grew up in, and yet it had never really felt like home to her. The drive out from New Orleans with Lily had been fun, more fun than the solo drive she'd taken to get to New Orleans. Sure, she'd done some sightseeing along the way, but road trips were so much more fun when taken with others.

Still, she was looking forward to getting back to New Orleans and getting everything unpacked. There was a locked chest her mother had kept in her closet that Emelise hadn't gotten around to trying to open before she'd packed everything up. Once she got back home she was going to change that. What could be in it that was so important her mama had kept it locked? She wasn't sure how she was going to get into the thing, since she didn't have the key for it, but she'd figure something out.

"Homeward bound," Lily said as they headed away from Phoenix. "So are you really ready to close this chapter of your life, Eme?"

"More than ready. Phoenix never really felt like home. I think deep down my leopard knew where she belonged and it wasn't in Arizona."

"Maybe she did," Lily said and turned her attention to the road since she was driving the first leg of their trip. "So, do you think Mal will take you up on the offer and come down to New Orleans once you've got the club open?"

"I don't know but I hope so. Even if he just visits, I think Venus will be a big hit at the club." She snickered. "Especially if I announce her using her full stage name."

Lily arched a brow. "Okay, I'll bite. What's her full stage name?"

"Venus Flysnatch," Emelise said with a straight face.

Lily stared at her for a few seconds, then jerked her attention back to the road as she busted out laughing. "Oh my gods, that's great. Where in the hell did Malcolm come up with that?"

"Back when he was still with a Pride, they had…expectations. In order to be part of the Pride, any Pride, he had to settle down with a female shifter and have babies. He was trying to conform even though he knew he wasn't straight. The only time he ever got an erection on his own was if he pictured some hot, naked guy in his head. Otherwise she had to give him a hand job. A few months into the relationship he discovered she had a bad habit of spreading her legs for any guy that wanted to dip his wick in her. Malcolm said she was like a Venus Flycatcher, pretty but deadly to a man's ego. When he created his alter ego, he decided to go with a pun on that because he knew she'd heard about him calling her a Venus Flycatcher and if she ever saw the show she'd know the name was a jab at her."

"Oh, wow, poor Mal. I can't imagine how defeated he must have felt. First he has to completely suppress such a core part of himself in order to be accepted and then he finds out the woman he's with is a serial cheater? At least he got an awesome stage name out of it."

"Yeah, he said he went through a lot of upheaval during it, but that was the catalyst that made him decide to leave the Pride and embrace who he really was." Eme settled in for the drive. She'd hired a contractor who would be going in later in the week to start the remodel of the upstairs part of the club, Gage had agreed to restore all the wood to it's original glory, the electrical work was almost done, and the mason would be going in after the upstairs remodel was completed. Soon enough she'd be able to open the doors and her dream would become a reality.

Caine

Caine was enraged, and it was taking every ounce of willpower to not lay into the five members of his Pard kneeling in front of him. When Declan had informed him that Lily and Emelise had decided, on the spur of the moment, to drive to Phoenix, not even sparing a thought to the fact they had to go through Red Moon Clan territory to do so, he'd almost lost it. Then he found out that Emelise told the leopards, who were helping her get the club cleanup and remodel done, to just go ahead and show up and not mention it to Caine unless he specifically asked about her. He'd gone ballistic. "You should have come to me, immediately."

All five were kneeling submissively in front of their Alpha. They knew they'd done wrong by not coming to him immediately. "You're right, Alpha, we should have said someting. We, none of us, we didn't really tink about why she didn't want us sayin' anyting even though we knew she was your mate. I mean, I thought it was odd she asked us to not say anyting unless you asked but I didn't tink to really question it." Josiah, the one who'd decided to be the 'spokesperson' for the small group, swallowed nervously while he waited for his Alpha's decision. He knew Caine could punish all of them for not coming to him about her leaving.

Caine looked them over and growled with frustration. They were all barely out of high school; he couldn't really expect them to think like grown men who had some real world experience. "Get out of here. In da future, if someone says 'Don't tell Caine', you come and tell me right away."

"Yes, Alpha," they said, almost in unison, before they rushed away.

Caine watched them go before he stripped, shifted, and went out into the bayou to roar his frustrations with his mate into the air without disturbing the Pard. By the time he got back, he felt less like he was going to rip someone's head off and went inside to send a text to Declan, asking him to notify him when Eme and Lily were due to be back in New Orleans, then he went back to work. There was much he still needed to do in order to be ready for the coming battle with the Red Moon Clan.

The moment Caine awoke, he began preparing for the impending attack from the Red Moon Clan. Declan was certain it would happen that night, and there were a number of Pard members who would be at risk if they remained at the compound. Declan was opening his secured headquarters to those members of the Pard and Caine needed to get everyone organized.

His first order of business was to get his lieutenants together. He sent a text to Remy Delacroix and Beau Lafluer, then went to make coffee.

"Mornin', Caine."

Caine nodded at Remy, who'd entered after knocking. "Mornin'. As soon as Beau gets here, we'll get started. Coffee's fresh." He motioned to the pot.

"No'ting better den fresh coffee in da mornin'," Remy replied and fixed himself a cup. Moments later, Beau arrived, and got himself a cup as well.

"Now dat you're both here, we have some plannin' to do. Declan's openin' his headquarters to da Pard, for da ones who won't be joinin' da fight. We need to get ever'one moved quickly. Dey should take what dey need to be comfortable while dey wait for word on how da fight goes."

"You got it, Alpha. We'll get da women, children, and elders to safety."

"Don't go assumin' none of da women are gonna wanna join da fight," Caine admonished Beau.

"If da choice is helpin' keep da little ones calm or fightin', I tink most of dem are gonna choose da first option," Beau countered.

"Maybe, but if any of dem want to fight, den dey will be welcome to do so." Caine knew Beau's reasoning wasn't steeped in sexism even if it sounded like it was. "Let's get dis done. We've got a fight to get ready for."

As the day progressed and the compound emptied of all but those leopards who wanted to fight to defend their home, Caine's thoughts grew heavy. He knew there was a very real chance some of his people could end up seriously injured or dead. Of all the neighboring shifter groups he'd dealt with, the Red Moon Clan was the only one that refused to discuss any issues that arose between them. Caine never really understood that kind of mentality. Why would a person prefer to fight when doing so could lead to death? Shaking the thought from his mind, he focused on the growing darkness.

He watched as the last boat returned to the compound, carrying Declan and his team. Every one of them had a grim look on their faces and Caine wondered if his face mirrored theirs. "Dis ends tonight, one way or another," he said to Delcan when the wolf stopped in front of him.

"With the Pard coming out the victor. Failure isn't an option," Declan replied.

"I do like your tinkin'." Caine smirked before he headed to where his Pard waited for him. "Y'all know what's at stake here." He went on to explain just how important it was for them to win in the coming fight. It was Declan's speech, though, that really galvanized the Pard.

Caine watched the faces of his Pard. He'd not been the least bit surprised when a few of the women decided they were going to stay and fight. One of them was Sabine. She was a doctor but she was a leopard first, and that meant fiercely protecting home and hearth from attacks. When Declan gave them the option to leave and head into New Orleans, pride filled Caine when not a single leopard made a move to leave. Every single one of them looked determined to do whatever it took to protect their homes.

After Declan's speech, each group moved off into the growing darkness and Caine stepped up to Declan. "If da Alpha gets past me, take him out. Don't wait for me to catch up to him, because if he gets past me, it'll only be because I'm already fightin' one of his lieutenants."

He moved away from Declan after the wolf agreed. Standing in the shadows cast by the trees, Caine stared out at the swamp. Soon, soon the fighting would begin. Soon blood would be spilled and lives would be lost. He sent up a silent prayer that none of his own people lost their lives just as the traps Nikolai had set up went off. Within moments, shapes began to move through the darkness and Caine put all thought aside. He needed to focus. He let his leopard out just enough to quicken his reflexes. The first jaguar to come at him was soon unconscious with a gash to his temple, compliments of Caine's claws. He didn't have time to pause to make sure he didn't kill the jaguar because another came at him, and he took that one out as well.

Caine lost track of where everyone was as he worked his way toward the one jaguar he really wanted to fight. Lucas Cormier. The Alpha of the Red Moon Clan needed to die. They might go easy on the weaker members of the Clan, but not Lucas.

Finally. Finally he was face to face with the Alpha of the Red Moon Clan. "Dis ends now."

The fight between them was quick, but brutal. Caine knew it wasn't going to be easy. Lucas wouldn't be Alpha if he was weak and unable to protect his position. However, Caine had something Lucas didn't: determination. He was determined to protect his Pard and their home. The only way he could do that was by winning.

When he landed the killing blow, he'd expected to feel a sense of satisfaction and was surprised to realize that what he felt, instead, was remorse. Such senseless, needless death. It could have been avoided if only the other Alpha hadn't been so stubborn. He closed his eyes, for just a moment, in silent respect for the lives that were lost, when a snarl had him turning. The jaguar was too close and Caine knew he didn't have enough time counter the attack. When Declan put himself between them, earning a nasty gash across his chest, compliments of the jaguar's claws, Caine knew he owed the wolf his life. In that moment, he made a decision. For the first time since the Pard took up residence in New Orleans several generations ago, The Big Easy was going to belong to more than one shifter group. He was going to offer Declan part of the Pard's territory for him to create his own pack.

Emelise

The second day of their return drive, Lily drove in the morning, so it was Emelise who was behind the wheel as they neared their destination. All she could think about was getting home and finding a corner to curl up in. She wouldn't even care about sleeping on the hard floor, she was that tired.

"Come crash at my place tonight, Eme. We can get the Pard to help you unpack tomorrow," Lily offered.

Emelise considered it but she waved it away once they'd stopped the U-haul truck and gotten out. "No, it's fine, I can rough it for one night." And then, of course, things went from bad to worse, figuratively speaking. Sauntering toward them, in a way that made things low in her body tighten, her skin warm, and dampness pool between her thighs, was the one leopard she didn't want to see. Okay, maybe she did want to see him but she really couldn't handle him, and she could see by the hard look in his eyes that he was pissed.

When Caine reached her, Emelise straightened her shoulders and lifted her chin to look at him. "Don't start. We can talk another time,

I'm too damn tired to do this right now." Even her voice sounded tired and she knew the exhaustion was evident on her face.

Caine

Caine was there, outside Emelise's apartment building, with several members of the Pard, when the truck pulled up. He'd watched from the shadows while Eme and Lily had a brief conversation, then climbed out. Even from where he'd stood, he'd seen how tired his mate was from the long drive. It had tempered his anger quicker than anything else could have. Seeing the exhaustion on his mate's face had almost made his anger disappear completely, but not quite. He was just as livid with Lily for being so thoughtless and careless, as well.

As soon as Emelise slid out of the truck, he'd moved into view so she could see him before he'd approached her. He wanted to take her in his arms and ravish her mouth but he also wanted to shake some sense into her. He did neither of those things. "Tomorrow, dinner at da compound. We'll discuss your impulsiveness den." He motioned for the leopards to get busy with the truck, and Lily's car, which was towed behind it, was unhooked so she could head home.

Emelise opened her mouth—he was sure she was going to tell him to go to hell—but that wasn't what came out. "Okay."

Caine smirked at the look on her face. She looked like she'd just realized she got herself caught in a trap. It was so damn cute he wanted to kiss her. His smirk increased as he stood back and listened to the banter between Emelise and Lily.

"What's with the grumpy look?" Lily asked her friend while she waited for her car to be unhooked.

"I just got wrangled into having dinner with Caine at the compound."

Lily laughed softly. "Ouch. Have fun with that," she teased before she turned toward her car so she could leave. "I'll call you tomorrow, Eme, after we've both gotten some sleep," she said, then looked at Caine. "Yeah, yeah, I know, you're mad at me too. You can chew me out later. I'm beat. Night, Eme."

"Night, girl, thanks for going with me."

"I'm glad you made it home safe, Angel," Caine murmured near her ear, once Lily was gone, before he went to help unload the truck. He felt Emelise's eyes on him before she went into the apartment building and upstairs to unlock her apartment door for them.

Caine carried a number of items inside before he let the others take care of the rest of it. He wanted to get a good look at the apartment his mate had picked out. "I tink da place suits you. You leavin' the walls da color dey are or paintin' dem?"

"I'm going to be painting them. I'm thinking shades of turquoise for the front of the apartment and maybe warm yellows for my bedroom."

Caine smirked. "Wantin' something relaxin' in dere, yeah?" he teased. "I tink turquoise is a good color for out here; it'll fit wit' your furniture." Her sofa and chairs had a mix of blue, black, and silver colors in it.

"Well, yeah, the bedroom is a place to relax and sleep; of course I want calm colors in it."

"I can tink of other tings da bedroom is good for," Caine growled.

Eme's cheeks pinked at his words. "Don't even go there. I am so not up for your teasing tonight, Caine. Mentally or emotionally."

That got his attention. The trip out to Phoenix wasn't all pleasant and it brought out his protective streak. He gripped her elbow and guided her to the sofa to sit. "What happened?"

Emelise shook her head. "It's not that something happened, Caine. I grew up there, I just lost my mama a month ago, it just took an emotional toll on me. I put up a good act, pretending like it didn't bother me any to sell the house I grew up in and move, but it did hurt, a little. I don't regret it; Phoenix never really felt like home, but that house, it was where all my good memories with my mama were made."

Caine slipped his arm around her and pulled her close. "I'm sorry for your loss, cher," he hushed. "Losing a parent is never easy and dere are no words dat can really be said to ease da pain. You don't have to hold it all in wit' me, Angel. I won't tink less of you for letting your grief out."

"Truck's unloaded," Josiah said once they'd carried the last box in.

"Go on back. I'll be along later," Caine said and watched them go. He could feel Emelise shaking as she fought her grief. He had a feeling she didn't want to cry in front of the others. She needed to let it out though before it ate her up inside.

Emelise

Emelise had watched as Caine had moved around her apartment, checking out every nook and cranny. She'd had to admit she liked seeing him in her space, not that she would tell him that. She'd also liked the way his jeans clung to his ass when he moved. He had a very nice ass. His T-shirt was snug across his chest and the sight of it made her mouth water. She really wished he was somewhere else because she couldn't handle any more emotional turmoil right now.

"I am so not up to your teasing tonight, Caine. Mentally or emotionally."

Why had she admitted that out loud? What had she been thinking? She didn't want to talk about the grief that was clinging to her. If she started crying, she wasn't sure she'd be able to stop. The one thing she'd not even admitted to Lily yet was that she'd not allowed herself the time to grieve properly. She'd only shed a few tears after her mother died and then she'd pushed it down so she could take care of all the things she'd needed to do.

She was almost numb as she let Caine ease her down onto the sofa. Before she could stop herself, the words tumbled out. That was when the shaking started. She'd felt the tears hovering on the edge, she'd known any minute they were going to start falling, and once they did, she wasn't going to be able to stop them. It had barely registered when Caine had sent the others away, leaving them alone in the apartment. When his arms tightened around her, the dam broke and a sob escaped her. One sob turned into more and before she knew it, she was clinging to his shirt and shaking with the force of her cries.

Caine's arms tightened around her until he moved and pulled her onto his lap. He didn't speak platitudes, he didn't tell her it would be okay, he didn't even shush her as she sobbed in his arms. All he did was hold her and give her what comfort he could.

Emelise wasn't sure how long she sat there clinging to him and crying before the sobs finally died down to sniffles. His shirt was wet with her tears, and she could just imagine how rough she looked now with her eyes all red and puffy. When she pulled back, he loosened his arms and she lifted her head to look at him. "Thank you."

"Anytime, Angel. You needed to grieve." He pressed a gentle kiss to her temple. "Let's get you tucked into bed." He stood, scooping her up in his arms as he did so.

Eme squeaked a little. "I can walk, Caine."

"Mmmh, but I want to carry you, cher." He'd made sure the others had made her bed so she could just crawl under the covers, so once he got to her room he set her on the edge of the bed and knelt to remove her shoes. Then he reached for her shirt.

"I can undress myself."

"Relax, Angel. As much as I want to run my hands over every inch of your luscious body and make you beg, tonight isn't about dat. I just want to help you get comfortable so you can sleep."

She bit her lip. "Okay. I have pajamas in my suitcase by the door."

He moved to get the suitcase and when he turned, he sucked in a breath. She'd removed her shirt and jeans and stood there in just a lace bra and panties. He stared, for just a moment, before he opened the bag, got her pajamas out, and handed them to her, then set the bag aside.

Emelise swallowed at the heat in his eyes when his gaze traveled over her. Would he resist the temptation her being mostly naked presented? When he didn't try to take advantage of her, she couldn't help but smile a little. He was keeping his word. When he held the clothes out for her, she quickly covered herself and moved to crawl into bed.

Caine moved to her bedside and held the covers back for her to crawl in. "Sleep, Angel," he growled softly before he pressed a gentle kiss to her lips.

Eme almost asked him to stay. Almost. But she wasn't sure if she'd be able to resist him if he slept next to her. "Thank you, Caine, for not pushing anything tonight."

"You're welcome, cher. Tomorrow, all bets are off," he told her with a wink before he headed to her door. "I'll lock da door behind me, don't worry." He turned her bedroom light off for her.

Eme listened to him move across her living room floor, then listened for the door to close and lock behind him. Her hand touched her lips briefly as if she was trying to hold in the feel of his lips on hers, then she let her eyes close and sleep claim her.

Chapter Five
Emelise

Eme woke the next morning with her head hurting a bit from all the crying she'd done the night before, but her heart felt a little lighter. She'd kept her grief so bottled up, but she now realized doing so had been the wrong thing to do. If nothing else, Caine had at least helped her to let some of it go.

A smile flitted across her face when she remembered the gentleness and strength in him when he'd held her on his lap and let her cry herself out. A shiver worked it's way down her spine when she recalled the heat in his eyes when he'd turned with her suitcase in hand to find her standing there in bra and panties. She knew it was a big temptation for him and part of her had wanted him to give in.

Still, when he kept his word and helped her to get dressed, then tucked her into bed, she'd been grateful. She might have enjoyed the sex, which was debatable since she'd not really enjoyed sex up to now, but she would have had morning-after regrets because it wouldn't have been a direct result of the attraction between them but more her raw emotions. Somehow he'd known that and he'd left without even a real kiss good-night.

Emelise spent the day unpacking boxes and putting things away. Anything that would go on the walls would wait until she'd had the chance to paint, but everything else could be put where it belonged. Despite spending the day unpacking, there were still unopened boxes cluttering up her living room. She knew it was going to take more than one day to get her new place organized, but by the time she stopped so she could shower and decide what to wear to dinner, she'd made a big dent in things.

She'd gotten all of her clothes put away and, standing there, looking in her closet, she was torn. Did she want to wear a dress, a skirt, or pants? Each had their own pros and cons. She finally settled on a boho-style dress that looked like different types of lace sewn together in strips. The skirt of it dipped down to a point in front and back and rose up on the sides in a V almost to her knees. The bodice hugged her breasts and thin straps held it on her shoulders.

The hardest thing to decide on was what to wear on her feet. Her mama used to tease her about her shoe collection. It was almost an addiction, her need for so many shoes. It took fifteen minutes of trying on different pairs before she finally settled on a pair of black boots that stopped just below the knees. The leather boots were a combination of lace-up and three-buckle design and a front view revealed a bee broach and sprocket details. It was sexy and stylish, with a little bit of a funky look, thanks to the boots being more Steampunk than sexy chic. Even with the four-inch heel, Caine was still going to be several inches taller than her.

After applying a little makeup, she stared at herself in the mirror. Now for her hair. What to do, what to do? Put it up or let it hang down? She thought about all the times she'd seen Caine, and realized that he'd never seen her hair down. Any time he saw her she'd had it pulled up. She left it hanging loose down her back where it reached just below her shoulder blades, added a little mousse to it to smooth it out, and called it done. She didn't stop to question why she wanted to look good for him when she kept telling herself she didn't want or need a man in her life. "Here goes nothing," she said under her breath and headed out to meet Remy at the docks for her ride to the compound. She really did need to get her own damn boat.

Caine

Walking out of Emelise's apartment that night had been one of the hardest things he'd ever done. Every single protective instinct he'd had was screaming at him to stay there, wrap her in his arms, and hold her throughout the night in case she needed him. He'd left because he wasn't sure he could have stayed and not press for more than just holding her in his arms. He craved her the way a junkie craved their next fix. Every time he saw her, his hands itched to strip her and caress her skin, his mouth watered at the thought of tasting her sweet nectar, and his cock hardened and throbbed with the need to be buried deep inside her. No, he wasn't so sure he could have held her in his arms and not pushed for something more. So he'd left, letting her know that it was the only reprieve she had because, come morning, he was going to really begin pursuing his mate.

Awaking with renewed resolve, Caine got his morning started while the sky still had that pre-dawn darkness to it. His first order of business, after fixing a quick breakfast, was to make sure his home was as inviting as possible. As a single male, he admitted that his home had an overabundance of masculine influences and almost no feminine ones. What would make Emelise feel comfortable and relaxed? He didn't have the answer to his question so he did the only thing he could think of; he enlisted the aid of both Lily, via text, and Sabine. Why Sabine and not Eliza, when Eliza was related to Emelise? Because Sabine, despite being born and raised with the Pard, had gone away for college so she had more experience with what women away from the bayou were interested in. He thought someone with more outside influences might have better ideas.

Lily, apologies for the early morning text but I am in need of some advice. I want things to be perfect when Emelise comes to dinner tonight and you know her best. Any advice you can offer will be welcome.

He sent the text, after reading it a few times, then went in search of Sabine. He knew it might be a bit before he heard back from Lily.

Caine knew Sabine would already be awake. She'd always been an early riser; even when she was a child, she was awake early enough to watch the sun come up. This morning found her curled up on the swing she'd recently added to the small cottage next to her childhood home, with a cup of coffee in one hand and a muffin in the other. "Good mornin', Sabine."

"Good mornin', Caine. What brings you by dis early in da day?"

Caine rubbed his brow a moment. "I am in need of some…assistance. My mate is coming to dinner tonight, and I am not too proud to admit that my home is less than inviting to the feminine eye."

Sabine arched a brow at him. "You come to me and not her kin?" Her dark eyes studied her Alpha with curiosity.

"Dat, I do. Dey may be her kin but dey haven't lived away from da bayou da way you have. My mate is…eccentric. Growing up away from here, she's experienced tings most here haven't." He knew that in some ways his Pard was isolated from the world beyond New Orleans.

"Ah, dey don't have da worldly experiences she does, but I do. Now I understand." Sabine laughed softly. "Let me see what I have to work wit'." She got up to follow him to his home.

On the way to his home his phone vibrated, and Caine took it out to see Lily had responded to his text. She must have to work the morning shift if she was up this early.

Good morning, Caine. Don't sweat the early text; it's all good. As for insight on Eme, her favorite colors are red, black, gold, and turquoise, which I'm sure you've probably figured out. Unlike me, her favorite flower is a rose; I know, so common, but it's about the only 'common' thing about Eme. Don't be overbearing because she'll tell you to fuck off. Let's see, she loves blues and jazz, which is a given considering the club she's opening, but she also really enjoys classical music, and don't tell her I said anything, but she loves to dance. She took dance growing up and she's really good at it. Her favorite sweet treat is cheesecake, with any kind of fruit topping. She's been raised to believe that you can't depend on others, romantically, to stick by you. When she was four her mother fell in love, he moved in with them, and both Eme and her mom thought he'd be there forever. He was the only father Eme ever knew. He left when she was ten; it devastated both of them, and it jaded Emelise about relationships with men. You've got your work cut out for you, Caine. She'll be pissed when she realizes I told you about Sean Scotsdale abandoning them when they believed he was in it for the long haul, but I felt you deserved to know why she's fighting the attraction she feels for you so hard. Good luck!

Caine read over the long text several times. Emelise and her mother were abandoned by the man they believed loved them. That explained her resistance to getting involved. He needed to change Emelise's perception, but he had a feeling it wasn't going to be easy. *Thanks for the information, cher. I forgive you for taking off to Phoenix without an escort when it was so risky going through the Red Moon Clan's territory.* He couldn't very well stay angry when she was trying to help him win over his mate.

That done, he turned his attention to Sabine. He watched as she moved through his home while shaking her head. "Just tell me whatever it is you're tinkin'."

"It's easy to see you're a bachelor. Dis entire house is one big man cave. Do you trust me to make some changes wit'out makin' it feel like someone else's home?"

"What do you need to do?"

"Go shoppin'."

Caine groaned but handed over his credit card. He wanted the house to be welcoming for Emelise and if that meant a little change in décor, so be it.

Sabine chuckled. "Don't look so scared; I won't do too much damage," she teased and left.

Caine decided to focus on work until she returned. Regardless of his desire to make things perfect for his dinner with Emelise, he still had work to do. There were bills to be paid, he had a Pard to look after, and he'd offered to send monetary aid to the Red Moon Clan now that they were allies. Shit, he still needed to talk with Declan, to formally thank him and his team for their assistance with the jaguars, and present him with the offer he'd come up with as proper thanks.

When you have some free time, I need to speak with you. Let me know when you can come out to the compound and I'll have Remy bring you.

Declan's response came almost immediately after Caine's was sent. *I can come out this afternoon. Be there at 2.*

See you at 2, then. With that piece of business done, he spent the next two hours working until Sabine returned from her shopping trip.

When she got back, Sabine had several bags with her. She handed Caine his card and went to work. She changed out the lamps in the living room because they were dark and rather bland, to something that helped to brighten things up. She'd also gotten some colorful throw pillows for his leather sofa and an area rug to put on the hardwood floor. A few changes to decorations on the walls, including a couple of paintings, and she was done.

Caine watched her work and when she was done, he had to admit the house felt a bit brighter. "Thank you, cher."

"So you approve?"

Caine chuckled. "You were right—it needed some changes."

Sabine patted his arm. "Good luck in wooin' your mate, Alpha."

It was Caine's turn to head out and do a little shopping. He had a dinner to prepare, and he needed to be back at the compound before Declan's arrival at two.

Declan

Declan had spent the night making good on his word to Lily about how she wouldn't be getting out of bed any time soon once she'd gotten back from Phoenix. When they'd both awakened that morning, the passion hadn't eased any, and he'd spent another hour pleasuring her very responsive body. Now with the sun hovering overhead in the sky, before it started it's slow descent towards the western horizon, he headed to the Pard's compound to see what Caine wanted.

"You and Lily seem to be getting' along better," Remy said as he headed the boat toward the compound.

"That's because we are. That doesn't mean she isn't making me work for it though. The woman is still stubborn as hell, but that's one of the many things I like about her." Like, hell, he was in love with the she-wolf but he wasn't ready to admit it out loud.

Remy laughed. "Dat's a good ting, considerin' she's your mate."

"True. Listen, since we have a few minutes, there's something I wanted to talk to you about. I know you have a carpentry business with your brother, and you're free to decline the offer I'm about to make, but I want to make it anyway. I've decided to start my own private security company, doing things similar to what we did when the jaguars came after the Pard, along with other things like offering bodyguards to people when needed. I wanted to offer you a position. You're a damn good fighter, you're fast on your feet, you know how to move in silence, and you've got an integrity that I respect. Don't give me an answer right now. Just think on it," he said before Remy could respond one way or the other. He didn't want the man to make a quick decision and regret it later.

"Dat's a mighty fine offer," Remy said with a nod. "I'll tink on it and get back to you." When they reached the dock at the compound, he tied off and hopped out. "Lemme know when you're ready to go back," he said and headed to his home.

"Will do," Declan said before he hopped off the boat and made a beeline for Caine's house.

"I see you're right on time," Caine said when he met Declan at the door. "Can I get you a drink before we talk?"

"Some of that sweet tea that seems to be so popular here in the South would be great. I had no idea tea could taste that good."

Caine chuckled. "Dat it can, when it's sweetened just right." He got two glasses, complete with ice, handed Declan's to him, and headed to his study. "Sit," he said once he was behind his desk.

Declan got comfortable and took a drink of the tea before he cocked a brow at the leopard across from him. "What's on your mind, Caine?"

"I've been tinkin'. You and your team were a great asset during da trouble wit' da jaguars. I wanted to thank you for your help by offerin' part of Black Water Pard territory to you, as your own territory."

Declan blinked. "Come again?" Had he heard Caine right?

"You heard me right," Caine said. "Dis is Lily's home, you're an Alpha in your own right, you should have your own territory. New Orleans, as well as the surrounding area, will be split between the Black Water Pard and your Pack. Ever'ting east and nor'east of da eight hundred block of da French Quarter will be yours. Da Pard's territory will continue nor'west to Baton Rouge."

"That's…quite the thank you, Caine. I'd be a damned fool to turn down such a generous offer. Looks like the Black Water Pard has gained another ally. The Ghostpoint Pack. It just seems to be a fitting name now that we're going to officially be a Pack." He knew there were other 'misfits' out there, shifters who wanted to belong to a pack, a group, but for whatever reason weren't welcome among their own. He'd reach out to them, give them an option to join, under a few conditions, of course.

"I agree, it is a fittin' name. I tink dis is da beginnin' of a very long friendship," Caine said as he walked Declan out.

"I think you're right," Declan agreed. He couldn't wait to share the news with Lily and his team. No, not team, his Pack.

Chapter Six
Emelise

Emelise stepped off the boat, when they reached the compound, and had to take several deep breaths to calm her nerves. Why was she feeling so nervous? It was just dinner. With Caine. A man who drove her crazy and made her body come alive in a way it never had before. There was no reason to be nervous. Yeah, if she kept telling herself that, maybe her mind, and her body, would eventually believe it.

She made her way to the path that would lead her to Caine's home and stopped to stare at the gorgeous man coming her way. Every other time she'd seen Caine, he was wearing jeans and a T-shirt. Tonight he was dressed completely differently. Black slacks hugged his ass and legs and helped to draw the eye to his waist, and lower. He paired the slacks with a short-sleeved button-down shirt in deep blue. The color brought out the blue in his eyes and made them appear darker. The first three buttons were undone, giving a nice peek at his chest, and Emelise found herself wanting to undo the rest just to see all that gorgeous skin and hard muscle exposed to her hungry gaze. This dinner was so not a good idea.

"Good evenin', Angel," Caine growled softly when he reached her.

Eme had to suppress the shiver his growl elicited. "Good evening, Caine. You look…amazing. You bayou boys clean up well."

Caine laughed. "Dat we do, cher, dat we do." He offered her his arm. "You are absolutely stunning tonight."

Emelise blushed a little at the compliment. "Thank you." She slid her hand into the crook of his arm. Her fingertips brushed his forearm, where the sleeves to his shirt were rolled up, and a jolt of electricity went through her. Yeah, this was a bad idea, but she was here; there was nothing she could do about it now.

Caine

Caine had watched the boat approach and had gazed at his mate as she'd stepped off. She'd taken his breath away and he'd had to give himself a mental shake to get moving. The way her dress draped her body and drew the eye to her very lovely breasts had his cock stiffening with need, and he'd stifled a groan. It was going to take a lot of willpower to not pounce on her the moment he got her alone. He craved another taste of her lips, ached to feel her body pressed against his. Tonight he wasn't letting her get away until he made her scream his name in pleasure.

Once at her side, Caine had offered his arm to keep from embarrassing them both by ravishing her in front of Remy. The warmth of her small hand on his skin caused goosebumps and he shifted closer to her as they walked. "How are tings goin' wit' da club?" He was genuinely curious about it.

"They're going well. The contractor has been hard at work, getting the upstairs remodeled. He says it'll be finished by the end of the week, and the electrician can come back in to finish the wiring. If all goes as planned, we'll be opening our doors in a month." She was so excited that it showed in her voice. "I've already started advertising for help and some of the local musicians have voiced an interest in checking out the acoustics in the club once it's open."

"Dat's great, cher. Your dream is comin' along nicely."

"It is. I can't wait for it to be finished. It's going to be great, I know it."

"A'course it will," Caine replied, voice filled with conviction.

Eme arched a brow at him. "It's nice to have your vote of confidence, but I have to wonder why you feel so sure of it."

"Because, Angel, you are a woman who is determined to succeed and dat makes a world of difference." Once at his home he opened the door and ushered her inside. He hoped that soon it would be their home and not just his. He'd let her make any decorating changes she wanted if it meant she was there in his arms every morning for the rest of their lives.

Emelise

Eme wasn't sure what to expect when they reached his house. She really didn't know much about him beyond the fact he was the Alpha of the Pard and he could be an arrogant pain in the ass when he wanted to be. She found she was looking forward to getting to know him. She really was in so much trouble. When she stepped into the house, she arched a brow. "I wouldn't have taken you for a man who liked vibrant colors," she said, motioning to the paintings on the wall.

Caine chuckled. "To be completely honest, cher, I'm not. I was informed dis mornin' dat my house was one big man cave and needed to be lightened up a bit so I let one our females do some shoppin'."

Emelise laughed. "One big man cave. Now *that* I can see. I don't want you changing who you are out of some misguided belief that you need to do it to impress me or some shit, Caine. Whoever picked all this out, she has a good eye for color, but it doesn't really feel like it's you. It feels more like things an ex left behind and you've just not gotten around to removing them." A spike of jealousy went through her at that thought. Who was this female who went shopping for him?

Caine smirked at her. "No, cher, it's not someting an ex left behind and dere's no'ting between Sabine, who went shoppin', and me other den I'm her Alpha. She's da only one of da Pard, in our generation, who has really left da bayou, and I wanted da opinion of someone who had more experience with the world outside of New Orleans." He leaned down before she could get away from him and brushed his lips across hers. "It's cute dat you're jealous, Angel. Stay right here, I have someting for you. " He winked and went to the kitchen.

Emelise was mildly embarrassed by the fact he'd heard the jealousy in her voice. She hadn't planned on that. While he stepped away from her, she moved around the living room. She could tell which influences were from this Sabine, and yes she still felt a little spike of jealousy at the thought of another woman buying things for Caine's home, which was totally ridiculous. She should definitely not be feeling jealous. So what if he was her leopard's mate? He was a man—he'd probably fucked a lot of women, and as the past taught her, she couldn't count on him sticking around once he got what he wanted.

Caine returned to her with one arm behind his back. "Dese are for you, cher," he said and held out a bouquet of Black Beauty roses.

Eme's eyes widened and a soft gasp escaped her. "Oh, wow, they're gorgeous." She took them from him, lifted them to her nose, and breathed in the soft scent clinging to them. "Thank you. They're Black Beauties, aren't they?"

"Dey are. How'd you know dat, Angel?"

"Black Beauties are my favorite of the large tea roses," she admitted. "Another of my favorite type of rose is the Rosa Mundi. It's a gorgeous Gallica rose that comes in a variety of colors splashed across the petals like paint." She blushed a little. She adored roses; you name them she liked them. The only other thing she'd ever wanted to do, besides open a club of her own, was own a greenhouse filled with roses.

Caine

Caine found himself more and more intrigued by his mate. She was a bit of a paradox to him. She was tough, independent, stubborn, strong, and then she would say or do something that exposed a sense of vulnerability in her that she quickly covered up with bravado. Finding out she was such an avid fan of roses made him want to give her a bouquet every day. "Someting tells me dis is more den a passing fancy for roses." He offered her a crystal vase for the flowers and watched as she placed them in it with a hint of reverence.

Eme looked up at him and her cheeks were slightly pink. "You are too fucking perceptive for my own good. I used to talk about building a greenhouse in our backyard, back in Phoenix before my mama died, so I could grow my own roses, maybe come up with my own hybrid."

"Dere's no'ting stoppin' you from doin' dat, cher. Dere's plenty of land here where you could build your own greenhouse." Yes, he was trying to tempt her into moving to the compound so she'd be closer to him.

Emelise shook her head. "You aren't going to give up on trying to get me out here, are you?"

"Not a chance, Angel. Dis is where you belong, wit' me, wit' your Pard." He reached out and caressed her cheek. "I understand your need to be independent, but dat doesn't mean I'll stop tryin' to get you in my arms every night. I have every intention of makin' you beg for my cock before I have you screamin' in pleasure."

Emelise

Emelise couldn't believe how easy it was to talk to him. She'd never shared her secret wish for her own greenhouse with anyone but her mother and yet she'd told him about it as if it was common knowledge. How the fuck did he get past her defenses, past her walls, so damned easily? Was it because he was her mate? Or was there more to it? Did she really want to risk getting her heart broken by letting him in?

His admission, and the very naughty thoughts his words put into her head, combined with his growl, made Emelise blush as a shiver worked it's way down her back. "There you go, ruining a perfectly good conversation again by putting kinky thoughts in my head," she said and was rewarded with a startled look from him. That was the first time she'd admitted he put those thoughts in her head.

Caine chuckled. "Oh, dat's good to know, cher. Dat means I'm makin' headway." He ushered her toward the table where dinner was waiting for them. He held her chair for her before he took the seat across from her.

Emelise wasn't sure what to expect in regards to their dinner. Would he cook it himself or order from a restaurant? Looking at the platters of food on the table, she still wasn't sure which it was. "Did you cook all of this yourself or did you cheat and get takeout?"

"No'ting on dis table was bought from a restaurant."

Eme blinked. "You cooked all of this? How in the hell did you find the time to do that?"

"A combination of wakin' up while it was still dark out and determination, cher." He'd made steak, steamed crab legs, scallops sauteed in garlic and butter, shrimp etouffee, asparagus cooked in butter with creole seasoning, and for dessert, he made both bananas foster and blueberry cheesecake.

She looked at the food, then looked at him. "It's a damn good thing we've got such high metabolisms or I wouldn't be able to eat half of what you fixed. It all looks delicious. I had no idea you could cook."

"I am a man of many talents, cher."

"I see that." She filled her plate and took a bite of her steak before she turned her attention to him. "I've only recently realized I know very little about you, Caine."

"What would you like to know? I'll tell you anyting and ever'ting."

"When did you become Alpha of the Pard? What led you to decide to challenge the old Alpha?"

"Da old Alpha, Zachary Eitenne, he was a hard man who cared more for his own comforts den he did da Pard. Da compound you see today, it wasn't always in such good condition. Da yards were unkempt, many of da houses needed repairs, some had leaky roofs and holes in da walls. It was worse den an inner-city slum." There was anger in his voice as he spoke of the conditions he'd had to grow up in. "Eight years ago I decided it was time dat Zachary was removed as Alpha. He'd let his self go; he was soft, weak, because he didn't tink anyone would ever challenge him. I defeated him easily and once he was gone, I focused on makin' dis a safe place for da Pard to live. Anyone who couldn't afford to pay for dere own repairs, I took care of it for dem."

"You took care of it? How?"

"I'm an investor. I'd already made quite a bit of money by da time I became Alpha."

"Ah. That makes sense. Mamere Eulalie said he was the reason my mama left here, after she got pregnant with me, because he would have forced her to abort, and if she'd tried to come home with me once I was born, he would have killed me."

"Dat's true, he would have. He didn't like anyone who wasn't full leopard. He only interacted wit' humans when he had to for business. Or when he had an itch he needed scratchin'."

Emelise shuddered. "I'm glad he's no longer here." She tipped her head at him. "Are you an only child? Where are your parents?"

"I am. My mama died when I was a babe; Papa ended up drinkin' his self into an early grave. He couldn't handle losin' his mate."

"I'm sorry. That couldn't have been easy to go through."

"Tink no'ting of it, cher. It was a long time ago. Now it's your turn to tell me a bit about you. What was your childhood like?"

Emelise's face lit up a bit at the question. "My childhood was great. I mean, sure, there were times when money was tight, but Mama always managed to provide the things I needed. Sometimes she had to work extra hours at the diner to do it, but her boss would let me hang out there when I was little, and after school, as I got older, on the days she had to work late. She always encouraged me to chase my dreams, no matter what they were, and she told me to never let anyone try to hold me back. Mama had to grow up fast, you know? She was sixteen when she got pregnant with me; she was on her own, she had no support system whatsoever, and yet not once did she make me feel like she'd wished she'd never had me."

"You and your mama were close?"

"We were. We didn't have anyone but each other, not after…well, not after the only father I ever knew decided six years into their relationship he no longer wanted a ready-made family."

"Dat was a really shitty ting for him to do to you and your mama," Caine said with a growl in his voice.

"Yeah, well, he's a man, what do you expect?"

Caine cocked a brow at her. "No, he was a boy. A man wouldn't have abandoned da woman and child he claimed to love. You have a very poor opinion of men, cher. Is dat why? Because of what he did?"

"Not just him. I've learned that lesson on a more personal level, too." She looked down at her plate a moment before she turned her attention back to him. "If there's one thing I've learned about men, Caine, it's that they cannot be counted on to be there when you need them the most."

Caine got up and moved to her side before he pulled her out of the chair and into his arms. "Dat is untrue, Angel. Whoever made you tink dat, dey weren't worthy of you to begin wit'. If it takes a lifetime to make you see dat, den I'm up for da challenge," he said and claimed her mouth in a heated kiss.

Emelise felt weak in the knees when he kissed her. Her fingers curled into his shirt and a soft noise escaped her. She should push him away—she even moved her hands to do that—but her body decided to betray her and instead she wrapped her arms around him and leaned into his body.

Caine

Caine had watched his mate as she'd enjoyed bites of food in between talking. The way her eyes lit up and the little pleased noises that had come from her told him she'd really enjoyed everything she'd tasted. Every time she'd licked her lips he'd felt himself harden. He'd wanted her, desperately. He'd wanted to peel that dress off her body and kiss every inch of exposed skin.

The animated way in which she had talked about her childhood had brought a smile to his face. She'd grown up without a Pard, and without a father, but her mother had done the best she could and she'd given Emelise unconditional love. That was what a parent should give their child but he knew there were many parents out there who didn't. His own father was one such parent. He'd blamed

Caine for the loss of his mate because she'd had complications during childbirth that eventually led to her death. He was never outright cruel to his son, but he was never very affectionate either. He'd loved getting to know more about her, loved getting to see little glimpses of her past. There were so many layers to his mate, much like an onion, but where onions were often strong and bitter, Emelise was soft and sweet.

It wasn't until Emelise outright said all men were pretty much worthless, when it came to counting on them to be there, that he'd decided it was time to start changing her view on his entire gender. Sure there were some men who took off when things got tough, but not all did, and he sure as hell wasn't the kind to walk away from his woman.

It didn't matter that they were in the middle of dinner. He needed to start changing her view of men, immediately. He moved to her side and pulled her out of her chair. The moment their lips touched, Caine pulled her closer to him and let her feel how much he wanted her. The way her body molded against his, it was as if they were made for each other. The noises escaping her as he deepened their kiss made him harden even more than he already was. He lifted her up and when her legs wrapped around his waist, he growled against her lips. "You're drivin' me crazy, cher," he said and kissed her again. Her body fit perfectly with his.

Emelise

Lost. She was completely and utterly lost. The feel of his arousal against her sent shivers of anticipation down her spine, and Emelise felt dampness pooling between her thighs. For the first time in her life, she really and truly felt aroused and it was both startling and a little scary. It scared her that her body responded on such a deep level to even the slightest touch from him. She didn't want to lose herself in him, didn't want to lose sight of who she was as an individual, and she feared that was exactly what was going to happen if she let him burrow his way into her heart. The problem was, no matter how hard she tried to keep him at a distance, he slipped past her defenses. How the fuck did he do that?

When Caine lifted her up, Emelise wrapped her legs around his waist. The position pushed her dress up to her thighs and placed his very hard cock against her heated mound. A strangled sound escaped her and her hands gripped his hair. Was that needy sound really coming from her?

"Tell me what you're tinkin', Angel," Caine growled against her mouth before he trailed kisses down her throat. He nibbled on her collarbone and smirked when she shuddered against him.

Did he really expect her to form a coherent thought? It took her several seconds to respond. "I've never felt such…need before."

Caine lifted his head to look at her. "What do you mean, cher?"

She wanted to look away but his gaze held hers. "I mean I've never really gotten much from sex. The only fucking orgasms I've ever had have come from a vibrator."

Caine

When Caine heard those words he froze. "Is dat a joke, cher?" His voice was gruff with need.

"Do you really think I'd joke about something like that, Caine?"

"Oh, Angel, you have been missin' out. You must have been wit' boys who didn't know how to please a woman. A man knows how to make his woman scream in pleasure."

Their dinner was all but forgotten as he headed toward the back of the house to his bedroom. He was going to show his mate just how much she'd been missing out.

Emelise snorted. "Uh huh." There was skepticism in her voice.

Caine smirked. He wasn't going to try to convince her with words. No, as the saying went, actions spoke louder. He carried her into his room and laid her down on his king-size bed before he crawled onto it with her. His hands slid over her body with the thin material of her dress between them. "By da time I'm done wit' you, cher, you're goin' to know exactly what I'm talkin' about." He slid his hands beneath her dress to slowly move it up her body. As her skin was revealed to him, he dipped his head and trailed kisses over her body. When the black ink he'd gotten a glimpse of was finally revealed to him, he trailed his tongue over the design. Roses with an intricate swirled design graced her right side from hip to just below her breast. The entire thing was in black ink and it was beautiful. "Dis is beautiful work, Angel. What inspired it?"

Emelise's eyes closed as his lips trailed along her skin. She shivered and a soft whimper escaped her parted lips. "I got it after my mama passed away. Our mutual love of roses was one of the few things we had in common."

Caine lifted his head to look at her. "In a way you're honorin' her memory wit' this."

Eme nodded. "Yeah." She swallowed at the desire burning in his gaze.

Caine kept his gaze locked with hers as he finally got the dress up and off her body, leaving her in just her lace bra and panties. He leaned back so he could look her over before he ran his hands down her body. "You are absolutely beautiful, Angel."

A faint blush tinged her cheeks as she stared up at him. "You really think that, don't you?"

"I never say anyting I don't mean." His hands cupped her breasts and massaged them until her nipples were tight little peaks. He kept his eyes on her face as he lowered his head and suckled one through her bra while he lightly pinched her other nipple between his thumb and forefinger.

Emelise whimpered and arched her back, pushing her breasts into his touch. Her hands went to his shoulders and she clung to him.

Caine kept up the attention on her breasts with his mouth while his hand slid down her body to dip between her thighs. "So wet already, cher." Her panties were soaked from her arousal. He shifted the material out of his way and slid a finger into her. He'd intended to discuss the impulsiveness of her decision to go to Phoenix, but any thought of that was long gone as her hips bucked into his hand.

Emelise

She was on fire. That was how she felt from every touch of his fingers, every brush of Caine's lips on her body. He was burning her up and she wasn't sure she was going to survive it. Or maybe she'd be like the phoenix and be reborn. When he teased her nipples, pinching one between his fingers while his teeth nibbled on the other, Emelise thought she was going to go mad. Then he slid a finger inside her. Her entire body reacted to it and her hips bucked. She'd never felt anything so intense in her life. Not even her best vibrator could make her feel the way he did with just a single finger inside her.

"Dat's it, Angel," Caine growled against her breast. He worked his finger in her a moment before he slipped a second in to join it. The snugness of her sheath was testament to the fact she'd not had a lot of sex. As her movements increased so did the thrusting of his fingers before he moved his thumb up to caress her clit.

Eme moaned and writhed against Caine's hand as an orgasm rushed over her. When it broke she gasped and stared up at him. "Holy fuck," she panted, while her muscles quivered in little aftershocks. "I've never… Gods, Caine, I've never come that fast in my life."

"It's not over yet, cher. Not by a long shot," he told her. He leaned in and kissed her deeply before he trailed kisses down her body. He removed her bra and tossed it to the floor before his hands slid her panties down her legs. Those he shoved into the pocket of his slacks as he kissed his way down to her sex. Her legs parted for him and he pushed them farther apart before he buried his mouth against her.

Emelise's back arched when Caine's tongue delved into her wet heat. "Oh fuck…oh gods, Caine." A husky moan escaped her as her hands slid into his hair to grip it lightly. How in the fuck had she gone this long thinking sex was boring? How could she possibly have been so wrong? Or maybe she wasn't wrong, maybe it was just different with Caine?

Caine

Caine was determined to give his mate more pleasure than she'd ever known. Sure, she said she'd never orgasmed from sex before, but he wanted the pleasure she'd gotten from her toys to pale in comparison to what he was doing to her. Her taste, her scent, drove him crazy and his cock throbbed painfully in his suddenly too-tight pants. He was holding onto his control by a thread that threatened to snap at any moment. His mouth moved up to suckle her clit and he slid fingers inside her again. He needed her to find her release because he needed to be inside her.

"Caine…please…oh gods, please…" Eme writhed against his mouth.

"Please, what, Angel?"

"Please…please fuck me. I need to feel you inside me."

Caine groaned against her. "Not yet, cher. Come for me one more time." He curled his fingers to stroke her G-spot while he teased her sensitive clit with his teeth and tongue.

The combination of his tongue on her clit and his fingers against her G-spot sent Emelise crashing over the edge. She cried out as her entire body shook from the orgasm.

"Dat's my girl." Caine quickly shed his clothes. He gazed down at her as he moved up to position himself between her welcoming thighs. He kept his eyes locked with hers as he pressed into her one slow inch at a time. "Fuck, Angel, you're so snug. You feel so good." He dipped his head to kiss her heatedly.

Caine watched her face as he filled her. The stark hunger and the need in her eyes made him smirk a little. The tightness of her sheath around him, however, made him groan. "Fuck, cher," he hissed before he kissed her again. "You just hold on and let me show you how it's supposed to feel," he growled. And then he began to move.

Emelise

Eme had glanced down as he'd pressed his shaft against her and she'd swallowed at his size. He wasn't a small man. All she could think at the time was how in the hell was all of *that* going to fit inside her? He didn't give her time to question him before he was pushing into her. Her hands went to his shoulders and she clung to him as her hips arched to meet him.

Never in her wildest dreams could she have imagined sex would feel this good. She'd been completely honest with him before. The only orgasms she'd ever had, until now, were ones she'd given herself with a vibrator. Those orgasms paled in comparison to the ones he'd already given her with his mouth and fingers. How much more intense was it going to be when he pushed her over the edge while he was inside her? Hell, she hadn't even realized she *could* orgasm more than once.

Emelise gripped his shoulders and clung to him as they moved together. Each thrust of his hips sent him deeper into her and caused the fire burning in her to flare that much hotter. Soon she was whimpering and whining, and her nails raked along his back. She became a veritable wildcat beneath him.

"Oh gods…Caine…please…" She wasn't sure how much more she could handle before she completely lost it. Her nails left angry, red marks along his back and she writhed and bucked beneath him.

"Tell me what you need, Angel," Caine growled in her ear. He wanted to hear her say the words.

"Please…please make me come!" Later she might be mad at herself for giving in and begging, because she'd always told herself she would never beg a man for an orgasm, but right now the only thing that mattered was finding relief.

"Wit' pleasure." He slipped a hand between them to tease her clit while he pounded into her.

That was all Emelise needed to send her crashing over the edge. She nearly screamed his name while her inner walls clenched and spasmed around him, urging him to follow her in release.

Caine

The first time he'd kissed her he'd suspected that Emelise would be a wildcat in bed. She'd been too passionate in her response for her to be a meek lover. Even so, he'd not fully expected her to be as wild as she got. The feel of her nails raking his back was maddening. When she begged him to make her come he could do naught but comply. Her walls clenching around him dragged him over the edge with her and he roared his pleasure. He knew the Pard would hear him but he really didn't give a damn.

When she finally stopped quivering beneath him, Caine half collapsed atop her before he rolled and took her with him. He kept his arms around her so she was draped over him and dipped his head to nuzzle her. "Dat was magnificent."

Emelise lifted her gaze to his. "I had no fucking idea it could feel like that. That…I have no words."

Caine chuckled and dipped his head to claim her lips. "Dat's okay, Angel, you don't need any. Stay tonight." He nibbled lightly on her bottom lip.

She paused for several seconds before she responded. "Okay." The word was almost a whisper as she curled against him.

Caine tugged the sheet up and draped it over them before he ran his hand up and down her side, caressing her skin. "Sleep, cher. We can talk more tomorrow."

Before she could do little more than murmur a sleepy "M'kay," she was drifting off to sleep.

Caine held her and watched her sleep. He suspected that, come morning, she would try to find a reason to push him away again, but he'd had a taste of her now; he wasn't about to let his mate slip through his fingers. With renewed resolve to make her see that her belief, that she couldn't depend on him to be there when she needed him, was a false one, Caine finally allowed sleep to claim him, as well.

Chapter Seven
Emelise

Eme awoke to find herself half-draped across Caine with his arms wrapped around her. Her head was on his chest and, as she shifted against him, she realized he was already awake. She took a breath to calm her racing heart before she lifted her face to look at him. "Good morning."

"Mornin', cher," he replied and dipped his head to capture her lips in a gentle kiss. "I could get used to dis."

"Yeah, well, don't get your hopes up, Caine. I'm not moving to the compound."

"I can be patient, Angel," he informed her and nuzzled her lips. "I tink dat'll change in time."

Eme shifted to try to get up but Caine's arms tightened around her. "Where you tink you're goin', cher?" He trailed kisses along her jaw before he moved her onto her back and continued the kisses until he took a nipple in his mouth.

Emelise shuddered and her fingers found their way into his hair. Any thought of getting out of bed fled under the onslaught of desire coursing through her. Soon he had her writhing and whimpering and she'd all but forgotten what they'd been talking about.

Caine

Caine had awakened with the sunrise but for the first time in years he'd had no desire to get up and start working. No, he'd wanted to lay there and enjoy the feel of his mate in his arms. Her scent clung to his skin and had caused his morning arousal to become almost painfully hard. He'd known sex with Emelise was going to be great, but he was still blown away by just how intense and mind-blowing it had been. The combination of watching her let go while simultaneously clenching around him had sent him to another plane of awareness for a moment.

Caine had watched her sleep and, when he'd felt her stirring, he'd smiled. He'd been able to tell she was trying to pull away, trying to create some distance between them, but he wasn't going to let that happen. He'd captured her lips in a kiss and ran his hands over her body. It didn't take long for him to ignite the fire in her again, and he focused on fanning the flames for as long as he could.

It wasn't until much later that he finally let her out of bed. She was stubborn and proud; he knew he could only push so far before she pushed back. Still, the fact she was there with him, the fact she'd stayed the night, meant he was making headway.

They showered together—and damn if that wasn't a test of his willpower to keep it at just a shower—before he fixed them both breakfast. "Now, about dat little trip you and Lily just came back from." He'd waited until they were at the table with plates in front of them.

Emelise groaned. "I know you think it was foolish, Caine, but we were careful and I had to go get my things from storage. Besides, you don't fucking own me."

"I don't just tink it was foolish, I know it was. It's not about owning you, cher. It was dangerous. Da Red Moon Clan was targetin' ever'one who was associated wit' the Pard. Da jaguars from Declan's team, dey infiltrated da Clan and found dat out. Da Red Moon Clan knew who you were. Dey knew what hotel you were stayin' in. Dey even knew what room you were in. Dey knew when you were at da club, doin' clean up. You and Lily tink you weren't followed, but you were. Da ones followin' you were called back by dere Alpha because he'd decided to attack da Pard's compound. If he hadn't called dem back, dey would have forced you and Lily off da road and taken you both. Da Alpha would have used both of you as leverage against us. What would you have done, den?"

"It doesn't matter because it didn't happen." Her chin lifted in defiance.

"It does matter!" He all but growled at her. "If dey had gotten dere hands on you, tings would have gone very bad, very quickly. You're right, I don't own you, but you *are* my mate and I would have slaughtered all of dem if dey'd harmed you. I wouldn't have spared a single adult member of Da Red Moon Clan. Not. A. Single. One."

Emelise

When he'd finally let her out of bed, she'd felt a pleasant soreness between her thighs. If sex with him was going to feel that good all the time, she was okay with being sore. Because holy fuck, the man had rocked her world and then some. "Breakfast smells really good," she'd murmured when they sat at the table. She was looking forward to enjoying it and then he'd had to go and ruin things.

Okay, she understood his anger over her and Lily taking off, she really did. He was an Alpha so he felt all protective of them and shit, but he was acting like she and Lily were careless little girls who weren't capable of thinking for themselves and it pissed her the hell off. Then his words sunk in.

Emelise stared at him. He was serious. He genuinely meant what he was saying. "I'm sorry, Caine." She realized, looking in his eyes, that she'd nearly driven him crazy with worry about her at a time when he'd needed to be focused. "What happened, with the jaguars?"

She watched as Caine rubbed a hand down his face. It was pretty obvious to her that he hadn't wanted to talk about it just yet, but he'd brought up her trip, which in turn reminded her that the Pard had taken on the jaguars while she and Lily were gone.

"Da Alpha and his lieutenants, da ones who weren't incapacitated before da fight, dey died. Da Red Moon Clan has a new Alpha and da Pard has a new ally."

"Did…we lose anyone?" She was finally showing some interest, and she was ashamed to realize that, beyond using some of the younger males to help her with the club, she'd not given the Pard, as a whole, much thought.

"No, Angel, we didn't lose anyone. We had some injured, but dey healed fine."

Emelise breathed a sigh of relief. "Thank Goddess. I'm sorry I've been so selfish and self-absorbed. Here I am using some of the younger Pard to help me get the club ready, and I can't even bother to ask about the welfare of everyone else."

Caine shook his head. "Tink no'ting of it, Angel. You're not used to bein' part of a group so dis is all new to you. You'll do better wit' time."

"Thanks for the vote of confidence. I should get back into the city, soon. I have a lot of work to do. I'm thinking of buying myself a boat so I don't have to keep asking Remy for a ride. Would you be willing to teach me the route to get here?"

Caine

"A boat? You really do plan on stayin' in da city, eh cher?" At her nod he wanted to growl but sighed instead. "A'course I'll teach you da route. Dat way you can come and go as you please. Maybe it'll help you change your mind about livin' here."

"Don't bet on it."

"A man can hope, cher, a man can hope," he replied with a wink. "I'll take you back to da city."

"Are you sure? I'm sure I can get Remy to do it."

"I'm sure, woman. I'll take you back when you're ready to go."

"Okay. Far be it for me to argue with you over a little boat ride."

Caine chuckled. "Smart woman," he teased and laughed when Emelise stuck her tongue out at him. They sat on the sofa, sipping tea for a while, before he caught Emelise glancing at her watch.

"I really should get back. It's getting kind of late."

"All right, Angel. I wish you'd reconsider and stay but I'm not goin' to push." He took their cups to the kitchen, rinsed them out, then returned to her side. He offered her his arm before he escorted her out of his home and down to the docks where several boats were tied up. He helped her onto his boat, got her settled, and headed through the swamp toward New Orleans.

Emelise

Emelise watched him as he headed his boat toward the city. She'd only ever ridden in Remy's and Caine's was a little nicer. It had thicker padding on the seats and he'd put a canopy up to shield her from the sun. She could feel the humidity rising in the air and she reached back to pull her hair up off her neck. "It looks like it's going to be a hot, sticky day."

"Mmhmm," Caine said, then flashed a wicked grin at her. "I wouldn't mind someting else being hot and sticky."

Emelise felt her cheeks heat up. "You just had to go there, didn't you? Careful, Caine, I might start thinking you're a sex-crazed fiend."

"When it comes to you, Angel, I am."

Her blush deepened and she rolled her eyes. He was in a mood, that was for sure. When they finally reached their destination, she moved to step out of the boat.

Caine saw her intention and his hand snaked out to gently grab her arm. "Not so fast," he said and pulled her into his arms. He lowered his head and pressed his lips to hers. His tongue traced the seam in them until they parted and he deepened the kiss.

Emelise moaned against his mouth. Why oh why hadn't she been faster? Better yet, why wasn't she just staying right there and asking him to take her back to the compound? No, just fucking no. She didn't want to play house with him. Once the novelty of things with her wore off, he'd get bored and she'd be left alone. At least this way she wouldn't have to see him every day. "I really need to go, Caine," she breathed against his lips.

Caine reluctantly released her and stepped back. "I'm not leavin' til I know you're safe inside your car, Angel."

Emelise opened her mouth to argue but she shut it, shook her head, and made her way to her car. She glanced back at him to find his eyes locked on her. He didn't budge until she was in the car with the door closed. From where she sat, she watched him turn the boat around and head back to the compound.

She'd seen the reluctance in his gaze but she was glad he didn't push her to return with him. They'd had an amazing night, and she didn't want to tarnish the memory with an argument, which would have happened if he'd not backed off. Once he was out of sight, she turned her car on and headed for the club. She had work to do.

Chapter Eight
Emelise

Emelise stood in the center of her club and looked around. The second floor was officially a VIP section. The stairs leading up to it had been redone in a dark wood, that Gage had hand-carved with roses and vines on the front of each stair, and he'd had wrought iron rails custom-made to pair with the woodwork. They, too, had roses and vines and looked delicate but they were sturdy. The bar was restored to it's original glory and shone in the soft lighting of the club. There were a few minor things still to do, mostly just adding the finishing touches, but once she had the club fully staffed, she'd be ready to open the doors.

"It looks amazing, Eme," Lily said. She turned and grinned at her best friend. "You really did an outstanding job getting this place cleaned up and ready."

Emelise smiled. "Thanks, girl, but I didn't do it alone. If Caine hadn't sent some of the Pard to help, I'd still be cleaning." Her gaze went to where the man in question was talking with Declan. They were having a small party there in the club to celebrate it's completion. Caine was still trying to get her to move to the compound, preferably in his bed, and she still stubbornly refused to do it. It wasn't that she didn't want to be with him—the sex was insane—but she was an independent woman and she still feared that one day he would get bored and end things between them.

"True, but it was your vision, your dream, that got you to this point," Lily countered. She saw where Eme's gaze kept going and shook her head. "Still being stubborn about not moving to the compound?"

"I'm staying independent, thank you very much." Eme gave her a mock glare before she laughed. "Don't get me wrong, I enjoy being with him, but how do I know the novelty isn't going to wear off?"

Lily shook her head. "That's not how it works when you're mates."

Eme waved the comment away. "I don't want to talk about that tonight. This is about celebrating the completion of Scarlet Flux. Now all I need to do is finish hiring people to work." Her voice bubbled with excitement. "Oh, guess who I got a call from this morning."

"I don't know, who?"

Eme grinned. "Mal. He'll be down week after next for a visit. I'm hoping to convince him to stay when he gets here."

"That is awesome. I hope he brings Venus out and performs while he's here. He's definitely talented."

"I know, right?" Emelise saw Caine and Declan headed their way and wrinkled her nose. "Testosterone alert," she joked before she turned her attention to her mate.

Caine

Caine was just a little frustrated with his mate. He'd gotten her to spend the night on multiple occasions but she still wouldn't even consider moving to the compound. He knew she thought it was a way for him to control her but that wasn't the case. He simply wanted to know she was close, and safe. Anything could happen in the city, and heaven help anyone who broke into her apartment and hurt her. He'd rip them to shreds.

They were at Scarlet Flux to celebrate it's completion, and his gaze kept going to Emelise where she was talking with Lily. He should have been paying closer attention to the wolf next to him but he couldn't help himself. When she was near, she consumed his every thought.

"You've got it bad, Caine. Why don't you just ask her to marry you already?" Declan said after Caine's gaze shifted to Emelise for the sixth time since they'd been talking.

Caine's eyes snapped back to him. "She isn't ready for dat. She still won't stay at da compound. If she won't do dat, she's not going to agree to marriage."

"But you do want to ask, don't you?"

Caine decided to turn the tables on him. "What about you? When are you plannin' on poppin' da question?"

Declan shrugged. "When it feels right. Don't go changing the subject, Caine. At least I know it's what I want, where I want things to go."

Caine growled at him. "Yes, da answer to your question is yes, but she isn't ready yet. Enough of dis, we're here to celebrate." He ended the conversation there and turned to go to his mate's side.

Caine turned his attention away from the conversation he and Declan had been having and focused instead on Emelise. "Dis place looks amazin', Angel." He leaned down to kiss her cheek. "It doesn't even look like da same place it did a month ago."

Emelise flashed him a grin. "Thanks. I know, I'm a little impressed myself. Have you guys seen the VIP section yet?"

Declan cocked a brow. "VIP section? Is that what the upstairs is? I just assumed it was a regular second level."

"Nope, it's for VIP's. It has its own bar so it'll have its own Drink Mixologist and serving staff."

"Drink Mixologist? I like that. That's definitely more catchy than 'bartender'," Declan told her.

Lily laughed. "I agree. When Eme told me that was what she was going to call the position, I told her it was perfect because it's different and quirky, just like her."

Emelise stuck her tongue out at her best friend before she motioned them all to the stairs. The VIP section was a bit more intimate, in that it was closer together, and where the downstairs had a mix of tables and booths, the VIP section was just tables, with chairs tucked around them, that butted up against plush couches. The décor kept the black, gold, and scarlet color scheme but in a more expensive flair. The lights, the table edges, and even the trim around the bar were all edged in gold.

"Holy shit, Eme, this is…wow," Lily said. She sat on one of the couches and groaned. "Oh man, I could sleep on this thing, it's so soft. Please tell me I'm on the VIP list."

"Of course you are, girl."

"I was only kidding but I'm good with that," Lily said with a grin.

"You outdid yourself up here, cher," Caine said after he checked everything out.

"Thank you. And thank you for first putting the idea in my head."

"My pleasure, Angel," Cain growled and leaned closer. "I'd like to put other ideas in your head."

Eme blushed and rolled her eyes at him. "You can tell you're a male; all you can think about is fucking." She said it only half in jest.

"Only when it comes to you, cher." He enjoyed their banter.

"Get a room you two," Lily said, flashing a grin their way. "I say we crack open that bottle of wine you brought out, Eme, and get this celebration started." Members of the Pard would be stopping by to check out the club and congratulate Emelise, but for now it was just the four of them there.

Eme laughed. "Bite me."

She reached for the bottle of wine to open it, but Caine beat her to it and carefully opened it with the corkscrew. He poured four glasses and lifted his up. "To my stunnin', sexy mate and her club." He watched her face as he made the toast.

"To Eme and Scarlet Flux—may it be open forever," Lily said and tapped her glass against her best friend's.

Emelise smiled at both of them. "Thanks. I'll drink to that," she said with a wink that made all of them laugh.

Caine set his glass down and took her hand to lead her away from Lily and Declan. "Dis really is amazin', Angel. You far exceeded what I thought it was goin' to look like when you were done wit' da club."

Emelise beamed at the praise. "That was the point, Caine. I wanted this to really be something. I worked my ass off to achieve this dream."

Caine dipped his head and brushed his lips across hers. "Enjoy your success, cher. You've earned it, but not only dat, you deserve it."

Eme started to lean into him but voices drifting up from downstairs stopped her. "Looks like some of the Pard has arrived." She pulled away from him so she could go downstairs.

Caine groaned silently and watched her go. That happened far more than he liked: getting interrupted by someone or something.

Emelise

Eme was only partly grateful for the interruption. Part of her had wanted to stay upstairs in Caine's arms and forget the world around them, but the other part, the logical part of her, knew it wasn't wise. The heat between them was unmistakable, but heat and attraction a relationship did not make. He kept talking about having her move to the compound, kept trying to entice her by offering to build her a greenhouse, but not once did he say anything about a serious commitment. She didn't want to just be his go-to for sex when he was horny.

Downstairs, she found that Gage had escorted Mia, and their son, to check out the club. Mamere Eulalie was with them and trailing in behind them, was the rest of Mia's family, including sweet little Sophie. "I'm so glad y'all could come to check the club out before it opens," she said, flashing them a genuine smile.

"Oh wow, dis place is amazin'," Mia said. "Gage told me no one would recognize it for da old, rundown bar it used to be, and I didn't believe him but dis…Eme, you did a wonderful job here."

Emelise beamed. "Thanks. It's definitely been a labor of love but I'm thrilled with the end result."

"And well you should be, child," Eulalie said. "I tink your Mama would be proud if she saw dis place right now."

Eme smiled. "I'd like to think so, yeah. Let me show you around." She gave them a tour that included the VIP section upstairs.

Sophie held a small, wrapped package in her hands and followed her siblings quietly. She was usually full to bursting with excitement, but today she seemed a bit awed by the club and it tempered her usual exuberance. When they reached the second floor she finally spoke up. "We have a present for you, Eme," she said and bounced a little on the balls of her feet. "Mama said I could carry it as long as I was real careful wit' it."

Emelise knelt down so she was more eye level with her cousin and smiled gently at her. "A present? That's so sweet. I'll bet you took really good care of it."

Sophie nodded. "Uh-huh." She held the package out to her. "We hope you like it. Mama tinks you will."

Emelise took the small package from her before she stood and moved to a table to unwrap it. "I'm sure I will." Once she got the wrapping paper off she gasped. Encased in a handmade frame was an autographed photo of Ella Fitzgerald. "Oh…my gods. This…this is…how? Where did you get this?"

"Mamere Eulalie," Eliza replied. "She met Ella years ago and she thought it would be da perfect gift for your club."

"Beau made da frame for it," Sophie told her.

"Thanks, Beau. It's gorgeous. Thank you, so much for this. It'll go right over the bar downstairs where anyone coming in can see it," Emelise assured them.

Throughout the day, Pard members filtered in and out before finally it was time to lock the doors and head home. "I think it's safe to say today was a success," Lily said and gave Eme a hug. "Let me know if you need any help with the hiring. Emile's been letting me handle that at the coffee shop, since a couple of people quit, so I've got a little experience with that now."

"Will do, girl. Have a good night." Eme watched Lily and Declan leave. That left just her and Caine alone in the club.

"Dis was a good day, Angel," Caine said as he slid up behind her and wrapped his arms around her. "Come back to da compound wit' me. I'd like you to stay da night," he added and dipped his head so he could nuzzle her neck.

"I can't. I have to be here first thing in the morning. I have several interviews, and we both know if I stay, getting up early isn't going to happen." Yeah, he wanted her to spend the night so they could fuck, no mention of committing to her though.

Caine groaned. "Maybe dis club isn't dat great an idea after all," he teased and kissed her temple. "Tomorrow night den, cher. Dinner— I'll cook my gumbo for you dat you like so much."

"Oo, throw in some cheesecake and I'm there," she said with a wink.

"Done," Caine replied with a laugh. He escorted her out to her car, gave her a quick kiss, and got in his truck.

Emelise saw him sitting there, watching her, and waved before she pulled away from the club and headed home. She wasn't surprised that he waited for her to leave before leaving himself.

Chapter Nine
Emelise

Emelise was at the club first thing in the morning. Her first interview was set for nine am which gave her time to hang the photo her cousins and grandmother had given her and finish her cup of coffee. She knew it was going to be a long day, between interviewing wait staff, putting away stock, and finishing up last minute details like making sure the linens were where they needed to be; she had her hands full. She wasn't complaining though because she was looking forward to it all. Her dream had finally come to fruition.

By two that afternoon, Emelise was getting tired. She'd had several interviews and was waiting to hear back on references from all of them, and she had one last interview to give. She was also getting hungry but since her last interview was due any minute, that would have to wait.

"Hey girl, how's it going so far?" Lily asked as she stepped into Scarlet Flux. "I was on my way to work and decided to stop by to see how the interviews were going." In one hand she carried a takeout bag from one of the local diners.

Emelise eyed the bag and arched a brow. "Please tell me there's food in that for me."

"Of course. I know how you can be; you get all distracted and forget to eat," Lily replied with a laugh.

"Damn, girl, you know me too well," Eme said with a laugh of her own. "Thanks. It's going okay. I'm waiting to hear back on the references from the people I interviewed earlier, and I have one final interview to give, then I'm done for the day."

"The other interviews went okay then?"

"Yeah, they did. They have experience and they're available immediately. I just need to fill the last three server positions and one Drink Mixologist, and it's done."

"I still love that title. It's fucking awesome," Lily said. She pulled out a burger and fries and set them in front of Eme, then pulled her own burger from the bag, as well.

"I had to go with something quirky, you know that."

"Yeah, I know." She watched Emelise a moment. "Okay, so I have to ask, how are things with Caine?"

Eme sighed. "I don't know, to be honest."

"What do you mean?" She slid onto one of the stools at the bar and dug into her lunch while they talked.

"Don't get me wrong, girl, the sex with him is phenomenal. I mean, I had no fucking idea sex could feel like that; it was always so boring before. But you keep talking about this deep connection you and Declan have and…it makes me wonder if Caine and I really are mates because he doesn't seem to have the same feelings for me that I have for him. Sure he asks me to spend the night with him so we can have mind-blowing sex, but a relationship isn't just sex. There's no hint of any kind of commitment from him. And you wonder why I don't think a man can be trusted to be there when he's needed?"

Lily winced. "Oh, Eme, I'm sure he does feel the same way. Maybe he's reluctant to push you for anything, worried you'll push back and put those walls up again or something."

Emelise shook her head. "I don't think that's the case. I think it's just sex for him. He doesn't want me to spend the night so we can just curl up and watch a movie or something; he wants me to spend the night so we can fuck."

"He's an ass, then," Lily said and gave her friend's hand a squeeze. "Don't give up on that commitment though, Eme, because you deserve it."

Eme shrugged. "I'm used to men not being dependable." She tried to ignore the hurt she felt at thinking she meant so little to him.

Before Lily could say anything else the last interviewee arrived. "That's my cue to head out," she said and stuffed her trash into the bag she'd brought their food in. "We need to have a girl's night out soon—you, me, and Shelli."

"That sounds good; just let me know when you two have a free night," Eme replied and turned her attention to the guy who was applying for the Drink Mixologist position for the VIP section.

Caine

"Caine Bordeaux, you are an asshole."

Caine looked up from his desk to frown at the she-wolf standing in his study doorway. "And why is dat, cher?"

"Why is that? He asks why when he should know damn well why," Lily growled. "Emelise. That's why."

His frown deepened. "I'm not sure I know what you're talkin' about."

Lily stalked into the room and stopped when she reached his desk. She leaned forward and propped her hands on top of it so she could look him in the eye. "I'm talking about the fact you keep asking her to stay the night so you can fuck while leaving the impression that the *only* thing you want from her is sex."

"What are you talkin' about? Dat couldn't be further from da truth."

"Oh really? Then why did she tell me that the only thing you two do when you invite her to stay the night is fuck? There's no cuddling in front of the television, just food then fucking, which you could get from any tramp in the city. As far as she's concerned, you two can't really be mates because you obviously don't have any feelings for her beyond your leopard wanting to fuck its chosen female. Do you have any idea what your insensitive attitude is doing to her? She already believed men only wanted one thing from a woman and when they got tired of it they moved on, so what do you do? You reinforce that belief by *not* showing her any kind of commitment!"

Caine's eyes narrowed at her. "I've asked her to move to da compound, even asked her to move into my home, more den once, and she always says no."

"And have you told her how you feel about her? Beyond the whole 'I want to fuck you' thing?" Lily countered. "Caine, she didn't grow up with other shifters; she doesn't know the first damn thing about mates and how intense the connection is between them. You haven't given her any reason to believe you want her close for more than just easy access to a good fuck."

Caine stared at Lily for several minutes while his brain processed what she was saying. "Fuck," he hissed. "I've been givin' her space, lettin' her decide when to take tings to a deeper level. I didn't want to scare her off or make her pull away." He rubbed his brow. "You're tellin' me dat all I've done is make tings worse?"

"That's exactly what I'm telling you. She's afraid to let a man close because her only experiences with them has taught her they can't be counted on, and you not committing to her isn't helping her to change her mind. She thinks you only want her for sex, which means that eventually the newness will wear off and you'll move on to someone else."

He wanted to snarl at Lily for pointing out the stupidity of his actions, but he didn't because he'd needed the wake-up call. "Thank you, cher, for not bein' afraid to point out I'm bein' stupid."

"Don't thank me, Caine; just make things right with Eme. She loves you, you know. Oh, she might not be willing to admit it out loud, just yet, because she thinks it's one-sided, but she does love you. And that scares the shit out of her because it makes her vulnerable. It puts her heart at risk of being broken."

"I'll make dis right," he assured Lily. He had a lot of work to do before Emelise came over for dinner. How had he not realized she would take his reluctance to push for something deeper to mean he didn't have feelings for her?

"Good. I've got to get out of here before I'm late for work," Lily said and left.

Chapter Ten
Emelise

Eme packed an overnight bag and headed out to the compound. She'd told Caine she would have dinner with him and she knew if he asked her to stay, she would. Was she a glutton for punishment? She was in love with him but it seemed to her that all she was to him was a good lay. A soft sigh escaped her as she climbed into the small boat she'd purchased. She paid a docking fee to the marina in order to have easy access to the water so she could get to the compound whenever she wanted to. She'd found out that the docks, where she used to meet Remy whenever he picked her up, were owned by the Pard, and really, she could have kept her boat there but…maybe it was stubbornness on her part that caused her to use the public marina instead.

At least one part of her life was going smoothly. As long as the references checked out for everyone she interviewed, the club would be fully staffed. The last of the stock was arriving the following day, and everything was in order for their grand opening in two days. She was cutting it close, staff-wise, she knew, but she wanted to be sure everyone she hired was a good fit.

If only her personal life would fall in line, as well. She was still trying to figure out exactly how she'd managed to get herself mixed up in a purely physical situation when her heart wanted more. Better yet, why the fuck was her heart making this difficult for her? Purely physical was better; it meant she wouldn't have to face a broken heart when he moved on. With a soft hiss of frustration she put the thought out of her mind and headed into the bayou.

Caine

Caine was waiting when Emelise arrived. As always she took his breath away with her fresh-faced beauty and her carefree attitude toward life. "Hello, Angel." He leaned down to kiss her cheek. "Did you have a good day?"

"Hey. Yeah, I did. I'm waiting on the references from two of my interviews to come back, and if they come back clean, I'll be fully staffed. I know, I know, I'm cutting it awfully close to the grand opening," she said before he could comment.

Caine chuckled. "I had no doubt you would succeed, cher," he told her as he escorted her to his home.

"You always have such confidence in me. I don't get it."

"I already told you, Angel, your determination can't be stopped." He'd taken what Lily said to heart, and he knew Emelise expected a quick meal and then him trying to get her naked, but tonight was going to be very different. He opened the door and ushered her inside with a faint smirk on his face.

Emelise

Eme saw the smirk and arched a brow at him. What was he up to? That smirk said he was plotting something; she just wasn't sure what. Knowing him, it was something devious that would leave her weak and sweaty. She stepped into his house and blinked. Or maybe not. There were several vases of roses scattered about, but the real surprise was the fact they weren't alone. "Mamere Eulalie? Eliza? What are y'all doing here?" she asked because there, seated around the living room, were her grandmother and cousins, including Mia, Gage, and their infant son, Elijah.

"I invited dem to dinner," Caine told her once he got the door closed behind them.

"You did?" She gave him a puzzled look.

"A'course I did. Dey're your family; we should have family dinners from time to time, don't you tink?"

"Excuse us a minute," she said to them and opened the door to drag him back outside. "What are you up to Caine Bordeaux?"

Caine shook his head. "I'm not 'up to' anyting, cher. You're my mate, dat makes dem family, not just part of the Pard." He reached out and caressed her cheek. "I tink it's high time I show you dat dis between us is someting real, someting more den a physical attraction."

Emelise stared at him a moment. "Oh," she said softly. She swallowed a sudden bout of nerves. "Okay, then. Thank you."

"You're welcome, Angel," he murmured and gave her a quick kiss before he escorted her back inside.

"Sorry about that," Emelise said. "It's really great to see all of you."

"Ever'ting okay?" Eulalie asked her granddaughter.

"Yep. I was just a little puzzled by the sudden invite since this was a first for him." She was still a little thrown by his admission.

"Not to change da subject… Okay, I lied, it is to change da subject," Mia said, an amused look on her face, "but are you lookin' forward to da grand openin' of your club? It's da day after tomorrow, right?"

"Yes it is. I'm excited and a little scared because I have no idea how it's going to go."

"You know we'll all stop in to support you, or almost all of us," Eliza said. Her younger children wouldn't be able to go because it was a club that sold alcohol.

"I know, and you have now idea how much your support means to me. It's so crazy too because it was just me and Mama for so long; the realization that I have family who support my dream is a bit…staggering. After Mama died I didn't think I'd ever have that kind of support system again."

"Well, you're stuck wit' us, cher," Beau told his cousin.

Eme grinned. "I'm good with that."

"Stuck wit' me, too," Caine growled in her ear. "Who's hungry? Dinner's done."

They all sat at the large table and once again Emelise found herself caught up in their conversations. She loved listening to them talk bout things going on in their lives. Having Caine there to be part of it made it that much more right, that much more perfect. Not that she was willing to let *that* secret out. Nope, she was keeping that to herself, for now, at least.

Caine

Caine listened to their banter and realized he enjoyed having her family there. It had taken a few minutes for them to relax since he was their Alpha, but as soon as one of them started really talking, it was like the floodgates suddenly opened and soon the table was buzzing with all their chatter. When he glanced over at his mate, he couldn't hide the pleased smile that tugged at the corners of his mouth. She looked so happy with her family there enjoying dinner with them. This was what Lily was talking about. The happiness he saw in his mate's eyes while they had dinner with her family made him realize that he had been focusing more on the physical aspects of their relationship than the emotional one. It was time that changed.

It was fairly late when the Rousseau clan finally left, leaving Caine and Emelise alone. He went to her and wrapped his arms around her. "Dis was a good night," he said and kissed her temple. "I liked seein' you so happy wit' your family around."

Emelise smiled up at him. "I really enjoyed them being here. Thank you for this, Caine."

"You don't need to thank me, Angel. I was happy to do it. Let's go to bed; I want to hold you."

Emelise

Emelise'd had so much fun talking with her family that she hadn't even noticed how much time had passed. At some point they'd all moved back to the living room and begun a game of charades, which she really sucked at, but she still had fun with it. It wasn't until little Sophie was falling asleep, where she was curled up on the sofa, that everyone finally headed back to their own homes.

She'd cleaned up while Caine showed them out, then turned to watch him. He'd shown her a different side of him, one she hadn't realized existed. He knew how to have fun and he was wicked good at charades. "If we ever play that again, we're doing it as partners," she said with a laugh. They'd ended up on opposite teams, men versus women, and the guys had smoked them at it.

Caine chuckled. "Deal," he'd said and pulled her into his arms.

She'd leaned into him with the expectation of some steamy kisses so when he'd said he wanted to hold her, she was startled. "Just hold me? Really?"

"Yes, just hold you," he replied and pressed a kiss to her lips. "You drive me crazy, cher, but tonight I just want to curl up wit' you in my arms and fall asleep knowin' you'll be dere when I wake up."

Her heart skipped a little at the thought. "Okay then," she said and smiled at him. "Let's go to bed." She didn't doubt his attraction for her—she could smell it—but it meant so much to her that he was willing to put the physical aside sometimes just to be *with* her.

Once in the bedroom Emelise changed into the lounge pants and tank top she'd brought to sleep in, not that she usually got to do so, but she liked to have it close when she woke up in the morning. She crawled into bed. The pajama bottoms, Caine tugged on, hung low on his hips and made her mouth water. Morning. She could wait until morning. Then they could get all sweaty and shower together to clean up before she had to leave.

Caine

Caine had watched her change and had silently groaned. It was going to be hard falling asleep with her without letting his hands wander, but she deserved more from him than just lust. She deserved love and love wasn't always about fucking. It was about just being together, holding one another, being close as they drifted off to sleep. He wasn't going to screw this up.

He slid into bed with her and opened his arms. When Emelise curled against him, he pulled her closer and tugged the sheet up over them. "G'night, Angel," he growled in her ear.

"Good-night, Caine," she replied. She gave him a sleepy smile before she sighed and relaxed in his arms.

Caine caressed her side as she slowly drifted off. Watching her sleep he couldn't help but wonder, and not for the first time, what he'd done to be so lucky as to have this amazing, stubborn, strong woman in his arms, in his life. Whatever gods were watching over him, he was thankful to them for bringing her into his life. "I'll do whatever it takes to show you dat what we have is real, dat I'm not goin' anywhere." He whispered the words before he finally let his own eyes close as sleep dragged him into oblivion.

Chapter Eleven

Emelise

A whirlwind of activity flitted around the interior of Scarlet Flux. In ten minutes the doors would officially open for the first time, and Emelise was making sure everything was perfect. She kept fearing that something was going to happen to throw things off, or some glitch was going to pop up to ruin the evening, and it turned her into a bundle of nervous energy.

"Eme, relax, you've got this, girl," Lily said, watching her best friend run around frantically. "The place looks great, people are already lined up outside waiting to get in, the performers are ready to go, everything is going to go smoothly."

"But what if something doesn't? What if I've forgotten something?"

Lily looked at Caine as if to say 'Do something.'

Caine moved to his mate and gently gripped her arms. "You haven't forgotten anyting, Angel. Ever'ting is in place. Take some deep breaths. Dat's my girl. Now, don't you feel calmer?" he asked when she did as he suggested.

Emelise closed her eyes and took several slow, deep breaths to calm her racing nerves. "Yeah, I do. Thanks, baby."

Caine brushed his lips across hers. "Dat's what I'm here for, to help you wit' anyting you need," he told her.

Eme touched his cheek. "Okay, it's showtime." She nodded at the band. As she headed to open the doors and cut the ribbon, they started playing.

Derrick

Derrick Winton wanted to surprise his wife, Angie, for their anniversary. She loved blues, and when he heard there was a new club opening up on Decatur, he knew he had to take her to it. He escorted her in and chuckled at the grin that lit up her face.

"Oh, honey, this place is great," Angie said. "You always find just the perfect way to surprise me."

"I try, love, I try." His gaze moved around the club when it fell on a face that had his eyes widening in shock.

Angie saw the look on her husband's face and frowned. "Derrick? What's wrong?"

"I feel like I've just seen a ghost," he said after a moment.

She followed his gaze and blinked. "That young woman, she looks a lot like…"

"Adelaide." Angie knew about his first love, his high school sweetheart who suddenly took off, without a word, in their junior year of high school. It was like she'd disappeared off the face of the earth, and she'd never once contacted him to explain the reason why. Looking at the young woman, who looked so much like his first love, he had a very troubling thought. If she was the age he had a feeling she was, he had a daughter he'd known nothing about. "Maybe this is why she left."

Angie slipped her arm around her husband. "Let's go talk to her. But let me do the talking. You're likely to fall all over yourself," she teased to try and help him to calm down.

Derrick looked at his wife and shook his head. "You know me too well," he said. "Okay, you do the talking," he added.

Emelise

"Excuse me, Miss? Do you happen to be related to an Adelaide Rousseau?"

Emelise turned at the question. There weren't that many people outside of the Pard who knew that. She arched a brow at the older couple standing in front of her. "Yes, I am. She's my mama. How do you know her?" Maybe they went to school together or something, and the woman wanted to know if her mother was there too.

"I think...I think I might be your father."

Eme felt like she'd had the wind knocked out of her and had to lean against the bar behind her. Of all the things she'd been expecting to hear, that wasn't one of them.

Caine, noticing his mate's distress, moved to her side immediately. "What is it, Angel?" he asked and eyed the couple in front of her.

It took several seconds for Emelise to get her mind to function enough to respond. "I-I need…I need to find Lily; I need her to take over a moment."

Caine motioned to Remy. "Go get Lily; she's upstairs," he said and watched his lieutenant rush off. "She'll be here in a minute, cher." He slipped an arm around her and it tightened at her shaking.

Lily

Lily was upstairs in the VIP section enjoying the music and the festive atmosphere. "Can you believe how busy this place is? If she keeps getting business like this, she'll be rewarded for her efforts in no time," she said to her mate.

"That woman has a damn good head for business when it comes to a jazz club, that's for sure," Declan agreed. He spotted Remy headed their way and cocked a brow. "What's up?"

"Dere you are. Caine sent me to find you; someting's goin' on downstairs. Emelise looks upset," Remy said once he reached Lily's side.

Lily frowned. "Someone better not be trying to ruin Eme's day or I'ma have to hurt them," she growled and headed to the stairs.

Declan gave Remy a questioning look but the Cajun shrugged to indicate he wasn't sure what was going on. "Fuck," he muttered under his breath and followed his mate.

"Eme? What's wrong? What's going on?" Lily asked the instant she was at he friend's side.

Emelise

When Lily reached them, Emelise turned to her. She knew she was pale, she could feel it, but she couldn't fill Lily in right then. "I need you to take over greeting people for a bit. I-I need to go to my office." Her eyes begged Lily to not ask any questions right then.

"Okay, sure, Eme, whatever you need. But I hope to get an explanation later."

"You will," Emelise promised before she moved away from the bar. "Follow me," she said to the man who she was almost certain was right when he suspected he might be her father.

Eme kept hold of Caine's hand until they were in the hallway leading to her office. Once there, she moved closer so she was tucked under his arm until they reached her office door. Once she was sitting behind her desk and the couple were seated across from her, she turned her attention to them. "Why do you think you might be my father?"

"How old are you?" the man asked in response to her question. "You're, what, twenty-five? Going on twenty-six?"

Eme nodded. "Yes. Oh gods, you're the reason Mama left New Orleans."

"I don't understand. Why is Derrick the reason your mother left here?" the woman asked. "I know about Adelaide; we don't have any secrets. He knows who my first love was too."

Eme wished she could have talked with Caine about this beforehand but that wasn't an option. She had no idea if he was comfortable with people knowing about the Pard's existence because, while people knew in theory that shifters existed, their reactions when they met one were sometimes a bit unexpected. There wasn't any way to check with him first so she just had to go with it.

"If you're like most people, you know, in theory, that humans aren't at the top of the food chain, but you've never really given it a lot of thought because you've had no reason to."

She felt Caine move closer to her and when he rested his hand on her shoulder she knew he supported her decision to be completely honest with them.

"Unless you were faced with the physical proof, you could dismiss the claims that humans weren't the Alpha species as just conspiracy-theorist bullshit someone made up, because they don't want to live in the real world and instead prefer to live in a fantasy world, where all manner of creatures exist. The truth is, however, that it's not conspiracy-theorist bullshit. Shifters exist. We come in various types: wolves, bears, leopards," she said and motioned to her and Caine.

"When my mama started dating you, she knew she wasn't supposed to. She knew that her Alpha, the leader of the Pard—that's what leopard shifters call their group— wouldn't allow a real relationship with a human but Mama didn't care. She liked you, came to really care about you. I think you were her first love, too. That's not to say all shifter groups have a rule against humans and shifters dating, or even marrying, but her Alpha was, to be blunt, a prejudiced bastard. He felt humans were lesser and, as such, relationships with them weren't allowed."

The woman shared a look with her husband before she turned her attention to Emelise. "So, are you telling us that you two turn into animals on the full moon like in the stories?"

Emelise laughed. "No, not just on the full moon. But yes, we can turn into leopards. Haven't you wondered why, every now and then, there are echoes of what sounds like big cats in the bayou?"

The man looked at his wife before he nodded. "I have, yes, but this is a bit much to believe."

"Allow me, cher." Caine moved away from the desk and removed his shirt. "Don't worry, I'm not strippin'," he said with a wink. He didn't need to. As an Alpha, he could change just part of his body if he so wished, and that was what he did now. Fur flowed over the upper part of his body, his hands turned into paws, and his face shifted to that of his animal.

"Sweet baby Jesus," the man said, eyes wide. "That...and your mother could do that?" he asked, voice a little breathless from the spike of fear that went through him.

"Not that, no. Only an Alpha can change just part of their body and Mama wasn't an Alpha anything. But that's why she left. See, when she realized she was pregnant, she had to run away. If her Alpha had known, he would have made her get rid of the baby, and if she'd ever brought me back here, he would have killed me because I wasn't 'pure'. When a shifter has children with a human, there's no guarantee their child will be able to shift and he, well, like I said, he was a bigot."

"He was a cruel, sadistic bastard who cared not'ing for his Pard. Dat's why he's no longer here," Caine growled once he'd put his shirt back on.

"That too," Emelise agreed.

"Why didn't she tell me? Did she really think I would abandon her and our child?"

"I don't know. Mama was young, she was scared, maybe she wasn't sure how you would feel about being a daddy so young, or how you would react if I shifted in front of you without her there to explain everything. Mama never really talked about that and now that she's gone, I can't ask her any questions."

Emelise knew she'd just dropped something very heavy in his lap. She could tell, from his stunned silence, that he was trying to wrap his brain around everything he'd just learned. That was why his next words startled her

"Would you...be open to getting together to talk sometime? You have some siblings: three half-brothers and a half-sister; I'm sure they'd love to meet you too."

Eme swallowed. Did she want to meet them? She thought about it, thought about how lonely her childhood had been growing up, and nodded. "I think I'd like that."

"Great. I'll make sure you have both our numbers and you can let me know when you're up for it. We'll do this on your time."

"Maybe we should introduce ourselves," the woman said, because she'd realized no names had passed between them.

The man gave his wife a sheepish look. "Right. Sorry, I'm Derrick Winton; this is my wife, Angie," he said and offered his hand to his long-lost daughter.

"Emelise Rousseau. This is my mate, Caine Bordeaux," she replied and shook hands with him. It all felt so surreal to her.

"We'll go and give you some space," Derrick said. "I'm so glad to meet you and...I'm so sorry your mama died. I'm guessing when you said 'now that she's gone' you meant your mother passed away. She was something special. That night we spent together, I never once regretted it. I loved your mother, as much as a seventeen-year-old boy could love a girl, anyway."

"Thank you for that," Emelise replied and watched them go.

Caine

The entire time they were talking Caine kept close to his mate. He could feel her shaking, could hear the pain and fear in her voice when she talked about her mother, and all he'd wanted to do was wrap her up in his arms and protect her. This was one thing he couldn't protect her from though. This was her past, a past he knew had left an indelible mark on her life. The only thing he could do was offer his silent support.

In any other situation, had a member of the Pard shared the truth with humans about what they were, without first getting his approval, there would have been hell to pay, but this wasn't a normal situation. Emelise didn't have time to take him aside and discuss it with him first. Telling her father the truth was the only option she'd had available to her if she hoped to have any sort of a relationship with the man, and clearly she did.

As soon as the door closed behind them, Caine pulled Emelise into his arms. He felt her body shaking in silent tears and just held her.

His hand moved in little comforting circles on her back and he nuzzled her hair. A soft rumbling echoed in his chest in an attempt to soothe her. His heart was hurting for her.

Emelise

To say she was in an emotional turmoil would be putting it lightly. Her entire world had been thrown completely off kilter. She'd known, theoretically, that there was a chance she might run into the man who'd helped bring her into this world, but she'd never really given it concrete thought. In a city this big, she could go her entire life without ever seeing the same person twice, unless they happened to move in the same circles or live in the same area. Plus, there was no guarantee he'd stayed in the area; people moved away from their hometowns all the time. Yet, on one of the most important nights of her life, the man who'd fathered her, walked into her life and turned her world upside down.

She kept it together until her office door closed behind them. The instant Caine pulled her into his arms, the tears started. She couldn't stop them. Her body shook, and she wasn't sure if she was crying for all the lost years or if it was just because her emotions were overwhelmed.

Caine scooped her up and moved to sit on the small, leather sofa she had tucked into one corner of her office. There he held her on his lap and continued to soothe her until her crying slowly subsided.

Eme wasn't sure how long he held her like that before her cries quieted and the tears stopped. When she looked up at him, she knew her makeup was ruined. "Thank you."

"Anytime, Angel. Anyting you need, I'm here, cher."

Eme rested there in his arms a moment longer before she reluctantly pulled away, She used the bathroom in her office to fix her makeup and was grateful she didn't look *too* bad. Some of their guests would know she'd been crying, but she didn't have to explain that to anyone until she felt ready to. "I need to get back out there," she said and squared her shoulders. "This is my grand opening; I can't hide in here all night."

Caine chuckled. "Dat's my girl," he said. "Always so stubborn," he teased and offered his arm to escort her back out front.

Emelise was feeling a little…fragile as Caine escorted her back out into the club. She plastered on a smile for the benefit of her guests, but inside she was still shaky as they made their way to where Lily and Declan were. She could see the worry on Lily's face and it made her smile, just a little.

"Hey, you okay?" Lily leaned over and gave Eme a quick hug. "Do I need to kick someone's ass?" she teased.

Lily's comment, when she hugged her, caused Eme to burst into laughter. "Oh my gods, girl, how do you always know just what I need?"

"Because we're besties, duh," Lily countered. "Tomorrow, lunch, you and me," she said and left it at that.

"Definitely. Let's go to that new little cafe that just opened up: Little Eden Cafe."

"Sounds like a plan," Lily replied. "Now, let's go enjoy this fantabulous music." She looped arms with Emelise so they could move closer to the stage.

Eme laughed softly. Lily knew exactly what to say or do to pull her out of a funk. She was so grateful for her friendship.

Chapter Twelve
Lily

"Okay girl, start talking." They'd decided to meet at the cafe a little after one, and she'd managed to hold off until they'd both ordered sandwiches and taken a seat at one of the outdoor tables the cafe offered.

Emelise had slept a little fitfully because the conversation she'd had with Derrick and Angie, her father and, well, stepmother, kept replaying every time she drifted off. As a result, she was a little grumpy but it wouldn't be fair to take it out on her best friend. "Where do I start?"

"The beginning?"

Eme stuck her tongue out at her, then rubbed her brow. "Okay, so, you know the older couple I was talking with last night? He knew my mama," she said. She lifted her gaze to Lily's as she continued. "He's my biological father."

Lily stared at Emelise. "Oh, wow. Eme. That's…damn, that's got to throw things really off-kilter for you. I mean, you weren't really expecting to ever meet him, were you?"

"Not really. I mean, I knew theoretically it was a possibility, but people move away from their hometowns all the time, right? And New Orleans is a big city. I mean, what are the fucking chances that he or his wife would be such jazz fans that they'd make a special trip to come to my grand opening?"

"I'd say, not very high, and yet that's exactly what happened."

"Yeah, I know. And I don't know how to feel about it. He said he loved my mama, as much as a seventeen-year-old boy can love a girl, and that it had upset him when she took off. That doesn't really mesh with what Mama told me, but then Mama also was mistaken about the reason why her papa told her she wasn't welcome back here."

Lily listened and tapped a finger on the table. "Have you opened that locked chest yet? I remember you saying you needed to figure out how to get into it without damaging it."

"No, I haven't. Why?"

Lily grinned. "Gimme a sec," she said. "Oh, by the way, have you heard the news? Your mate gave Declan part of New Orleans for his own pack's territory. We're officially the Ghostpoint Pack, and it consists of me, him, and his team. For now. Until we can get other misfit shifters to join."

Eme blinked. "No, I didn't know that. That is fucking awesome, girl!"

"I know, right? Declan and I are looking into buying a house since my apartment is in Pard territory, meaning we'll have to move. It's okay though because I think I found the perfect house. Anyway, gimme a sec. I'm going to call Echo; she's one of the jaguars in our pack who infiltrated the Red Moon Clan in order to find out what they were up to. Declan says she's amazing with locks. You name it, she can open it, no matter what it is or how tight the security on it."

"That could come in handy," Eme said with a laugh.

"Like now," Lily said with a cheeky grin before she made the call. "Hey, Echo, it's Lily. I'm good, you? That's great. Listen, I have a favor to ask you. Emelise has this big locked chest her mama left that she doesn't have the key to. She wants to see what's in it but she doesn't want to damage it. Could you open it for her?"

"Can a soprano hit a high note?" Echo asked loud enough for Emelise to hear. "Of course I can. Just text me when and where you want it done and I'm on it."

"Thanks, Echo," Lily said and hung up.

Emelise snickered. "I like her; she's funny."

"She is. She's also deadly and wicked faithful to her team and her Pack."

"Hey, let's get this to go so we can go see what my mama felt was so important it had to be locked up."

"Sounds like a plan to me," Lily replied.

Emelise

Emelise was trying to be patient. They were waiting for Echo to arrive so she could unlock the chest for them. It wasn't extremely heavy, but at the same time, she knew it wasn't empty because she could hear things moving in it when she picked it up.

"Eme, pacing isn't going to make her get here any faster."

Emelise gave her a dirty look, then laughed. "I know, I can't help it. I'm just so curious to find out what's in it."

Lily's phone beeped and she grinned. "Well, you'll know soon enough, Echo just pulled up."

Emelise met the jaguar at the door. "Hi, you must be Echo. Emelise," she said and offered her hand.

"Nice to meet you. Make sure you keep that man of yours on his toes, can't let them get too complacent," she said with a snicker.

Eme laughed. "No, we can't." She motioned her in and closed the door behind her.

"Oh, this'll be easy," Echo said and sat down in front of the chest. She pulled a small case out of her pocket and took two thin tools out of it. Within a minute she popped the lock. "There you go. I haven't seen an old chest like this in years. The older locks can be tricky because they get a lot of buildup in them. That one was a piece of cake."

"Thanks," Eme said. "I really appreciate it."

"No problem," Echo replied. "I'll head out and give you some privacy to see what's inside."

Eme watched her go before she turned to the chest. She swallowed before she lifted the lid and stared down into it. As she started pulling things out, her eyes filled with tears. There were photo albums she'd never seen, and when she opened them, she realized they were ones her mother had put together before she was born. There were some little keepsakes in it, and the yellow blanket she'd taken Emelise home from the hospital in.

Then, on the bottom, beneath the baby blanket, she found a small bundle of letters. One was addressed to Eulalie, one to Buford, one to Eliza, there was one for Eme, and on the bottom of the list was a letter for Derrick. Eme looked at the front of each one before she set all but hers aside. With shaking hands she opened the envelope and removed the paper inside.

My sweet girl,

If you're reading this, then I know I am no longer here with you. I don't know why I am gone, or how long I was with you before I left this world, but that matters not. There are so many things I should have told you when you were growing up—things you needed to know, but I was afraid. Afraid to let my secrets out, afraid to cloud your view of the world.

For a long time, after I left New Orleans, I lived in anger and hurt. I lashed out at my parents by refusing to tell them about you until you were much older, and by letting you believe they never wanted you. I didn't think about the pain that might cause you. It was selfish of me, my sweet angel, and you didn't deserve that.

I want you to know, I am so proud of the young woman you're becoming. I see so much of myself in you: your drive and determination to succeed no matter what you do and your love of life. You are the best thing that ever happened to me, Eme, and I never once regretted my decision to leave home.

I know things were tough when you were little; I know you didn't always understand why we were alone and not with a Pard, or why you had to keep it a secret that you were a shifter, but I tried my best to guide you and I hope I did a good job.

In this envelope, there is a key. It goes to a safety deposit box at the Bank of New Orleans. In it you will find several things, including the deposit book for an account I opened there shortly before I left. If you present the bank with a copy of my death certificate, they will give you access to the box and it's contents. I've had money going into that account for years, money to help you achieve any goal you set for yourself.

I know you often wondered about your papa, wondered why I never spoke of him. He was my first love. His name was Derrick,

Derrick Winton, and he was something else. He was on the football team; you'd think a jock wouldn't notice the shy girl, but he did. I think he loved me too. When I left home, I couldn't tell him the reason why. I couldn't tell him I was pregnant. He was headed to college; he had such goals—I couldn't change his future by telling him he'd gotten me pregnant.

Then, when I knew he'd graduated, I wanted to tell him but I found he'd moved on. He had a wife, they had a baby, and it hurt to think maybe I'd never meant that much to him. That was when I met Sean, and we both know how that went. It took me a long time to realize that by not telling Derrick about you, I was hurting you, too. It was selfish of me to want to keep you all to myself, and when I think about the time you could have had with him, I feel ashamed. I hope you can forgive me, sweet angel, for keeping so much from you.

If you go to New Orleans and meet my parents, please, try not to hate them. They could only do as their Alpha commanded and he was a horrid beast. I hope you can find it in your heart to forgive them the way I never could. Be better than I was, my girl. And remember, I love you, Emelise Acadia Rousseau, my treasure, my pride, the one good thing I really did in this life.

Your loving Mama

Emelise read the letter several times while tears fell freely down her cheeks. "Oh, Mama, I love you," she whispered. "She was thinking about me, about my future, even before she had me. There's a savings account here at the Bank of New Orleans that is now mine. She'd been putting money into it all these years."

"Oh, Eme." Lily scooted over to her and hugged her. "Your mom really loved you; anyone who saw you two together would know that."

"Yeah, she did. I think she'd be happy if she knew I'd forgiven her mama for turning her back on us. It's what she wanted, for me to not hate them for it."

"Are you going to deliver the other letters?"

"Yeah, I am. Mama wrote them for a reason. Her papa isn't here to read his, but I'll give it to Mamere Eulalie."

"I'm glad I got Echo to come open this thing for you. You uncovered some really good memories here," Lily said, motioning to the photo albums.

"I'm glad you did too." They spent some time looking through the photo albums, before Eme put the letters away, until she could deliver them, and she walked Lily to the door. She didn't need to know what any of the other letters said—they weren't for her eyes—but the people they were written for deserved to read them.

Chapter Thirteen

Malcolm

This was, by far, the craziest thing he'd ever done in his life. And the most reckless. He'd told Emelise he was coming 'for a visit'. What he didn't tell her was that he'd decided to quit his job at The Inferno, pack everything he owned into an U-haul truck, and relocate to hot and humid New Orleans.

He wasn't too worried about the heat and humidity; he knew he'd acclimate fairly easily, thanks to his beast. Lions liked the heat. What he was worried about was working enough to support himself. Sure Eme had a club she'd just opened up, but would Venus be a hit in The Big Easy? That was the real question.

He'd played it smart, when making his decision to move. He'd gotten online, looked at real estate for sale in New Orleans, and found himself a house he liked. He had a nice little nest egg saved up, and it came in handy now to help him get his own place That way he wouldn't have to put things in storage when he got to where he was going. He just had to unpack. "Goodbye, Phoenix, hello Big Easy," he said as he pulled onto the I-10, which would take him right to the heart of New Orleans.

Four days after he left Phoenix, Malcolm looked around the house he'd purchased on N. Roman Street. It had four bedrooms and two bathrooms and was done up in earth tones. He liked the color scheme so that was one thing he didn't have to worry about changing. It was going to take him a while to completely unpack, but at least the truck was unloaded. Sure he had to move around stacks of boxes, but hey, at least they were organized stacks. It was time to make a call to Miss Emelise Rousseau. He could unpack more later. No, he wasn't procrastinating. Oh hell, who was he kidding? Yes, he was.

Emelise

Emelise was curled up on her sofa with a glass of sweet tea while Lily did the same in the chair across from her. "You're sure you're really okay?" A few days ago Gathering Grounds was robbed just as Lily was closing. The person responsible got away with several hundred dollars that she was in the process of taking to the safe.

"I'm okay, Eme. Okay, if I'm totally honest, I'm still a little unsettled by the incident, but I'm not hurt. I'm more worried about Declan than myself. He completely freaked out when I called him, after I called the police. I honestly think he was on the verge of trying to tell me I couldn't work anymore before I finally got him to calm down. What really scares me is, I think he picked up the guy's scent, and if he ever crosses paths with him…look out."

"Do you really think he'd do something to the guy?"

"I don't know. I hope not, because that would land him in jail."

"That would definitely not be a good thing," Emelise replied just as her phone rang. She glanced at the number. "Mal's calling. He must be on his way to New Orleans; he said he'd call when he headed this way," she said before she answered it. "Hey, Mal."

"Hey to you too, sexy lady," Mal said with a chuckle. "So, don't be mad at me but I didn't call you when I left Phoenix. I've actually been in New Orleans since yesterday."

"What? You've been here since yesterday and you're just now calling me? Do you have a side bestie I don't know about here in New Orleans?" It was obvious she was teasing. "Malcolm Savage, what am I going to do with you? Why didn't you call before?"

"Well…I have a little confession, Eme," Mal started. "I did something completely crazy. I quit my job at The Inferno, sold my house…and bought one here in New Orleans."

Emelise stared at her phone. "Holy shit! You **moved** to New Orleans? I thought you were just coming for a visit! This is awesome! Here I was trying to figure out a way to lure you into moving and you beat me to it. Get your ass over here; we need to talk. Oh gods, and I'll have to take you out to meet Caine, and you'll need to meet Declan—"

"Declan? Who is that?" Mal interrupted.

"Oh, that's right, you don't know about that. Long story. Come to my apartment; I'll give you the address, and Lily and I can fill you in on all that's happened since we talked last."

Malcolm laughed. "Okay. This should be interesting. I'm on my way."

Malcolm

Fifteen minutes after putting Emelise's address into his GPS, Malcolm pulled up to the curb just up the street from her apartment building. He took a moment to admire the outside of it before he hopped out and headed inside. He'd always been an architecture buff, and he knew he was going to *love* the architecture of New Orleans. Once he reached her door he knocked and waited.

Emelise opened the door seconds after he knocked. "Mal! Get in here, dude," she said and gave him a quick hug. "I can't believe you took a leap of faith and moved down here." She'd already grabbed a glass for him and poured him a glass of sweet tea.

Malcolm took it and sat in the other armchair. "Never fear, darlings, I have arrived," he said with a cheeky grin. "This place is nice; it suits you. It's got just the right amount of quirkiness to it."

Lily laughed. "I said pretty much the same thing when I first saw it. It's good to see you, Mal."

"Thanks. You too, babe. So, which one of you is going to tell me who Declan is and why I have to meet him?"

Eme laughed. "Get right to the point, why dontcha?" she teased. "Who he is is kind of a long story. You remember me telling you about Lily's mate? That's Declan. Okay, so who he is wasn't really that long of an explanation after all," Eme replied. "The reason you have to meet him is really the part that's kind of long. When Lily and I drove out to Phoenix last month, the Pard was having trouble with a neighboring shifter group. The Red Moon Clan was trying to take over New Orleans, trying to take Pard territory, and things got really rough. There was a fight, some of the jaguars died, and Declan played a huge role in helping the Pard win. Him and his team. He was Special Ops once upon a time. Anyway, to thank him and his team for all their help, Caine split off part of Pard territory and gave it to Declan for his own Pack. So there are two shifter groups in New Orleans, which means there are two Alphas for you to meet."

Malcolm listened intently. "Damn, that sounds like it could have gotten really bad. I'm impressed the leopard's Alpha gave up part of his territory though. That's unusual."

"Caine isn't like a lot of Alphas," Lily put in. "He's more open to talking through issues, whenever possible, and he honors those who aid him and his Pard."

"Sounds like a much better Alpha than the last one I had," Malcolm replied.

Lily studied him. "You know, since you're not a leopard and can't join the Pard, you should consider joining the Ghostpoint Pack. We're a bunch of misfits but we've formed a strong, close-knit group. Of course the others were already pretty close-knit because they'd worked together."

"Misfits? How so?"

"What else would you call a Pack made up of three wolves, two jaguars, a grizzly bear, and a Siberian tiger?"

He blinked, then laughed. "Misfits. That definitely fits. Huh, I've never been part of a group that had different shifters in it. Might be interesting. It does get a little lonely being solo."

"Yeah, it does," Lily agreed.

"We'll see how it goes," Malcolm replied after a moment. There was a reason he wasn't part of a Pride, a reason why he was an outcast who was shunned by most of his own kind. "Unless my getting to stay in New Orleans is dependent upon my being in the Pack?"

"Gods, no, you can stay regardless," Lily replied. "I just remember how much I missed getting to be part of a group, especially on the nights I went for a run. Once I moved here I was welcome to run with the Pard, but it wasn't quite the same as being with my own Pack."

Malcolm nodded. "I get what you mean, babe. We'll see if I mesh with the others first."

"Sounds good to me," Lily agreed.

"Did you really buy a house?" Emelise asked suddenly. "Because if you lied and you're staying in a hotel, you can just crash here."

"No need for that. I really did buy a house."

"Already? How?"

"I bought it even before I moved. As soon as I knew I wanted to move here and not just visit, I sat down and looked at houses online, found one I wanted, and bought it."

"You were smarter than I was. When I got here I had to stay in a hotel for a few days until I found this place," Eme said with a laugh.

"Well, you *were* still reeling from losing your mother and focused on chasing your dream of owning your own club," Lily pointed out.

"True, there is that." Eme waved her hands in front of her face. "Whatever, it's kind of moot now. I'll text Caine and see if he can come to the club tonight. You can check it out and meet him there.

That way Lily can drag Declan out to meet you at the same time. Kill three birds with one stone." She flashed a cheeky grin.

"Sounds like a plan to me," Lily replied. "I'm going to head out. See you tonight."

"I should go too. I've still got a shit ton of unpacking to do," Mal said with a groan.

"Been there and done that," Emelise said. "I'll text you later to let you know what time to stop by the club."

"Alright. I hope you're making that man work for it. You deserve to be be happy, Eme," Mal said before he left. He was looking forward to meeting Caine just so he could be sure the leopard was worthy of her.

Chapter Fourteen

Emelise

Emelise didn't have time to worry about how the meeting between Caine and Malcolm might go. When she got to the club there was a bit of an issue in the VIP lounge. The club hadn't been open an hour and some local socialite thought that because he was an 'important person' in New Orleans it meant he could do whatever he wanted in the club. What that boiled down to was him verbally assaulting the bartender and letting his hands wander to places they didn't belong every time the server got near him.

"Emelise, I agreed to be nice to the customers, especially the VIP ones on the nights I worked the VIP lounge, but I didn't agree to being felt up by some jerk who thinks he's God's gift to women," Sierra, one of the newer waitresses, said.

"That's not in your job description," Emelise replied. "I'll take care of this. I'm sorry you were subjected to that kind of behavior. I don't put up with it and I won't allow it in my club," she added and had to bite back a growl.

"Joe's pretty pissed too. The guy has been really ugly toward him, pretty much telling him he was shitty at his job when we both know that's not true," Sierra told her.

"I'll take care of that, too," Emelise said and headed upstairs. Sierra had gone downstairs to get away from the guy and his grabby hands.

Emelise sauntered upstairs and made a beeline for the bar where Joe was fixing drinks. "Hey, Sierra told me about what's been happening; point me in the right direction and I'll take care of this."

"Good, because if he touched Sierra one more time I was going to break his fingers for him," Joe replied. Sierra was his sister; he was *not* happy about the jerk pawing at her. He nodded with his head at the table where the troublemaker sat.

"I might do it for you," Emelise muttered under her breath before she headed his way.

Aaron Sutton was one of those rich men who thought that because he had money the entire world should bend over backwards for him. Emelise recognized him from a recent article that was done on him. When she stopped in front of his table, she saw his gaze trail over her before he finally met her gaze. "Oh, aren't you a pretty little thing. Come to take care of me, have you? Compared to you, the other waitress is a bit lackluster."

Emelise rolled her eyes at him. "No, I'm not here to 'take care of you', at least not in the way you mean the phrase. What I am here to do is ask you to leave. You've verbally assaulted one employee and what you did to your *server* can be considered sexual assault if she wanted to pursue a case against you."

He blinked at her. "Oh, that's cute. No one would believe it, sweetheart. Dressed the way she is, of course she's looking for attention of the male persuasion."

"I am only going to say this once more and if you still ignore me I'll take matters in my own hands. You need to leave. Now."

"No can do, sweetheart. I'm enjoying myself. Why don't you run along and find the owner. I'm sure he'll understand and tell you to mind your own business."

Eme gave him a mockingly sweet smile before she leaned down a little so she was in his face. "First, I'm not your sweetheart so cut the bullshit. Second, you're looking at the owner, and you harassing my staff *is* my business."

He looked her over again. "You don't want to get on my bad side, sweetheart," he said, deliberately using the endearment. "I can make or break this club. One word from me and you'll lose all of your business."

Emelise laughed. "I don't think so. You see that right there," she said and pointed to what appeared to be a glass globe over a light fixture. "That's a security camera. How much you want to bet if I looked at it I'd find you doing exactly what you were accused of: putting your hands where they didn't belong?"

His hand snaked out and his fingers curled around her wrist. "I will bury you and this fucking club."

"Get. Your. Fucking. Hand. Off. Her."

Caine

Caine had gotten the text from Emelise, asking him to come to the club because she wanted him to meet someone: a friend from Phoenix who just relocated to New Orleans. He knew that was Eme's way of letting him know the person was a shifter, otherwise why would she be so formal about the meeting? He wondered who it might be, but since she'd not talked about her life in Phoenix much, he was pretty much in the dark.

He reached the club and before he could ask where she was, he was pointed to the stairs leading up to the VIP lounge. Hmm, intriguing. Did she want him to meet whoever it was there?

He took the steps two at a time and when he reached the top, his gaze immediately searched her out. What he saw made his blood boil and a growl escaped him before he could stop it. He reigned in his leopard as he approached. "Get. Your. Fucking. Hand. Off. Her." There was so much controlled rage in his voice he was surprised no one looked their way.

Emelise

Eme's head snapped up when she heard her mate's voice. Oh. He was pissed, no, beyond pissed, that the guy had grabbed her wrist. She felt his fingers loosen before they fell away and she had to resist the urge to rub her arm where they'd been. "You are no longer welcome at Scarlet Flux. Your photo will be given to the entire staff to ensure you don't return. And if you try to damage my club's reputation with lies? Just remember, there is more than enough video proof of your actions, and I will see that Sierra presses charges against you for sexual assault."

He stood slowly and sneered at her. "Fine, whatever, this place isn't any good anyway," he said and lifted his chin in defiance.

Eme laughed. "You keep telling yourself that to make yourself feel better. Me, I know the truth," she said and watched him leave.

Caine watched him go, as well, before he turned his attention to his mate. "Are you alright, Angel?" he asked with a soft growl.

Eme shivered. That growl made her damn toes curl, it sounded so good. "I'm fine. I had it under control," she said and saw a flash of something akin to hurt in his eyes. "But thank you. I probably would have had to get physical with him if you hadn't shown up when you did, and that could have gone badly."

He pulled her into his arms and buried his nose in her hair for a moment. "Mmmh, I might have enjoyed watching you put him in his place."

Eme laughed softly. "You're incorrigible."

"I am, but you wouldn't want me any other way."

"Too true, too true."

Malcolm

Malcolm reached Scarlet Flux and arched a brow as he took in the brick facade. The club had a distinctly quirky flare to it even from the outside and he couldn't help but grin. It definitely reflected Emelise's personality. He stepped inside and closed his eyes to let the music wash over him. God, he loved jazz. He made the right choice in moving to the Crescent City; he just knew it.

After a moment he opened his eyes and moved to the bar. "I'm looking for Emelise; she wanted me to meet her here," he said to the guy behind the bar.

"She's upstairs in the VIP lounge," came the reply before the guy finished the drink order he was working on.

"Thanks." Mal headed upstairs just as some guy came stomping down them. The anger rolled off the man and Malcolm cocked a brow. What was that all about? He watched the guy go before he shrugged and turned back to continue up the stairs.

At the top of the stairs he stopped again. "Wow," he said under his breath. The VIP lounge overlooked the rest of the club, but while it kept the red, gold, and black theme the downstairs had, this section kicked it up a few dozen notches. It was luxurious, almost obscenely so. He took it all in for a moment before his gaze fell on Emelise being held by someone who had to be her mate. "Now that's a pretty sight," he said loudly enough for them to hear him.

Emelise heard his voice and immediately pulled out of Caine's arms. "Mal! You're here. It's that time already?" she asked and glanced at her watch. "Damn, I thought I had a little more time. Are Lily and Declan here yet? Did you see them downstairs?"

"I sure didn't…Eme," Malcolm replied. He'd started to call her 'babe' but changed it because he had a feeling her mate might take issue with it without an explanation that a) he called everyone that b) Emelise was more like the sister he never had, and c) he was batting for the same team. Women made great friends but when it came to lovers, not so much.

"Well, no worries, I'm sure they'll be here." She went to him and grabbed his arm to pull him over to where Caine stood. "Malcolm, this is Caine, Alpha of the Black Water Pard, and my mate," she said, adding the last at the last moment. "Caine, this is Malcolm. He's a dear friend from Phoenix; he just relocated to New Orleans and he'll be working here at the club." She looked at Malcolm. "You are going to perform, right?" she asked for clarification.

"Of course I am, darling! I'm looking forward to seeing what kind of a reception I get." He turned his attention to Caine. "It's nice to meet you. I've heard a bit about you."

"Don't believe a word of it," Caine said and winked at Emelise. "I'm sure she's told you I'm an overbearin' jerk."

Eme blushed and Malcolm laughed. "Something like that," he replied. "Don't worry, I won't hold it against you as long as you make our little Eme happy."

"I'll make her happy as long as she'll let me."

"Oh, I like you. You really do know Eme well, don't you?"

Emelise gave him a mock glare. "Why did I think introducing you two would be a good idea?" she groused.

It was Caine who chuckled this time. "Because it is, Angel. Someone has to keep you on your toes and, lord knows, dat ain't me," he admitted and kissed her temple.

Before Emelise could reply Lily and Delcan showed up.

Emelise

Emelise had felt a little torn over Caine's coming to her defense with the jerk, who thought having money meant he could treat others any way he wanted to. On the one hand it was sweet of him, but on the other hand it had made her feel like he didn't think she could handle it herself. Still, at the hurt in his eyes, she'd found she couldn't be annoyed with him. He really was a good man even if he did frustrate the fuck out of her sometimes. And annoyed the ever-loving hell out of her sometimes, too.

"Speaking of the devils," Emelise said when Declan and Lily entered the VIP Lounge. "I was just taking about y'all," she added at the looks she got.

"Y'all? You're really getting into this whole 'Southern' thing," Lily teased her. "Why were you talking about us?"

"Just wondering if you were here yet," Eme replied after sticking her tongue out at her best friend's teasing tone.

Lily laughed. "Love you, too, Eme," she said, then arched a brow at Caine. "Okay, what happened up here? You're all tense and even Mal looks a little on edge. You boys aren't fighting, are you?"

Caine gave her a look. "No, we're not fightin'. There was an issue when I first arrived but I took care of it."

"Oh, is that why that guy brushed past me in such a foul mood?" Malcolm asked. "I was wondering what that was about. Sorry, babe, didn't know I looked tense. I must have been picking up on Caine's tension," he added to Lily.

Beside her, Lily felt Declan tense and rolled her eyes. "Let me make the introductions. Declan, this is Malcolm, Eme's friend from Phoenix. Malcolm, this is Declan. Don't let his glare bother you; he's like that with any man who even looks at me. Kind of the way Caine is when guys look at Eme," she added.

Lily and Emelise both laughed at the comment. "True, they do both do that whole glaring thing, don't they?" Emelise said.

"They totally do," Lily replied.

Malcolm snickered then decided to put both the males at ease. "Don't worry, darlings, I have no interest in your mates beyond maybe some makeup advice," he said. "Women make excellent friends but they don't have the right equipment to get my blood pumping."

Both Caine and Declan just stared at him a moment before Declan burst out laughing. "Damn, you'll fit right in with our Pack. Echo and Sasha will definitely love you."

"Oh? Why is that?" Malcolm asked curiously.

"Because you can talk shop, so to speak."

"Have those two finally admitted they're hooked on each other yet or are they still pretending otherwise?" Emelise asked. The one time she'd met the two women together she'd known right away how they felt about each other.

"They're still stubborn as fuck," Declan replied.

"I don't get that," Emelise replied. "They're good together; you'd think they'd just get it over with."

"I think they're just worried it will ruin the friendship and they're unwilling to let that happen," Lily countered. She shared a look with Eme. "Maybe we need to play a little matchmaking."

Emelise grinned. "I was just thinking the same thing!"

"So you don't have an issue with me not being straight?" Malcolm asked Declan while Eme and Lily bantered back and forth playfully.

"Fuck no. Why would I? Look, I know lions have this ego thing going on, especially the Alphas, and their only focus seems to be on making babies, but that attitude makes it hard for anyone who thinks differently to feel like they're accepted and part of the group. I don't give a shit what gets you hard as long as it's nothing illegal," Declan replied. "You should come meet the rest of the Pack once you're settled in. Lily told me you just moved here, so take all the time you need."

"Thanks," Malcolm replied. He looked a little stunned by the open acceptance, considering his status as an outcast among lion shifters. "Not everyone is a bigot," Lily said before she grinned. "When are you doing your first performance?"

"Haven't gotten that far yet," Malcolm and Emelise said at almost the same time.

"How about we plan it for this Saturday? That'll give you four days to get things in order and meet with the band," Eme put in.

"This Saturday sounds perfect," Malcolm replied. "Well, darlings, I hate to cut and run but it's been a long day, and I still have some unpacking to do so I will catch all of you later," he added and left.

Eme watched him go before she turned her attention to what had happened earlier. "I really hope that jerk lets it go. I don't want to drag anyone through the mud, but if he pushes it, I have proof he sexually assaulted one of the servers." She had a bad feeling about it though. Woman's intuition? Maybe, or maybe just go old fashion understanding the way the human mind worked.

Chapter Fifteen

Emelise

"Gods-damned, motherfucking son of a bitch!" Emelise was seething. She was in the middle of doing inventory when she'd gotten a text from Sierra telling her to check a website that highlighted local businesses. There, bold as can be, was a post about Scarlet Flux. A very nasty post about it.

"What's wrong, boss lady?" Joe asked.

"Sierra sent me a text about this website that showcases local businesses; that fucker who was messing with her, he put up a really nasty post about the club."

"What the fuck? Is there anything that can be done about it?"

"I have no idea," Eme replied. "I'll contact the website owner and ask. What he did is akin to slander, and outside of getting Sierra to press charges against him, I don't know how to stop him from dragging the club down."

Malcolm was stopping in to set up with the band so they could rehearse and overheard her. "What happened, babe?" he asked. Eme repeated the situation and he cocked a brow. "Oh, that's easy, darling. Why don't you let me take care of this little problem for you, hmmh?"

She gave him a puzzled look. "Are you sure?"

"Positive. Soon enough you'll see that his comment has been obliterated." Malcolm knew how to deal with people like this Aaron

Sutton.

"Okay," she finally agreed.

Malcolm flashed a grin and got to work immediately. Networking was a beautiful thing, and half an hour later he'd reached out to literally hundreds of people who'd been to Scarlet Flux since it opened. Not only were people commenting on the ugly things he'd said, but others were posting positive experiences. One particular one stuck out and Mal sent a link to Eme. *Go to this link and read what this person had to say about your club.*

Eme had just finished with the inventory and shrugged. Might as well, right? She grabbed herself a bottle of water, sat at the bar, and opened the link to read it.

After a recent bout with cancer that left me feeling less than attractive (because, really, what woman feels attractive when she has to shave her head because her hair was coming out in clumps and she has perpetual bags under her eyes?) I finally let some girlfriends of mine talk me into going out. My usual haunts tend to be rocker clubs and biker bars—at least they were before I got sick—so when I was informed that the club we were going to, Scarlet Flux, was a newly opened jazz club I blanched. Jazz? Ugh.

That was what went through my mind. I was expecting it to be boring: bland colors with second-rate musicians who could barely carry a tune. I couldn't have been more surprised if the Pope had shown up at my door in a mumu dancing the polka!

The first thing you notice when you walk in the doors are the colors. The combination of crimson and black with hints of gold lend the entire space a sexy, seductive feel. It's classy, sophisticated, and yet comfortable at the same time. The entire downstairs is set up in an inviting way that draws the listener into the live music that is continuously playing. The seat cushions are thick and comfortable, the chairs are wide to accommodate nearly any size patron, the tables are solid and sturdy, and every piece of wood gleams.

There are no doubt handmade pieces scattered throughout the club. The intricate carvings, along the stairs leading to the upstairs VIP Lounge, are gorgeous, and I have it on good authority they were done by Gage Delacroix of Delacroix Carpentry and Architectural Design. The man is truly a master at his craft!

The VIP Lounge is the epitome of luxurious. Smooth floors reflect the lights that twinkle from gold-encrusted wall sconces and globed chandeliers. Each table is nestled against a thick, padded booth that is covered in crimson velvet. Comfortable chairs line the other side of the tables, and each piece has gold embellishments that catch the glow of the lights. The entire space makes you feel special, regardless of who you are.

And the music is phenomenal. I dare say Miss Rousseau has found the cream of the crop with the musical talent that graces the small stage every night. I won't be surprised if some of the musicians find themselves with record deals, thanks to her bringing their talent to the world.

If you are looking for a night out on the town and want to go to a club that combines class, style, amazing talent, and delicious drinks, Scarlet Flux is the ONLY place to go!

~Izzy Catalini

Emelise read over the blog post several times. "Oh. Wow." She had no clue who this 'Izzy Catalini' was but she really wanted to thank the woman for what she'd said.

"What?" Joe asked and when Eme showed him the post he whistled. "Dayum, that's one sweet blog post. Your buddy Malcolm definitely knows what he's doing."

"He's multi-talented, that's for sure," Emelise replied. "I wonder if 'Izzy' is short for Isabella. I may have to try and track this young woman down to thank her for her kind words. Anyway, thanks for the help with the inventory, Joe."

"Welcome. I'm going to head home—got plans for tonight with it being my night off."

Eme waved him off and went to her office. After a little digging she located an Isabella Catalini there in New Orleans. After a little more investigation she had an address and directions to get there. She wanted to thank the woman in person.

An hour after finding Isabella Catalini's address, Emelise found herself sitting in her car in front of a small house in the Lower Ninth Ward. It was a bit rough but then a lot of places were once you got away from the more tourist-prone parts of the city, such as the French Quarter and Garden District. Next to her on the seat was a basket that held a variety of fruits and cheeses. It was just a small token of her gratitude, really. "It's not going to deliver itself," she said under her breath before she climbed out of her car. Just as she reached for the basket, her phone vibrated, alerting her to a text.

Come to da compound for dinner, cher. I miss you.

Eme smiled a little at the message. It was nice getting little messages like that from him even if he still hadn't given her a reason to believe he was looking for commitment between them. **What if I had a hot date?** She couldn't help teasing him.

If it was wit' another man, he'd be dead, Angel, and you wouldn't do dat to some poor, unsuspectin' fool. Quit teasin' me, woman.

Emelise laughed and sent her reply to him. **But you make it so easy to tease you.**

Careful, cher, you don't want to rile da beast. Will you come to dinner?

She could practically hear the growl through the text and decided to cut him some slack. **I'll be there at six. See you then.** That done, she put her phone away, grabbed the basket, and went to the door.

The door opened a couple minutes after Emelise knocked and a small, dark-haired little girl looked up at her. "Can I help you?"

Eme blinked. She hadn't expected a child to answer the door. "Hi there," she said warmly. "Is Isabella home?"

The little girl wrinkled her nose at her. "Uh-huh. But Mama goes by Izzy, not Isabella," she said. She turned away from the door and raised her voice. "Mama, there's a lady at the door for you."

"I'll keep that in mind," Emelise replied and waited for Izzy Catalini to come to the door.

When Izzy got to the door, her eyes widened a little. "You're Emelise Rousseau, aren't you? You own Scarlet Flux."

"I am, and I do," Eme replied. "A dear friend of mine showed me the blog post you made about the club and I was really touched by it. I just wanted to come by, thank you in person, and give you a token of my gratitude," she added and offered up the basket.

"That's very nice of you but you didn't have to do that," Izzy said. Still, she took the basket from her. "Would you like to come in for a moment?"

"I don't want to interrupt anything."

"You're not. I was just fixing Lexi something for lunch. Would you like a glass of tea? Or we have raspberry lemonade."

"That lemonade sounds good, thank you." Eme took in the rundown appearance of the apartment and it hurt her heart to see. It was clean but it was obvious there were little funds to keep the furniture in good condition. "How long have you lived in New Orleans?" she asked because Izzy definitely did not have a Southern accent. No, she sounded more New York than New Orleans.

"Four years. We moved here when Lexi was two," Izzy replied. "And you? You don't sound like you're from here either."

Eme laughed. "No, I'm not, but my Mama was. I grew up in Phoenix. I moved here a couple of months ago."

"Oh? What brought you here?" Izzy asked.

"Like I said, my Mama was from here. She died from a car accident and I decided I needed a change, so I came to the city of her birth."

"I'm so sorry for your loss," Izzy said quietly.

"Thank you." Eme watched her. "What about you? What brought you south? I'm going to guess you grew up somewhere in New York."

"Good ear," Izzy replied. "As for what brought us here: Lexi's father. He moved us all here because his job transferred him here. Things didn't turn out exactly as planned though."

"I'm sorry to hear that," Eme said honestly.

"Thank you. It's for the best. He wasn't really that interested in having a family anyway."

"I saw in your post that you're fighting cancer. How are you?" Eme asked hesitantly.

"Depends on the day," Izzy replied. "Some days are worse than others, but its just me and Lexi so I make do."

In that moment Emelise made a decision. She wasn't sure what drove her to do it but she wanted to help the other woman. Maybe it was because she saw a bit of her and her mama in Izzy and her daughter. Emelise knew, first hand, how hard it could be growing up with only one parent. She pulled a pen and notepad from her purse and jotted something on it. Then she tore the slip of paper off and slid it over to Izzy. "Here. If you need anything, and I do mean anything, you just call. Even if it's just a ride or for someone to keep an eye on Lexi so you can get some rest. I mean it. Please. Growing up, it was just me and my mama, and I remember how hard it was for her to be a single mama. You have that along with fighting cancer. I want to help."

Izzy looked at the piece of paper before her eyes filled with tears. "Thank you. I don't…I don't know what to say."

"You don't have to say anything," Eme replied and gave her hand a quick squeeze. "You just call or text if you need help."

Izzy slipped the piece of paper in her pocket. "I will."

"Good. I should get going and let you and your daughter get back to your afternoon. I hope you enjoy the basket. It was really nice to meet you, Izzy."

"It was nice to meet you too, Miss Rousseau," Izzy replied.

"Call me Eme; it's what my friends and family call me and I'd like to think we're friends," Emelise replied.

"Okay, Eme. I'd like that."

She walked Emelise to the door and waved before she closed it behind her.

Eme waved back before she got in her car and headed home to change. She had a dinner date to get ready for.

Caine

Caine looked around and nodded with approval. There was more than one reason why he wanted Emelise to come to dinner. Yes, he missed her, more than he wanted to admit, but he had a surprise for her, as well. She still insisted on living in that damn apartment, but he was hoping his surprise might entice her to change her mind.

Glancing at his watch, he headed into the house to check on dinner before taking a quick shower. A smile flitted across his face as the memory, of the last time Eme had stayed the night, came to mind. They'd finally gotten around to christening the shower. Fuck, his mate was a wildcat in bed. Her fiery temper was matched by her fiery passion when he touched her. Just thinking about her made him almost unbearably hard and he groaned. He ended up relieving some of the pressure with his hand before he got dressed and headed down to the docks to meet his mate.

Caine watched as she maneuvered the boat up to the docks. He'd recently taught her the route so she could bring herself, and the first couple of times she'd had trouble docking but not today. She'd clearly been practicing. "You did dat like you've been dockin' a boat all your life, cher," he said as he approached her.

Emelise grinned at him. "Thanks. That's some pretty high praise," she said and when he reached her, she leaned up for a kiss.

Caine readily obliged her by leaning down and kissing her deeply. "Mmmh, definitely missed dat," he growled against her lips.

Eme laughed. "You're insatiable, mister."

"When it comes to you, dat is very true, Angel," he agreed. "I have a surprise for you but you have to let me blindfold you first. I don't want you to see it until I'm ready for you to."

Eme arched a brow at him. "Okay."

Caine kissed her again before he pulled a strip of material from his pocket. He placed it over her eyes, then tied it so it would stay in place. Then he wrapped one arm around her waist and curled his hand around her arm to guide her towards his home.

He carefully guided her around the house toward the back of the property. Once there he moved so he could watch her face, then leaned close. "You can take the blindfold off now, Angel."

Emelise

Emelise was genuinely curious as to what Caine was up to. Whatever it was, it had to be pretty big if he needed her blindfolded first. She tried to figure out where they were as he led her down the path, but she didn't know the lay of the land by heart the way someone who'd grown up there would have.

When they finally stopped and he murmured that she could remove the blindfold, she took it off and then stared. "Oh…my gods. Is this…? How? When did you get this done?" There, in front of her, was a fairly large greenhouse.

"Why do you tink I haven't pressed you to come for a visit da last couple of days," he replied with a faint smirk.

"You sneaky bastard!" She laughed, threw her arms around him, and leaned up for a kiss. "This is amazing. Thank you."

Caine's arms tightened around her as he returned the kiss. "You're welcome, Angel. I was hopin' you'd like it."

Like it, hell, I love it!" She pulled out of his embrace and went inside to check it out. There was a complete watering system as well as overhead misters. Rows of rich soil awaited planting and she turned and gave him a huge grin. "This is…I can start growing my own roses now."

"Dat's da idea, cher."

Emelise turned to look at him. "You really were listening when I told you I'd wanted to build a greenhouse, back in Phoenix." She knew there was a bit of awe in her voice. "I'm totally not used to that."

"I will always listen when you talk, Emelise."

She could hear the honesty in his voice. "You're something, Caine Bordeaux." She shook her head and moved toward the back door that led into his home. "Now, feed me; I'm ravenous." There was a joking tone in her voice and she flashed him a playful grin.

Caine laughed at her playfulness. "Can't have dat, can we?" He followed her inside and soon they were seated at the table enjoying their meal.

Eme was quiet while she ate, which was unusual for her. She had a lot on her mind including the young woman she'd met earlier in the day.

"You're quiet," Caine remarked halfway through their meal.

"Sorry. I've got a lot on my mind." She set her fork down and turned her attention to him. "Remember that jerk in the VIP section who was harassing one of the servers? The one who grabbed my wrist when I went to throw him out, and you got all up in his face?" She paused a moment and when he nodded at her, she continued. "He got on some website that highlights local businesses and said some pretty awful things about the club. Malcolm stopped by while I was bitching about it and that man worked magic, I swear. In no time he had a plethora of people on there countering all the negative bullshit the jerk spewed. One post really stuck out and I tracked the woman down. She's got a little girl and something about them reminded me of me and my mama. I think it's because it's just the two of them. She's had it pretty rough from what I can tell. She's fighting cancer and raising her daughter on her own. I don't know what happened with the little girl's father, I don't know if he's still around, but considering the rundown condition of their home, I'm betting he's not." She waved a hand in front of her face. It was a habit she'd had ever since she was little. "Anyway, now you know why I'm so quiet."

Caine

Caine had watched as Emelise had wandered around the greenhouse taking in everything he'd had done to make it perfect for her. He wanted to see her in there every day while she coaxed the roses, she loved so much, to grow. He wanted to watch her dig her fingers into the soil with a contented smile on her face.

He loved her. It hit him that the emotions he felt for her went beyond the mate connection. The connection between their animals was different from love. It was a base animal instinct. What he'd realized, watching her in the greenhouse, was that his emotions were much deeper than a base animal attraction. He was in love.

By the time they'd headed inside to eat, he was already plotting. He knew Emelise doubted men; he knew her past made her hesitant to trust that he would be there no matter what life threw at them. Would she accept a marriage proposal? Lily had said Eme doubted his desire for commitment; would proposing show her how serious he was?

As the Alpha, he was the one who was supposed to always be in control. Why then did he feel like the world was spinning away from him? For the first time in his life he felt like he had no control whatsoever. It unsettled him. The thought that Emelise might turn him down when he asked her to marry him actually had his pulse increasing, and he wasn't even ready to pop the question yet.

He'd pulled himself from his thoughts when he'd realized she was being more quiet than usual. His mate usually chattered about things going on with the club whenever they were together. "You're quiet." That was all he'd needed to say to get her to open up.

He listened intently and his hackles rose at the thought of someone trying to damage her business. "Did he leave a name on da article?"

"I don't know. I'd have to check. Not that it matters. I know who he is. There was an article about him in the paper not long ago. Why do you want to know?"

Caine shrugged. "Curiosity." The truth was he wanted to teach the bastard a lesson but he couldn't do that physically. If he could find out who it was and humiliate him publicly, that would appease his leopard. He was going to have to check the paper's online archive.

"Uh-huh. Why do I get the feeling that's not all there is to it?"

Caine laughed at that. "Because you know me well, Angel." It was almost scary how well she knew him.

"True, I do. I should get out of here. I do have a club to run."

Caine was reluctant to end their time together, but he hoped that soon enough she would be there in his arms every night. "I'll walk you to da dock," he told her and offered his arm.

"You can be such a gentleman sometimes, Caine. I think you do it just to throw me off balance."

"Maybe I do," he teased right back. He winked at her and flashed her a wicked grin. "Keepin' you off balance is a good ting, cher. I wouldn't be able to surprise you otherwise."

That made Emelise laugh. "True. Very true."

When they reached the dock Caine pulled her close and dipped his head to kiss her. "Maybe I'll stop by later after I finish wit' work; if I get done before da club closes."

"All right. You're still coming Saturday, for Venus's debut, right?"

"A'course, Angel. I wouldn't miss it." He reluctantly let her go and watched until her boat was out of sight before he headed back to his home so he could get his work done. Between his day job and taking care of the Pard, some days there just wasn't enough time in the day to do everything he wanted to do. He'd learned fairly quickly to take a moment to enjoy himself whenever he could.

Chapter Sixteen

Caine

Despite his desire to get away from work, Caine hadn't had the chance to head into the city since he'd surprised Emelise with the greenhouse. It was Saturday, however, and he had a promise to keep. He also had a plan to finally convince his mate that he was in it for the long haul. He would show her that not all men were like Sean Scotsdale, the man who'd broken both hers and her mother's hearts when she was a little girl.

At least he hoped his plan would work. When it came to Emelise, things didn't always go the way he planned them. Unpredictable and Emelise went hand in hand. In anyone else, that quality would drive him to utter madness, but in Emelise he found it endearing. Funny how loving someone could change the way you reacted to things.

On his way to Scarlet Flux, Caine made two stops: the jewelers and a flower shop. At the jewelers he looked over the special piece he'd had made, checked it for any possible flaws, then nodded in approval. "Perfect." He closed the small, velvet box and slipped it into his pocket, then left. At the flower shop he picked up a dozen long-stem roses in the darkest red he could find.

By the time he reached the club it was already packed. All week, Emelise had been advertising Venus's debut. New Orleanians were a rare breed in that they openly accepted anyone who was seen as 'other' whether that be a medium, a shifter, or a drag queen. He was delighted to see such a large crowd. He knew how much the club meant to his mate.

"Evenin', Caine. Eme is in her office; she got a phone call she said she had to take."

Caine cocked a brow. "Surprised to see you here tonight, Julius." The leopard was one of NOPD's finest, but he had some secrets he was keeping from his coworkers, not the least of which was that he was a shifter.

Julius shrugged. "I like da atmosphere here." He saw the look on his Alpha's face. "Okay. Truth, Emelise told me I needed to come to see her friend's performance. Gage, Mia, and da rest of da family are upstairs, but I wanted to be down here in case dere was any trouble."

Caine chuckled. "Dat's what I thought. My woman's good at gettin' people to do what she wants dem to do," he said with pride. He nodded at Julius and made his way toward the back of the bar to the hallway leading to Emelise's office. What could have been so important she would answer her phone so close to Venus's show?

Caine's mind raced as he headed for the closed door. The only family she had was already at the club. Well, no, not true. As far as he knew her father and stepmother weren't there tonight. Had something happened to her father or one of her half-siblings?

When he reached the door he paused before he knocked and then opened it and stepped inside. He didn't wait for her to tell him to come in because he was worried about her. The worry increased when she didn't even seem to notice his entrance. "Angel? What's wrong?"

Emelise

As more and more people had come into the club, ordered drinks, and found places to sit, Emelise couldn't help but grin from ear to ear. All week she'd been using her own flare for advertising to push Venus's debut at the club. A favorite among their patrons, she'd been told, was the most recent one.

Looking for something different for your Saturday Night out in the Crescent City? Come to Scarlet Flux. There you will find yourself surrounded by a dark romantic ambiance that will make you feel like you've been transported to your favorite Anne Rice novel. That is only the beginning. The enchanting, alluring, and captivating voice of the ever-seductive Venus will lure you in the way sirens of old lured sailors into their arms. You do not want to miss the debut that will turn the Big Easy on it's ear.

She'd thought about the ad and couldn't help but smile. It was one of her best. She'd done some of the advertising for The Inferno when she'd lived in Phoenix but she'd had to curb her artistic flare. Now that she was the one calling the shots, she could be as artistic with her advertising as she wanted to be.

Eme had just greeted her cousins, whom she'd bribed into coming to the show, when her phone vibrated. A quick glance at her phone had her frowning. "I need to take this. Y'all go on up to the VIP Lounge," she'd told them and headed to her office.

By the time she reached her office, the call had already gone to voicemail. With trepidation she dialed her voicemail and pressed to listen to the new message. "Hi, Emelise, it's Angie. I'm just calling to let you know we're going to have to reschedule the family dinner that was planned for tomorrow. I know this is short notice but, well, call me back and I'll explain."

Her frown deepened as the message ended. Something was wrong. She heard it in Angie's voice. She ended the call and immediately dialed her stepmother's number. "Angie? What's wrong? I could hear it in your voice—something's up," she said as soon as the other woman answered.

"It's your father. He was having chest pains so I called an ambulance. They're running tests now but it will be a few hours before we know anything."

"What hospital are you at? I'll come right away."

"No, you don't have to do that. We know you have a big show going on at the club tonight. Just come after it. Like I said, it's going to be a few hours before we know anything so you don't need to rush right over. As soon as he's moved into a room, I'll text you the information. We're at Tulane Medical Center."

Emelise closed her eyes. "You text me the instant you know anything and as soon as I can get away from here, I will."

"I'll text you, Emelise. You have my word."

It wasn't until she'd hung up that she realized Caine had entered her office and was standing next to her. She lifted her gaze to him and there were tears glistening in her eyes. "My father is in the hospital, at Tulane Medical Center. He was having chest pains, but Angie said not to rush over because they're still in the ER and it'll be a while before they know anything." She was torn between wanting to be there to introduce Venus and rushing off to the hospital.

When a sob escaped her, despite her resolve to hold it all in, she felt Caine's arms wrap around her. With her face tucked into the space between his head and shoulders she let a few tears fall. "I just met him; I can't lose him now."

"I know, Angel." Caine tightened his arms around her and let her cry.

After several minutes, Emelise pulled back and wiped her eyes. "Thank you." She took several deep breaths and stepped back. "I must look a wreck," she grumbled before she grabbed her makeup bag out of her purse to make sure she didn't go back out with raccoon eyes. That was when her eyes fell on the roses resting on the desk. "You brought me roses." A soft smile flitted across her face. Even when she felt like her world was unraveling, he managed to ground her in some way. "They're beautiful."

"Not as beautiful as you." Caine lifted his hand and touched her cheek gently. "Do you want to go to da hospital now?"

"No. I can't do that to Venus. This is her big night. I have to be here to announce her. Besides, you haven't heard her full stage name." There was a mischievous gleam in her eyes.

"Den let's get back out front so you can introduce her." Caine slipped his arm around her waist as they headed for the door.

Eme leaned against him until they reached the bar. Then she stood up on her tiptoes, kissed his chin, and pulled away to go to the stage. "For those who are new here, welcome to Scarlet Flux. I hope y'all have been enjoying yourselves so far." She waited for the applause to stop before she continued. "Tonight it is my pleasure and honor to introduce you to an amazing performer. I lured her away from her long-time gig in Phoenix, Arizona, where she performed at The

Inferno several nights a week. Without further ado, I give you the enchanting and seductive Miss Venus Flysnatch."

Malcolm

Malcolm had arrived at the club in the late afternoon to go over the set one last time with the band. He'd wanted the show to be perfect. He was a mess in his private life but when it came to his professional life, he was a perfectionist. "That was perfect, guys and gals," he said with a wink to the band. "Thanks for putting up with my need to be sure we have it down pat."

"It's all good, Mal. At least you're dedicated to your music. You wouldn't believe some of the singers we've worked with who only put in half-ass effort and expected things to be great," the bassist said with a roll of her eyes. "Tonight should be great. You'll knock 'em dead."

Malcolm laughed. "That's the plan. Figuratively speaking, of course." With that he headed into the dressing room to begin the process of transforming himself from Malcolm Savage, lion shifter, to Venus Flysnatch, Blues Sensation. Few who saw him in drag ever recognized him out of it.

Hours later, Venus waited in the wings, listening to Emelise introduce her. She doubted any of the humans caught the strain in Eme's voice, but she knew every shifter there would hear it. Too bad she'd have to wait until the show was over to find out what was wrong.

"Without further ado, I give you the enchanting and seductive Miss Venus Flysnatch."

With those words Venus sauntered out into the club and took the small stage. She lost herself to the music at the first notes of *I Just Want to Make Love to You* written by Willie Dixon and performed by Blues greats such as Etta James and Muddy Waters. That segued into *A Sunday Kind of Love* which was followed by *Misty Blue* and *Something's Got A Hold On Me*, all of which were songs made popular by Etta James. Then she changed things up a little and sang Aretha Franklin's *Rolling in the Deep*, *Chain of Fools*, and *Respect*. She finished her set with Bonnie Raitt's *Thing Called Love* and *Love Me Like A Man*. Next was *Sweet Home Chicago*, followed by *The Thrill Is Gone*, *I Can't Quit You Baby*, *Shake Your Money Maker* and she closed the set with *It Hurts Me Too*.

By the time Venus left the stage, she was ready for something cold to drink and flying high on the applause she'd received. She made her way toward the bar and her gaze fell on a very attractive redhead leaning against the bar. He was a few inches shorter than Venus's own 6'4". He was toned in a way that told Venus he worked out, and it made her want to undress him just to see what he looked like under the snug-fitting slacks and dress shirt he wore. His scent hit her and she arched a brow. Leopard.

The way her lion suddenly reared its head, making it difficult to hold onto her persona, was almost enough to make her turn around and head to the dressing room to change. Almost. "Well, aren't you a spot of sunshine in the dark," Venus purred at the leopard before she leaned over the bar to order a drink. "Corona Extra." With a wink at the redhead, Venus took her drink and headed to the hall, leading to the backstage area and the dressing rooms.

"Fuck. Fuck. Fuck." The instant the dressing room door was closed, Malcolm dropped the Venus persona and growled with frustration. Of course he'd had the misfortune of running into the one shifter that could make his lion take notice while he was in drag. After his performance, the redhead, whoever he was, probably assumed 'Venus' was a real woman, and he'd be disgusted when he realized Venus was just a drag queen.

Staring at himself in the dressing room mirror, he felt despondent. As bad as homophobia was in the human world, it was even worse in the shifter world, depending on the flavor of shifter. Once upon a time he'd pretended to be straight just to be accepted in the Pride but that had gone horribly wrong. He'd ended up being shunned by the Pride, any Pride, and it had left him feeling defective and despondent. It had taken time to pull himself out of the deep depression he'd spiraled into, and he had no desire to go down that dark path again.

Malcolm drained his beer quickly before he focused on removing the wig and makeup. Fifteen minutes later he was stepping out of the dressing room in a pair of snug-fitting jeans and a T-shirt that hugged his upper body. Part of him hoped the redhead was still there but the other part hoped he'd left.

Emelise

Despite being anxious to leave and get to the hospital, Emelise waited until Malcolm was done. It was his debut as Venus, and she refused to slip out the door without seeing how the show was received first. The thunderous applause that echoed and swelled throughout the club, when Venus stepped off the stage, brought a grin to her face despite her worry. "Let me congratulate Malcolm on the show, then we can get out of here," she said to Caine who stood with his arm wrapped protectively around her.

"You got it, Angel."

She smiled, just a little, and leaned into him, before she pulled away, so she could head toward the hall Malcolm would have to exit to get into the club. When she noticed her cousin, Julius, standing there, she arched a brow. "Hey. What are you doing hanging around here?"

Julius turned his attention to his cousin. "Waitin' for Venus to come out. Don't worry, I know Venus is a drag queen," he said before she could say anything. "Just want to tell him he's got an amazin' voice." He leveled his gaze at her. "You're upset. What's wrong?"

She shook her head. "Tell you later. I'm heading out of here in a minute but… Ah, here he is now." She saw the way Malcolm froze, for a fraction of a second, when his gaze fell on Julius, and it piqued her curiosity. *Later, Eme, you need to get to the hospital*, she silently admonished herself. "Hey, Mal, that was so great. I have to leave. Derrick, my dad, had to be rushed to the hospital with chest pains, but I didn't want to go without congratulating you on a smashing debut."

Malcolm flashed her a grin. "Thanks, babe," he said with a wink in Caine's direction. "Venus seems to be a hit in the Big Easy." Then he sobered a little. "Shit, I hope he's okay."

"Thanks." At his comment about being a big hit, she smiled a little. "As if there was any doubt. Oh, Malcolm, this is my cousin, Julius. Jules, this is Mal. Okay, introductions done, I'm out of here. I'll call you tomorrow to fill you in," she added to both of them before she let Caine lead her out into the humid night air.

Eme stared out the window as Caine drove them to Tulane Medical Center. Her fingers restlessly played with the hem of her shirt, and every now and then she shifted in her seat. The tension in the car was thick enough to cut with a knife. To say she was scared was putting it lightly. Terror, at the thought of losing her father so soon after meeting him, almost had her frozen in her seat.

"We'll be there soon." Caine reached over and took her hand in his.

"Thank you for coming with me." Eme kept her voice soft out of fear it would break if she spoke too loudly.

"Dere's no place I'd rather be den at your side, Angel."

She could hear the fierce honesty in his voice. Gods, he was making her love him and that terrified her. If she lost her heart to him and he walked away, she knew it would shatter her and she'd never be able to put the pieces back together.

Caine

Caine had watched her from the corner of his eye as he drove. His leopard wanted to snarl at the helplessness he felt. Protecting his mate from harm was his number one priority, even before the Pard. This pain, this fear, was something he couldn't protect her from though. It made him feel powerless and that enraged his leopard.

He reached over and took her hand in his before he entwined their fingers together. He wasn't going to tell her everything would be 'okay' because they had no idea what had caused the chest pains. The most obvious answer was heart attack but there were other conditions that could cause it too. It damn-near broke his heart when she thanked him for being there. Her distrust of men and their ability to commit made him want to hunt down the man, who'd initially caused it, and hurt him. "Dere's no place I'd rather be den at your side, Angel." No truer words were ever spoken. He would move heaven and earth to be at her side whenever and wherever she needed him. He felt the outline of the velvet box in his pocket. Inside it was a pendant he'd had custom made for her. Caine decided that, once they reached the hospital parking lot, he was giving it to her before she got out of his car.

Caine found a parking spot as close to the Emergency Department entrance as he could and turned off the car. "Wait. Before you get out, dere's someting I want to give you. I'd planned a bit more of a romantic setting but dis will have to do." He pulled the box from his pocket and held it out to her. "I know you have a hard time trustin' men—I even know why dat is—but you thanking me for being here, it shows me dat I've not been diligent enough in showing you just how much you mean to me. I am in love wit' you Emelise Acadia Rousseau. Dis pendant is a symbol of how long dat love will last."

When he opened the box, he revealed a gorgeous, handcrafted Infinity pendant. It was white gold with a trail of diamonds along one side of the symbol. The other side had a heart carved into it with a gorgeous emerald stone resting in half of the heart. The color reminded him of her eyes.

Emelise covered her mouth and a soft sound escaped her. "Caine…it's beautiful," she whispered.

"I hoped you'd like it. I'm not goin' anywhere, Angel. You and me, dis is for life, whether you believe me yet or not." He helped her to put it on, then brushed his lips across hers. "We'll face whatever we find in dere together."

Eme curled her fingers around the pendant for a moment before she nodded. "I love you, too, you know."

A soft growl escaped him. "Dat's good to know." He kissed her again, then reluctantly let go so they could get out of the car. As soon as he'd rounded the back of the car to her side, he slipped his arm over her shoulder and pulled her close. He loved that she was petite enough he could tuck her against his side without difficulty.

As they neared the entrance to the doors leading into the hospital, he felt her take a deep breath before she released it slowly. He could almost feel her resolve to be strong, no matter what the news might be.

Chapter Seventeen

Emelise

She hated hospitals. Nothing good had ever come from visiting one. The tension in the air, from so many sick and injured people and their worried families, made it hard for her to breathe. As soon as the doors closed behind them, she stopped and closed her eyes. Memories, of the last time she was in a hospital, threatened to overwhelm her and a soft mewl escaped from between her lips. Caine's arms wrapping around her grounded her and brought her back to the present. She needed to get herself under control. Taking several deep breaths, she let each one out slowly before she opened her eyes. "Thank you. I hate hospitals." She felt the heat of embarrassment on her cheeks.

"No'ting to be embarrassed about, cher. You've had some bad experiences in hospitals."

Emelise gave him a faint smile. "I suppose." She refused to let the memories take hold again. "Let's see if we can find Angie."

A few minutes later found her sitting in a chair next to her stepmother. All four of her half-siblings were there, as well. "Have you heard anything yet?"

"Not yet but we should any time now." Angie turned her attention to her children. "I know we were going to do this officially tomorrow but since we're all here... Guys, this is Emelise. She's the sister your dad told you about. Emelise, this is Connor, Gavin, Jaxon, and Ava."

"Hi." Eme nodded at each of them. "You can call me Eme. It's nice to meet all of you; I just wish it was anywhere else."

"It's nice to meet you, too, finally. Dad's told us a little about you. He didn't really explain why he was never told about you, though." Connor, the oldest of the four and several years younger than Emelise, watched her closely.

"That's a bit hard to explain. See, Mama never told me much about her side of the family, and she never once talked about who my father was. I didn't know until he and your mama came to my club on opening night. I could wish it was different all I want, but that won't change the past. I just hope I get to know all of you now that we've been reunited. It was just me and Mama when I was growing up so this whole having lots of family members thing is new and a little overwhelming sometimes."

"I like you." Ava was the youngest. "You're spunky." She gave Emelise a shy smile.

Caine chuckled at Emelise's side. "Dat she is."

"Oh, crap. I'm so sorry. I'm forgetting my manners. This is my…boyfriend, Caine." He was more than that, but she wasn't up to going into detail there at the hospital, and she didn't think it was appropriate to call him her 'lover' considering Ava wasn't even in her teens.

"It's all right, Angel. You've been a little distracted. Nice to meet y'all." He nodded at her siblings before he noticed a doctor headed their way. "Looks like dey might finally have some answers."

Emelise tensed at his side and leaned into him when he tightened his arm around her shoulder.

"Mrs. Winton? I'm sorry to keep you waiting so long. Your

husband had a blood clot that broke off from a larger clot we found located in his right knee. Records show he had an injury to that knee a few years ago. Sometimes blood clots can form without there being any visible indication, as with your husband, which can make it difficult to catch before there is trouble. We're giving him blood thinners to break down the clot and will keep him overnight to monitor his condition. He will have to be on blood thinners for six months after his release, and he needs to follow up with his regular physician."

"Oh, thank God. I was so worried he'd had a heart attack," Angie whispered. "Can we see him?"

"He's being moved to a room in ICU. If you'll follow me I'll show you to his room so you can wait for him there."

They all followed him to the elevators and stepped inside. Emelise felt almost weak with relief. She wasn't an expert, but she knew a blood clot in the heart could have killed her father just as easily as a heart attack could have. But that didn't happen and she had time to get to know him, after all. She hadn't even had the chance to give him the letter from her mother yet. Eme would have never forgiven herself if he'd died without having had the chance to read it.

Emelise quietly followed behind her stepmother and siblings. It was still a little overwhelming for her to know she had such a large family when for so long it had been just her and her mother. When they reached the hospital room, she hovered near the door to give the others some privacy.

Derrick lay in the bed with a disgruntled look on his face. "All this fussing over me; I'm fine," he grumbled.

"You're not 'fine', Derrick. You could have died." Angie held her husband's hand tightly. "I'm just so glad you didn't try to hide it like you usually do when something is bothering you."

He sighed. "I'm sorry, love. I just really dislike hospitals."

From the door, Emelise couldn't help but snicker. "Good to know I'm not the only one who doesn't like them."

"Emelise? Don't you have a big show at the club tonight?" He and Angie had planned on going before he'd started having the chest pains.

"I did, yeah. It ended a little bit ago. The club is in good hands. I trust my manager to close it up after the last customer is gone." She stepped into the room and moved to the bedside. "There's something I've been meaning to give you. I was going to do it tomorrow at dinner, but since that's on hold and I'm here now…" She pulled the sealed envelope from her bag. "I found this in a chest Mama had locked tight."

Derrick took the letter and just held it.

"We're going down to the waiting room, give y'all some time together," Emelise said before she moved to go to the door. She didn't want to barge in on their family time.

"Please stick around? I think you should be here when I read this," Derrick told her.

"Sure," Emelise agreed. She was quiet as she took a seat in the waiting room down the hall from his room.

Derrick

Half an hour later, Derrick was still holding the letter Emelise had given him. He'd cuddled with Sophie and joked with his sons, to try and ease the worry he saw on their faces. He hated that he'd put such fear in his children's eyes.

"Go ahead, honey. Read it. You've been holding onto that letter since Emelise gave it to you. Maybe the answers to some of those questions you have will be in there. I'll take the kids down to the cafeteria for a little bit and give you and Emelise some time together."

"Thank you, love."

"You're welcome." She leaned down and gave him a gentle kiss. "I'll send Emelise in on our way to the elevators."

Derrick was waiting when Emelise knocked. "Come on in."

"Angie said you were ready to read the letter my mama left you."

"I am. Why don't you sit?" He waited until she sat in the chair beside the bed, with Caine standing behind her, before he took a deep breath and let it out slowly. "Well, here goes nothing." He opened the envelope and took out the sheet of paper that was folded up inside it.

Dearest Derrick,

If you're reading this then I'm gone and our daughter has done what I asked of her. I'm sure you have questions that I'm not here to answer in person, but I'll try to answer the ones I think you'll have within this letter.

By now you've met Emelise and you'll know she's a bit of a firecracker, just like her mama. If I know our girl, she's told you everything she possibly can, including the fact that we're shifters. I can just imagine your surprise. Oh, you knew, theoretically, that we existed—everyone does—but it's so very different when you get to see it, isn't it?

For the longest time, after I left, I thought about trying to get in touch with you. I admit, I kept some tabs on you because I wanted to know you were okay. I loved you and I didn't want my papa to blame you for me taking off. When I found out you'd gotten married, I knew you'd moved on, as you should, and I made myself let you go. There was always a place in my heart for you, though. You were my first love and you gave me the greatest gift a woman could ever ask for: an amazing daughter.

I'm sorry I never told you about her. When I realized I was pregnant, I panicked. I ran away because I knew my Alpha would make me get rid of the baby. He was a cruel man. Humans were beneath him and being with one, that was a sin in his eyes. I was sixteen and scared and I didn't know how to tell you any of my secrets. I was afraid you'd want nothing to do with me or our baby. I was worried you'd be afraid of me. Or worse, that you'd be disgusted because I wasn't human. So I ran and I kept the truth from you.

I know I should have contacted you, once Emelise was born. I started to. On more than one occasion I wrote a letter to you but fear kept me from sending them. Fear and shame.

Then you moved on. You started having babies with your wife. I told myself you didn't need Emelise; you had them. It was selfish of me to keep her to myself. It took away your chance to know your daughter when she was a little girl; it robbed you of your chance to watch her grow up into such a wonderful young woman. And it took away her chance to know her father while she was growing up.

Please know that I didn't maliciously set out to hurt anyone. I didn't keep her from you out of spite or anger. I was a selfish girl who was too scared to admit she'd messed up by running in the first place.

I'm not proud of the choices I made. I'm not proud of the pain I know my choices have caused both you and our daughter. Emelise deserved better and so did you. All I can do is ask for your forgiveness.

~Adelaide

By the time he finished reading, there were tears sliding silently down his cheek. "Oh, Adelaide, how could I possibly hate you when you gave me a gift too?" He shook his head and looked up at Emelise. "Although I wish I'd gotten to watch you grow up, I'm glad I have the chance to get to know you now. Thank you for giving me this. It did answer some questions. You know your mother didn't keep my identity from you to hurt you, right?"

Emelise

Emelise watched as her father read the letter her mama had left him. She wondered what it said, but she would never invade his privacy by asking. At his question she nodded and smiled a little. "Yeah, I know. She wrote me a letter too. She also had one for both her parents. I gave them to her mama since her papa is gone. Mama didn't mean to hurt anyone. She was sixteen, pregnant, and scared out of her mind. She did the best she could for me though and really, the way she raised me, it helped to make me the woman I am today. I don't know that I would want it any other way."

Caine leaned down and nuzzled her neck a moment. "I wouldn't want you any other way, Angel. You're perfect just as you are."

Emelise smiled back at him. "Thanks." She turned her attention back to her father. "We should get out of here and let you rest. I'll go find Angie and let her know we're leaving so she can come back. You need to focus on getting better because we still have that family dinner to do."

Derrick chuckled. "Yes, ma'am."

Eme leaned down and kissed his cheek. At the door she turned and waved good-night then, headed to the elevators. Once they were on the ground floor it didn't take long to find the cafeteria. "Hey. We're heading out of here. Would you like us to drop the kids off at your house? Or they could crash at my apartment," Emelise offered to Angie, so that Angie wouldn't have to leave Derrick's side.

"Or dey can come out to da compound since I have more room den your tiny apartment," Caine offered.

Angie looked at her children for their input.

"I'm seventeen, I don't need a babysitter," Connor pointed out.

"Who said anything about a babysitter? Have you guys spent any time in the bayou before?" Emelise gave her younger brother an arched look.

"Not a whole lot, why?"

"Would you like to? Because that's where Caine's house is. He and his community have some land out in the bayou. It's really pretty out there. You know, I'll bet you know some of them and don't even realize it. You're only a little younger than my cousins, Adele and Auguste."

"You're cousins with Adele?" Connor perked up at that.

Eme knew that look. He had a crush. "Yep, I sure am."

"I think it would be fun to go out to the bayou," Ava said shyly.

Gavin and Jaxon both shrugged. "Sounds like fun," they said almost in unison.

"Looks like you have your answer," Angie replied. "Thank you for doing this, Emelise."

"I want to. It'll give us time to get to know each other a little. Come on, guys. We can go to your house first so you can get whatever you need for tonight and tomorrow. Call if there's any change."

"I will." Angie turned to her children. "Be good and have fun, okay? Your dad's going to be fine." She hugged each of them in turn.

"Don't worry about us, Mom, we'll be fine. Tell Dad goodnight for us?" Connor was ever the spokesperson for the four of them.

"Of course." Angie watched her kids follow Emelise out before she went back to the hospital room and her husband.

Emelise was glad Caine's 'car' was an SUV because it had plenty of room for everyone. "You direct, Caine will drive, and we'll go to your house so you guys can get some clothes and whatever else you need for tonight," Emelise said once everyone was settled in the SUV.

"Do you think we'll get to see any alligators?" Ava asked once they were on their way.

"Maybe. You like gators?" Emelise glanced back at her.

"Yeah, they're really cool."

"They're also very dangerous," Jaxon pointed out to her.

"I know that. I wouldn't get close to one. I still think they're cool."

"You will definitely enjoy da bayou, cher." Caine glanced back at her. "Dere are lots of cool tings, not just gators."

Eme had a thought. Did Derrick and Angie fill them in on what she was? She sent a quick text off because she didn't want something to happen to scare one of her half-siblings. *Angie, do the kids know I'm a shifter? I need to know how much I have to protect them from while they're with me.*

They know. Derrick wanted there to be no secrets. Expect Gavin and Ava to ask to see one of the leopards. They were really fascinated by it all.

That can be arranged. I'm glad they're not totally freaked out by it. She couldn't believe how accepting people were in New Orleans. It was so different from Phoenix.

She and Caine waited in the vehicle while Connor and the others headed into their home to pack a bag. Once that was done they headed to the docks. Emelise had spent so much time at Caine's house that she'd left some clothes there in case she needed them. Now she was glad she did.

"Dad said you were a shifter. Is that true?" Gavin leaned forward in his seat as much as the seat belt would allow.

"Yes." Eme waited to see where he was going with the question.

"How did that happen? I mean, Dad isn't a shifter."

"No, he isn't. My mama was though. She died a little while ago. There was no guarantee that I'd be able to shift but I got lucky."

"What do you mean?" This time it was Jaxon who spoke.

"When a shifter and a human have a child together, there's a chance the child won't be able to shift. He or she might have some of the other characteristics that mark them shifter—faster healing, greater speed and strength, that kind of thing—but they can't shift to their animal form. Others are completely human."

"How often does it happen that a shifter and a human have a kid together?"

Emelise was a little surprised to hear Connor ask the question. He'd seemed very disinterested in the discussion.

"Honestly, I don't know but I'm betting it's a good bit. Everyone wants to be happy, after all, and sometimes you can't find that one person who seems to fit with the animal in you." She glanced over at Caine. "And sometimes you get really lucky."

"Will you change for us?" Ava piped up. "Or shift or whatever it's called."

"Sure, I can do that. I'll have to do it in a different room though because I'll have to get undressed first." Her leopard was a bit smaller than Caine's so it might be best if she was the one who shifted. "We call it shifting." She smiled back at Ava. She was adorable. Between Mia's newborn son, Elijah, little Lexi Caterini, whom she'd met the other day, her cousin Sophie, and now Ava, Emelise found herself longing for little ones of her own. What in the fuck was wrong with her? She shook her head and pushed the random thought away.

At the docks she let Caine help her onto the boat. "Watch your step so you don't slip." She reached out to steady Ava as she hopped down off the side of the boat. "Seriously, be careful, Ava. You don't want to fall into the water."

"Sorry." Ava gave a sheepish smile and settled down next to Emelise for the ride out to the compound.

"It's okay. You're just excited." Emelise remembered that age. Ava was on the cusp of 'teenage-hood'; still a child but rapidly speeding toward the hormonal upheaval that came with being a teen and learning to spread her wings.

When they reached the compound, Ava slipped her hand into Emelise's and walked tucked close to her side. She was excited but at the same time she was shy.

"I have an idea. My cousin Sophie is eight, so she's a few years younger than you, but I'll bet she would love to come over to our house for a slumber party. What do you think, Ava?"

"That sounds like fun!" She grinned up at her.

"Hey, babe, you go on to the house with the boys; Ava and I are going to stop and invite Sophie to a slumber party." Emelise blew Caine a kiss and steered Ava down the path that would take them to Eliza and Ephram's home.

Eliza was sitting on the front porch when they came up the walk. "Evenin', Emelise. Who you got wit' you?"

"Evening, Eliza. This is my half-sister, Ava. Ava, this is my Mama's cousin, Eliza. We were wondering if Sophie would like to come over for a slumber party."

"Hello dere, Ava." Eliza smiled warmly at the girl. "She probably would. Lemme go get her."

Five minutes later Sophie came barreling out of the house with a bag on her shoulder. She had clothes in it, along with her pillow and a stuffed tiger she slept with all the time. "Mama says you're havin' a slumber party!" She grinned at Ava. "Hi! I'm Sophie," she said while she waved.

Ava giggled. "I'm Ava. Emelise said we could have a slumber party."

"That's right. We'll do whatever you two want." Eme wanted to take Ava's mind off the fact their father was in the hospital.

"Sophie, you mind Emelise and have fun wit' your new friend." Eliza followed her daughter out onto the porch. "If she's any trouble, you can send her on home."

Emelise shook her head. "I'm sure we'll be fine. See you tomorrow, Eliza," she said and ushered the girls off.

Back at the house Emelise soon found herself playing dress-up with the girls. They then built a fort with blankets, which Caine helped to fortify because it kept falling, and then they made s'mores in the microwave. When Sophie and Ava were tired, Eme read them a bedtime story and waited until they'd both fallen asleep before she finally joined her mate out on the back porch.

Jaxon, Gavin, and Connor had been joined by some of the boys in the compound, including Emelise's cousins Auguste and Dempsey, and they were playing a game of football. "Are you refereeing or letting them play dirty?" Eme asked as she slid onto Caine's lap.

Caine chuckled. "Dey don't play dirty. It's good to get dere minds off of dere papa bein' in da hospital."

"Yeah. That's why I had Sophie come over for a slumber party. Maybe next time I'll plan something, and they can have a few friends over, as well, so it's not just the two of them."

"You plannin' on doin' dis a lot, mmh?"

"Yeah, I think I am."

Caine

It wasn't until much later, when the boys were playing footbal,l and little Ava, accompanied by Sophie, were asleep, that he had the chance to spend some time with his mate. "You're enjoyin' dis, havin' dem here, aren't you?"

Eme nodded. "I am. You were right. Bringing them out here was the better option. They would have been miserable at my apartment."

He chuckled. "I know I was right." He winked at her and continued, "You know, I'd had other plans for our evenin', Angel, but havin' dem here, where dey can let dere minds relax from worryin' is more important. Dere your family."

Emelise rolled her eyes at him. "Ha-ha, very funny." She glanced over to where the boys were playing football. "Yeah, they are. Thank you. I know you had other plans for our night, but thank you for supporting my offer."

"I will always support you. Dat's what you do when you love someone." He watched her face a moment. "Move in wit' me, Angel." Okay, that wasn't exactly the way he'd planned on asking her to do that. He'd had this idea in his head to be all romantic with her but it was already out there.

Emelise blinked at him. "I don't know, Caine..."

"You practically live here anyway. How often do you sleep at your apartment?"

They both knew the answer and it wasn't very much.

"You love it here, you know you do." He caressed her cheek. "But more importantly, I love gettin' to fall asleep holdin' you every night and wakin' up to you every mornin'. I know you have a hard time trustin'—I even know why dat is—but dis, what we have between us, it's not goin' to fade and I'm not goin' to walk away. It isn't just because we're mates, either. Yes, my leopard wants you here, why wouldn't he? But I want you here, as well. Dis decision, it's coming from both parts of me, cher. Da human and da leopard. Dis isn't just about us bein' mates. I want to watch as da sunrise kisses your skin each mornin'. I want to watch you dancin' around da kitchen while you cook. I want to be dere when someting makes you mad so you have someone to vent to. Move in wit' me, Angel."

He wanted so much more than that but he didn't have the ring. Still, everything he'd said was what he'd planned to say when he proposed. "No, don't just move in wit' me."

Fuck it. Ring or no ring, he was showing her how much she meant to him. "I'd planned to do dis next weekend but it can't wait. Don't just move in wit' me. Marry me, Emelise. I love you. I want you by my side for da rest of our lives. I want to grow old wit' you, cher. You drive me crazy both in bed and out of it, but it's a good kind of crazy. From da moment you came into my life, you've lit up my world. I didn't even realize I was livin' in such darkness until you came along. You've changed my life, my world, for da better. I don't have da ring—it's bein' made—dat's why I was waitin' til next weekend, but dis can't wait. I needed to tell you ever'ting I was feelin', ever'ting I was tinkin'." Caine sat there, holding his breath, as he waited for her to answer.

Emelise

If someone had told her, when she woke up that morning, that her emotions were going to be run through the ringer, she might have stayed in bed. Or told them to go fuck themselves. Or both. Yeah, both sounded about right. First she finds herself facing the fear of possibly losing her father so soon after finding him. She gets to the hospital and is bombarded by her memories of the last time she was at a hospital when she learned of her mother's death. Then, of course, she is overwhelmed by nervousness upon meeting her half-siblings and worrying about what they think of her. But this, this took the cake.

She'd sat there on Caine's lap listening to him, listening to all the reasons why he wanted her to move in with him, and she'd hesitated. Moving in together was a big step, but if history told her anything, it was that living together didn't mean it was for life. His next words blew her away. Emelise lost sight of everything else around them. All of her senses narrowed until the only two people who existed were her and Caine. The football game going on in the backyard faded out of existence. The girls sleeping in one of the spare rooms under a sheet fort, gone. The chirping of cicadas, the croaking of bullfrogs, the hiss of gators, the buzzing of insects—all of it disappeared.

Emelise felt tears stinging her eyes. She'd been so afraid of letting him into her heart because she didn't know if he wanted a commitment with her, and now here he was asking her to marry him. He said the one thing that let her know it was coming from him and not his cat. *This isn't about us being mates.* He wasn't being guided by the connection of their animals. "You mean it? It's not your cat talking? This is all you? Because, I swear to all that is holy, if this is coming more from your leopard than it is from the human part of you, Caine, I just might have to hurt you. I don't want to get married just because we're mates." She needed to know for sure.

"I really mean it, Angel. Dis is all me. You would make me da happiest, and luckiest, man in da world if you said yes."

Eme laughed softly. "I'm sure every man who has ever married feels the same way," she teased before she grew serious. "Yes. It scares the hell out of me but you make me crazy too. I want all those things, too, Caine. I want to wake up with you every morning; I want to fuss at you to stop working so hard when you get caught up in your office and forget to eat." She bit her lip a moment. "I want to watch you playing in the backyard with our children. Yes, I'll marry you."

"*Woohoo!*"

Emelise blushed clear to her hairline. She'd completely forgotten that they weren't alone. She looked over to where Dempsey and Auguste were grinning at them. "I take it you two approve?"

"Hell yeah we do! We've all been waitin' for dis'. You're a good influence on him, Cuz," Auguste said and Dempsey echoed him.

Emelise laughed. "That's good to know." As much fun as she knew the boys were having with their football game, it was getting late. "You two should get on home. It's late."

"Uh-huh, you just want to be alone," Auguste teased. He winked at her. "But, yeah, it is late. Dis was fun. You should come out again. We can get a few more together and have a real game," he added to Connor, Gavin, and Jaxon.

Connor looked to Emelise. "Do you think we could do that?"

Eme smiled. "Of course. You guys will be welcome any time."

"Cool. See you later, then," Connor said to Auguste and Dempsey before he ushered his brothers inside. They would take quick showers before heading to bed.

Caine wrapped his arms around Emelise and nuzzled her neck. "When do you want to pack up all your tings and move dem here?"

Emelise leaned back against him and sighed. "I don't know. I like being in my own place. When Mama was still alive, she was always so worried about something happening to me that I couldn't bring myself to move out of the house I grew up in. The few months I've been here, this is the first real freedom I've had and it's not going to be easy to give that up."

"I don't want to take your freedom from you, cher. I just want to wake up wit' you every mornin'." He kissed her jaw. "Dere's no rush. We'll go at whatever pace you're comfortable wit'."

"Thank you." She turned in his arms so she was facing him. "You know, I'd resigned myself to the fact I would likely never find my mate. Living in Phoenix, there weren't that many shifters there, other than a group of coyote shifters. Talk about an annoying group of people. They were a bunch of tricksters, I swear. It's like they heard native tales about Coyote—in them he is a trickster who frustrates all the other spirit animals—and they decided to emulate him."

Cain chuckled. "I've met a couple coyote shifters during Mardis Gras. I tink you're right about dem emulating da spirit animal."

"Anyway, as I was saying, I'd resigned myself to most likely never meeting my mate. Yet, here we are. It's crazy and scary and thrilling all at the same time."

"I know what you mean, Angel. I didn't think I would ever meet mine either. None of da females in da Pard were my mate and as Alpha, I couldn't just go to other Pards to search for one."

"Am I a bad person for sort of being glad my mama isn't here anymore? I never would have come to New Orleans, never would have met you, if she was still alive."

"No, cher. Or, if it does, then I'm just as bad. Come on, let's go to bed. You've had a rough day."

"Yeah. I've definitely had better." She let him lead her inside and down the hall to his bedroom. She paused to check in on Sophie and Ava, then, once they were in the bedroom, she stripped and crawled into bed. She curled up in Caine's arms when he joined her and half draped herself over him. "Good-night," she murmured softly.

"Good-night, Angel." Caine pressed a gentle kiss to her temple and caressed her side, which soothed her into slumber.

Chapter Eighteen

Emelise

The following morning, Emelise was awake before anyone. After a quick shower she called Angie at the hospital. She wanted to check on her father and ask her what the kids liked for breakfast because she didn't want to fix something they wouldn't eat. Once she was off the phone, she headed to the kitchen to get started.

By the time everyone else was up, she'd made blueberry pancakes, sausage, scrambled cheesy eggs, hash browns, and beignets. She surveyed the spread she had set out on the table with a satisfied nod. There was coffee for her, Caine, and Connor, and juice for the others.

"Wow. That's a lot of food."

Eme turned to the speaker and smiled a little. "Well, there's a lot of us to feed this morning. I called your mom when I got up so I would know what you guys liked. Dad is doing better and will be going home later today. The doctor had originally said he might have to stay a few days for observation, but they're confident he's on the mend enough to go home today."

Connor heaved a heavy sigh. "Thank God." He looked at Emelise a moment. "I wanted to thank you for inviting us to stay with you and Caine last night. I don't think I could have taken Ava's mind off Dad being in the hospital, not the way you did. You were really good with her."

"You don't have to thank me for that, Connor. We're family. I want to get to know all of you. Yeah, it would have been nice if we'd gotten to grow up together instead of meeting now, but it is what it is. As for Ava, she's a sweetheart."

Jaxon and Gavin came down the hall together with Ava and Sophie following them. "Something smells good. Please tell me we have sausage?"

Eme laughed. "We have sausage, Jaxon."

"Awesome." Then he changed gears. "Have you talked to our mom, yet? How's Dad doing?"

"Yeah, how's Daddy? Is he okay?" Ava bit her lip in worry.

Emelise went to her and knelt down so she was eye to eye with her. "I talked to your mom before I started breakfast. I wanted to be sure I didn't make something you guys either wouldn't or couldn't eat. Dad is doing much better and he'll get to go home later today."

Ava sniffled. "Really? You're not just saying that?"

"Really and truly. Do you want me to call your mom so you can hear it from her?"

"No. It's okay. I believe you." Ava brightened. "Can we see you change today before we have to leave?"

Eme had partially hoped she'd forgotten about that. "Of course, sweetie. But, we have to eat first before it gets cold."

"Dat sounds like a good idea to me." Caine was leaning against the opening between the living room and dining room, watching them. "Breakfast smells delicious, Angel."

"Thanks. Take a seat, guys; let's dig in."

There was light banter over breakfast. Mostly it was talk between Connor, Gavin, and Jaxon about the football game they'd played the night before. "I have a question." Gavin looked to Emelise and then

Caine before he continued. "Last night, when we were playing ball, did Auguste and Dempsey go easy on us because we're human?"

"Yes and no." Caine decided to field this one. "Dey can't hit you as hard as dey can each other because dey could have hurt you. But when it came to ever'ting else, no, dey didn't go easy on you. Well, besides dere speed. Dey moved a little slower too, but Auguste is used to dat since he's on da football team at school. He's followin' in his big brother's footsteps."

"Okay. Cool. I was just curious about that."

Once the breakfast dishes were done, Emelise went into the bedroom and stripped. She wasn't going to get undressed in front of her siblings just so they could see her in her leopard form. Her fur was on the paler end of the color spectrum. It was such a pale yellow it was almost white, but not quite, and her black spots stood out as a result. When Caine opened the door for her, she padded out on four legs, her movements slow to keep from scaring anyone.

Four pairs of eyes stared at her with a mixture of wonder and trepidation. It was sweet little Ava who moved first. "Wow. Can I touch her?" She looked up at Caine.

"A'course, cher. Emelise can understand you and she would never, in a million years, hurt you."

Eme huffed softly at Ava and gently butted her with her head.

Ava giggled and began petting her. "Oh. So soft." When Emelise licked her cheek, she giggled even more.

Connor, Gavin, and Jaxon finally moved closer and touched her too. "Wow, you're right. Her fur really is soft. This is so…weird. Cool, but weird." Connor shook his head. "If someone had told me a month ago that I'd be petting a leopard that was also my half-sister, I never would have believed them."

"Yeah, me either," Jaxon put in.

"Why don't we let Emelise shift back? Since Miss Ava wants to see some gators, why don't we give you a tour of da bayou?"

"Yes!" Ava hopped with excitement.

"Can I come?" Most of the other children in the Pard were boys, and Sophie was lonely for another girl to play with.

"A'course you can. Run along and let your mama know, and come right back." Caine gave her an encouraging smile.

Eme slipped into the bedroom, shifted back, and got dressed again. "I'll grab some bottles of water to take with us in case anyone gets thirsty. And the insect repellent for those of us who don't turn furry. For some reason, the mosquitoes don't seem to like us very much."

"Why do you have repellent then?" Connor gave her a confused look.

"We don't really have a big mosquito problem in Phoenix so I wasn't aware I didn't need it until I'd already bought it." Emelise shrugged. "I didn't want to just throw it away and now I'm glad I didn't."

Twenty minutes later they were all settled in the boat. Ava sat on one side of Emelise while Sophie sat on the other. The boat moved slowly through the water and, every now and then, Caine pointed out things of interest to them. When the boat slowed even more until it was barely moving, he pointed to the nearby shore. "Dat gator, right dere, we call him da grandaddy of gators." The reptile was huge. He was easily as long as the boat they were in. "He's a wily old ting. More den a few gator hunters have tried, and failed, to catch him." He chuckled. "Myself included."

"You're a gator hunter?" Eme arched a brow at her mate because that was news to her.

"Not so much dese days, but once upon a time, I was. Almost lost a hand to one of da buggers, once. Decided I was done wit' tryin' to catch dem. I had other tings to worry about at da time." Like defeating Zachary and becoming Alpha.

"Learn something new every day."

"How do you catch an alligator?" Gavin gave him a puzzled look.

"It's a dirty job, and a dangerous one. Dat's all you need to know. Don't you go tinkin' you can catch one yourself."

Gavin looked embarrassed. "I wasn't. Not really. I was just curious."

"You just keep it at dat."

Just as they were returning to the compound, Emelise's phone vibrated. A quick glance showed she had a text from Angie. *Derrick was just released and we're heading home. You can bring the kids back any time. Thank you, again, for letting them stay with you last night.*

She sent a quick text back, assuring Angie she'd enjoyed having them over and that she would bring them home soon, before she turned her attention to her siblings. "That was your mom. They're on their way home now so, whenever you guys are ready to go, we'll take you back."

They returned to the house where Emelise helped Ava to pack the bag she'd brought with her. The ride back to New Orleans was quiet. Even though their father was released to go home, he was going to have to take it easy for a bit.

"Hey, guys. Did you have fun hanging out with Emelise and Caine?" Angie smiled warmly at her kids and when Ava cuddled up to her, she hugged her close.

"Uh-huh. Emelise invited her cousin, Sophie, over for a sleepover and we built a fort out of tents and got to sleep in it. And today, we got to go see some alligators in the swamp!" Ava grinned up at her mother. "And Emelise shifted to her leopard and let us pet her. Her fur was so-o-o soft, Mama."

"I'm glad you had so much fun, Ava. Did you guys remember to say thank you?"

All four of them looked sheepish before they turned to Caine and Emelise and almost in unison, said "Thank you."

"You're welcome. I loved having you guys over." Eme was genuine about it.

"Emelise said we can come back any time. We played football with two of her other cousins and next time we go, they said they'll get more to play so we can have a real game." Jaxon grinned. "It was a lot of fun."

"I'm glad. Okay, I know you want to see your father," Angie said and moved out of the doorway so they could go inside. "Please, come in, Emelise, Caine."

Eme followed her inside and waited until the others were done greeting their father before she approached him. "Hey. I'm glad you're feeling better."

"Me too. Angie told me you let the kids stay with you last night. I hope they weren't any trouble?"

"No, not at all. It was fun. We've invited them to visit any time they want to."

Derrick reached out for her hand and when she let him take it, he squeezed it gently. "I'm glad you're getting along with them. We've still got a lot of catching up to do, kiddo."

Eme felt tears stinging her eyes and blinked several times. "Yeah. We do. But right now, I'm going to let you rest. I've got some stuff I need to get done." Like call Lily and Malcolm, and hell, Julius, and fill them in on how her father was doing. She also had a couple of interviews for the soon-to-be-open bartender position in the VIP Lounge. And she wanted to check in on Izzy Catalini. She hadn't been able to get her, or her daughter Lexi, out of her mind.

"All right. Come by soon though, so we can talk more. I want to hear all about your childhood."

"I will." She leaned down and kissed his cheek before she let Caine lead her out of there.

"So…Caine proposed to me last night." When she'd called Lily to fill her in on how her father was doing, Lily had invited her over for lunch. She'd tried to wait until after they were done eating but Emelise just couldn't keep it to herself.

Lily blinked. "Oh my gods. You said yes, didn't you? Wait, where's your ring? I know that leopard did *not* propose and not bother to get you a ring. Alpha or not, I will kick his ass for that."

Eme laughed. "No need to kick his ass. I'll have my ring this weekend. He wasn't exactly planning on asking me when he did it. He had this big, romantic plan to propose once he had the ring, but…it just kind of happened."

"Tell me. I want the deets!"

Emelise laughed. "Well, I'd invited my siblings to stay the night because I didn't think they should be alone. Sophie came over for a sleepover with Ava, and while I got them settled down, Auguste and Dempsey came over and got into a football game with Connor, Gavin, and Jaxon. Caine was watching them when I went out on the porch.

It started with him suddenly asking me to move in with him, but then he dropped the bomb and proposed. It was so spontaneous and so fucking perfect. I know most women envision a big, romantic deal complete with candlelight and music, but I've never needed anything like that. As long as it's from the heart, that's the only thing that really matters. I swear, girl, when he started talking, everything else disappeared. It was like he and I were the only two people in existence. It was…perfect."

"I am so happy for you, Eme. I know this scares you…"

"It scares the fuck out of me," Emelise interrupted.

"I know. Like I said, I know this scares you, but that man is wrapped so tightly around your little finger he's not ever going to stray. You're it for him, girlfriend."

"What about you and Declan? Do you think he'll ever pop the question?"

Lily shrugged. "I don't know. I like to think so, when he's ready. We're still feeling our way around being a couple who are also the Alphas of a Pack comprised of several species of shifters. He's also working on getting his personal security company up and running so he's got a lot on his plate at the moment. I just have to believe that when he feels like the time is right, he'll propose."

"He will. Have faith. That wolf's been hung up on you from the moment you two met. Between him and Caine, I don't know which one is worse."

They both snickered. "They're probably about even." Lily sighed softly. "Ugh. I'm having way too much fun just chilling here. It makes me wish I didn't have to go to work even though I love my job."

Emelise laughed softly. "I know what you mean. Part of me wants to blow off the interviews I have to give today, but I'll need a new bartender soon so I have to get to it."

"We need to get together again, soon. We should plan a day to go shopping or something."

"I agree. You pick the day; I'll make the time. I'll see you later, Lil."

"See you, Eme." Lily walked her to the door where they hugged before Emelise left.

Caine

When he'd awakened that morning to an empty bed, Caine had cocked a brow. He'd expected to find his mate still curled up against him. Then he'd caught the scent of food cooking and had heard voices coming from the front of the house. A smile had flitted across his face. She'd gotten up before everyone so she could fix breakfast. Damn, he loved that woman. He'd taken a quick shower and made his way toward the kitchen. He'd found Emelise in the dining room with her siblings and leaned against the wall to watch her.

Emelise took his breath away every time he looked at her. He knew she didn't think of herself as some great beauty. He knew she thought she was too short, didn't have enough curves, to be a woman men would chase after. But fuck, he got hard just looking at her. When she finally suggested they sit down to eat, he'd spoken up. "Dat sounds like a good idea to me. Breakfast smells delicious, Angel."

Over breakfast his gaze had kept going to her. He still couldn't believe she'd said yes. He'd been half afraid she would turn his proposal down. Who would have thought Caine Bordeaux could be brought to his knees by such a petite beauty? She had no idea just how much control she had over him. All it would take to destroy him was for her to walk away. It scared the hell out of him to know she had that much power.

It wasn't until much later in the day, after they'd taken her siblings back into New Orleans, that he turned his attention to work. He had an email from Ryan Vallier, Alpha of the Red Moon Clan. Opening it, he frowned as he scanned it.

Caine. Just wanted to give you a little heads-up. A couple of my people have had a run in with some bears comin' down from Mississippi. I'm sendin' someone to try and set up a meetin' with their Alpha to find out why the fuck they're comin' into our territory. ~Ryan

Caine tapped his fingers on the top of his desk before he responded to the email.

Ryan. Contact Declan. One of his pack is a Grizzly. I think it would be wise to have him there. ~Caine

That done he went through the rest of his messages, then got to work on the Pard finances. He had a short list of repairs that needed supplies, and he needed to double-check the finances before he sent someone to purchase everything.

Caine was just logging out of the account on his computer when his phone rang. "Caine Bordeaux."

"Mr. Bordeaux. My name is Evan Connelly. I am calling you on behalf of Samantha Markus."

Caine frowned. Samantha Markus was an old flame, one he'd had a brief, but steamy romance with, that ended badly when he found her in bed with another guy. "What can I do for you, Mr. Connelly?"

"Miss Markus hired me several months ago to oversee her will and estate. She was diagnosed six months ago with inoperable brain cancer, and she wanted to be sure that everything was in order for when she passed."

"I'm sorry to hear dat. I wasn't aware she was sick."

"I am aware, Mr. Bordeaux. The reason I am calling you, sir, is in regards to your daughter."

Caine made a noise. "Pardon me? I don't have a daughter."

"I assure you, Mr. Bordeaux, that you most certainly do. After Miss Markus was diagnosed, she had DNA testing done to verify that the other gentleman, with whom she'd had relations at the time she became pregnant, was not her child's biological father. If you contest the claim, DNA testing can be done to prove it, but Miss Markus insisted that, once you meet with the child, you will know that she is yours."

Caine's mind was in turmoil. How had she assumed he would know just from meeting the child? It took a moment for his mind to connect the dots. The child must be able to shift. Samantha knew he was a leopard shifter; he'd refused to be intimate with her without telling her so she could decide if she wanted to continue the relationship. "Where are you?"

"We are staying at the Wyndham, in the French Quarter."

"I can be dere in an hour." He hung up and stared at his phone. How was he going to tell Emelise about this? He'd just asked her to marry him and now he was going to have to focus on helping a child, his child, cope with the loss of the only parent she knew.

Cain hesitated for only a moment before he sent Emelsie a text. He wanted, needed her at his side. *Angel, I need you to meet me at the*

Wyndham in the French Quarter in an hour. It's...important. He waited with baited breath for her to respond.

What's wrong? Of course I'll meet you there, but what's wrong, Caine? I know something is. I can feel it.

He closed his eyes a moment before he replied. *I'll explain when I see you. I promise. See you in an hour, Angel.*

Okay. I'll be finished with interviews by then but if I haven't, I'll cancel them. See you soon. Love you.

I love you too, Angel. More than I though possible.

Caine shut down his computer, ran a hand through his hair, and headed for the docks. He was nervous as hell. He had no idea how Emelise was going to feel, knowing he had a child with another woman.

Chapter Nineteen

Emelise

Emelise finished with her last interview for the day feeling less than hopeful. So far, everyone who'd applied just didn't fit the position. Some of them had the deer in the headlights look when she told them they would potentially see celebrities in the VIP Lounge and had to maintain a professional attitude, no going full-on paparazzi. Others weren't able to pass the 'fix me a random drink or two' test. They wanted her to suggest something. She needed someone who was creative, a quick thinker, able to do the job without a ton of guidance. Someone who knew what the fuck they were doing. Was it really so wrong to want someone who knew their way around a bar for fuck's sake?

The instant she was behind the wheel of her car, her mind shifted gears. She was anxious to get to the Wyndham and find out what was going on. Something was certainly up. Unless Caine was pulling a surprise on her, but she didn't think that was the case. He'd known she had interviews so she doubted he would have made plans this early in the day.

Halfway there she found herself caught behind a car accident and growled in frustration. "Fuck it. I'll walk the rest of the way." She found a spot to park, locked her car up, and continued on foot. If someone had asked why she felt so on edge, she couldn't have answered. She just knew that something was off.

That feeling intensified when she stepped into the lobby of the Wyndham to find Caine pacing near the counter.

Caine

Caine arrived at the hotel a little ahead of Emelise and glanced at his watch. He kept glancing at it while he waited for her to arrive. Then he started pacing. She was late. She was never late. On top of everything else, he was now worried something had happened to her. He'd called the lawyer to inform him he was running a little behind but would be there soon. He didn't want to do this without his mate at his side, damn it.

"Caine? What's wrong?"

At her voice, relief filled him. "Thank God. I was beginnin' to worry someting happened to you, Angel."

"There was a traffic jam, thanks to an accident. I decided to park and walk the rest of the way. Caine, you were pacing and I can see the tension in the way you're standing. What in the hell is going on?"

Caine ran a hand through his hair. "Dere's someting I need to tell you. Five years ago, I was involved wit' someone. It ended badly when I caught her in bed wit' someone else."

"Okay? Caine, I'm not stupid. I know you've had other women in your bed before we met."

"It's not dat, cher. See, I got a call earlier from a lawyer. Samantha—dat was her name—she found out six months ago she had brain cancer. She just died…and left it to her lawyer to inform me…I'm a father."

Emelise blinked at him. "Come again?"

"I'm a father. I have a daughter."

"If she was fucking around on you, how do you know she's yours?"

"Samantha had a DNA test done with da other guy. Since she was only sleepin' with da two of us and he's not a match…"

"Please tell me you're going to get DNA testing done to be sure? Because, come on, Caine. If she was screwing one guy behind your back, how do you know she wasn't screwing others?"

"The lawyer said that Samantha assured him I'd know when I saw her dat she was mine. Dat can only mean one ting. She's a shifter, a leopard shifter. Da other guy, he was a shifter too, but he wasn't a leopard. He was a member of da Red Moon Clan."

"Wait. So if she had DNA testing done on the other guy, why didn't she ask you for your DNA?"

"I don't know. I plan on askin' dat when we get upstairs."

"Okay. Let's go, then."

"Thank you, Angel."

Eme slipped her hand into his and squeezed it at the emotion in his voice. "Caine, I love you. You don't need to thank me for being at your side while you meet the daughter you never knew about."

Caine leaned in and pressed a kiss to her temple. "Still, thank you for bein' here wit' me." He guided her to the elevators and they headed up to the third floor. Once they reached the door, he took several deep breaths to calm his cat, then knocked on the door.

The door opened moments later and an older, slightly overweight man stood there. "You must be Caine Bordeaux. Evan Connelly," he said and offered his hand.

"Pleasure. Dis is Emelise Rousseau," Caine said, introducing Eme to the man.

"Ma'am." He inclined his head in greeting. "Please, come in." He stepped back and motioned them inside.

On the bed, farthest from the door, a little girl sat curled up, her arms clinging to a large stuffed animal. It was clear, from one look, that she was frightened and very sad.

"Mr. Bordeaux, please, have a seat. There's some paperwork I need to go over with you."

"In a minute." Caine approached the bed and then knelt beside it so he was more eye level with the little girl. "Hello dere, sweetheart."

A pair of pale blue eyes blinked out at him through a mass of blond curls. Her nose twitched and she tipped her head curiously at him. "You smell like me," she whispered.

"Dat, I do, little one. I know all dis is confusin' and scary, and you're sad because you lost your mama, but it's gonna be okay. I'm gonna take care of you."

She sniffled. "How come?"

"Because, little one, I'm your papa. If I'd known about you, I'd have already been here wit' you." He kept his voice soft and gentle as he talked to her.

Slowly the death grip she had on the stuffed animal loosened. After a few minutes she let it go and crawled across the bed to Caine. "Promise?" She whispered so softly even Caine had a hard time hearing it.

"Promise, little one." When she moved to the edge of the bed, he picked her up. Her little body shook and his arms wrapped protectively around her.

Emelise

When Caine had dropped the bombshell on her, Emelise had been stunned. He had a child, a daughter, with another woman. Sure, she knew he wasn't a virgin, hell, neither was she, but a child? She'd envisioned being the one to give him his first child and someone else had already beaten her to it. She couldn't help the bit of resentment she felt.

She was quiet as they'd approached the hotel room. When the door opened she'd smelled the child's fear and sorrow. Emotions weren't always that easy for her to detect, but the little girl's world was shattered and as a result, her emotions had heavily scented the air in the room.

Emelise watched Caine with the child. One look at the little girl and she could see the resemblance. She had the same pale blue eyes, the same nose. And those curls. They hung down to her shoulders like spun gold. Seeing her, the resentment disappeared and was replaced with shame. The poor thing had her entire world upended and she'd felt resentful? What was wrong with her? "Mr. Connelly, is it? Why don't you show me the paperwork while Caine gets to know his daughter? I'm his fiancée. As such, I will eventually be the little girl's stepmother."

"Of course. I've got the file here on the table. Her name is Hailey Bijou Markus. Everything is in order for Mr. Bordeaux's signature."

Caine finally joined them with his daughter clinging to him like a lifeline. He read over everything before he put pen to paper. He wasn't stupid; he wasn't going to just sign without going through every single piece of paper. "Dis says she has a trust fund set up dat she will have access to when she turns eighteen. I wasn't aware Samantha was doing so well."

"Miss Markus invested in a couple of tech companies that brought her a healthy return. She set up the trust fund right away. Her medical bills ate into a big chunk of her estate, but what's left will be given to you, per her will. I've brought some of Hailey's things. The rest will arrive in a few days. The house is being packed up as we speak. All personal items will be placed in storage until such time as Hailey is old enough to go through them; the rest will be auctioned off and the proceeds will be placed into the trust fund."

An hour later, after he'd read every piece of paper the lawyer brought with him, everything was signed, and Caine was officially, and legally, the sole guardian of his daughter. He was a father. That was something he was going to have to get used to. "Hailey, dis is Emelise," he said, introducing his daughter to his mate. "She's goin' to help me take care of you."

Emelise gave him a look. The way he worded it made it sound like she was going to be the girl's babysitter or something. "What your papa is trying to say is that I'm going to be your new mommy. I won't ever take the place of your mama—you'll always be her little girl even though she's not here anymore—but I'm going to love you just as much as she did."

Hailey sniffed. "You smell like us, too."

Eme smiled gently. "That's right, sweet pea. You're not alone. I lost my mama not too long ago, too. I know you're sad and I know it hurts, lots and lots, but you're not alone."

"Okay." Hailey looked like she felt soothed by their presence and her eyes looked glassy with sleep.

"You carry her; I'll get the bags," Eme said quietly. She could tell the child was exhausted.

"All right, Angel. Let's go home."

"Yeah. Hailey needs some rest."

Caine

Caine held his daughter tight while Emelise helped him with the two bags the lawyer had brought with him. He was grateful Emelise was there with him. He wasn't so sure he could have been as calm if he'd been alone. It infuriated him to know that, if she hadn't gotten sick, Samantha would have kept his daughter from him, indefinitely. As it was, she waited until she was dead for him to find out about her existence. Being angry wouldn't do anyone any good, though, so he mentally shrugged it off. It didn't matter now. All that mattered was helping his daughter to heal.

When the lawyer held the booster seat out to him, Caine grabbed it with one hand, then nodded at the man and walked out the door. At least he didn't have to worry about getting a ticket for not having her properly restrained in the car. He started mentally going through everything he had at the house. Was there anything that could put her in danger? He didn't think so, but it was hard to be sure. He'd never had a young child in his home before.

He glanced at Emelise once they were in the car headed for the docks. "You're awful quiet, Angel."

"I'm sorry. I'm trying to process all of this." The confession came out just above a whisper.

"I know it's a lot to take in."

"Don't. Don't start getting worried, Caine. I'm just…I guess, I'm just a little hurt knowing someone else got to give you your first child. It's stupid and selfish because that little girl just lost her mama and her whole world has been upended, and I'm feeling slighted because someone else got to bear your first child."

Caine reached over and took her hand in his. "It's all right, Angel. You're entitled to your feelin's."

"No, it's not all right, Caine. It's selfish. I never thought I was a selfish person."

"Stop it. You're da least selfish person I've ever met. You're allowed to be upset, Emelise. If, and when, we have our first child together, it will be amazin'. I didn't get to be dere for all of Hailey's firsts, but wit' our baby, I will be."

Emelise smiled over at him. "You're right. Gods, my heart broke for her when we stepped into that room."

"I know. Mine, too. We'll help her to heal, though, together." In the morning, he would contact the lawyer, he had on retainer, to start the paperwork for them to adopt Hailey. Even though he was her legal guardian, he wanted the paperwork to reflect more than that. He wanted it to reflect that he was her father and that Emelise was now her mother.

Emelise

Over the next several days, when Eme wasn't at the club, she split her time between packing up her apartment and helping Caine get Hailey settled in her new home. It was late evening, Hailey had just fallen asleep, and Emelise and Caine were curled up together on the sofa. "I want to do something to introduce Hailey to everyone."

"What do you have in mind, Angel?"

"I was thinking we could have a big cookout. I can invite my Dad, Angela, and the kids, we can have the Pack join us…and I'd like to invite Izzy Catalini and her little girl, Lexi."

"Dat sounds good to me. When would you like to do it?"

"This Saturday, if possible. If not then next Saturday." It was only Tuesday so there was a good chance everyone would be able to attend.

"All right, Angel. We'll invite ever'one over for a cookout dis weekend."

Emelise leaned up and kissed his cheek. "You're the best."

"No, cher, dat would be you. You're da one who thought of da idea in da first place."

"True, I did. I'll make you a deal," she said and she moved to straddle his lap.

"What's dat?"

"I'll share the title with you if you kiss me." She flashed him a cheeky grin.

Caine laughed at her. "Dat I can do, Angel. Dat, I can do." He slid a hand into her hair, pulled her face close to his, and kissed her deeply.

"Let's go to bed," she breathed against his lips.

Caine growled and nipped her lips. "Mmmh, I do like da way you tink, cher."

His growl made her shiver. When he stood with her in his arms, she laughed softly and nuzzled his neck. "You're a man, of course you do."

Caine playfully swatted her ass before he tossed her onto the bed. He joined her but before things got too heated between them, soft whimpers caught their attention.

Emelise wanted to sigh in frustration but she couldn't. Hailey had been through so much. If she needed to be comforted, then that took precedence over sexy times with her mate. "I'll go get her while you take care of the tent in your pants." She winked at him and headed for the bedroom door.

"Dat tent is your doin', woman."

She knew that once she was out of the room he would try to think of things that would cool his lust so that when she returned with Hailey, he wouldn't be sporting an erection.

When Emelise slipped into Hailey's room, it nearly broke her heart to see her curled into a ball in the middle of the bed. Every protective instinct she had went into overdrive. "Shh, it's okay, pumpkin." She went to the bed, scooped Hailey up, and carried her down the hall to her and Caine's bedroom. When Hailey's little fingers curled into her shirt, Emelise hugged her even closer.

By the time Emelise entered the bedroom with his daughter in her arms, Caine had himself under control. He pulled the covers back so Eme could crawl into the bed with Hailey snuggled up between them.

"You know, this is good practice for us." When Caine gave her an arched look she grinned. "For when we have one of our own."

"I can't wait to see you wit' your belly swollen wit' my child."

"Don't go getting ahead of yourself there, mister. We haven't even said 'I do' yet. There will be no babies until after that."

"We need to set da date, den."

Emelise laughed softly. "Aren't you Mr. Impatient?"

"To make you my wife? Yes, I am."

She rolled her eyes at him. "Good-night, Caine."

He leaned over, careful not to wake the little girl who was now sound asleep between them, and kissed his mate. "Good-night, Angel."

Chapter Twenty

Emelise

By Wednesday afternoon, Emelise had invited everyone, except Izzy and Lexi, to the cookout. Since she'd been wanting to check in on the other woman anyway, this was the perfect opportunity to do so. She pulled up outside of the house and couldn't suppress the smile that flitted across her face. After she'd told Caine about Izzy and her daughter, and the rundown condition of the house they lived in, he'd taken it upon himself to fix it up. He'd paid for all of the repairs himself under the condition it be done anonymously. Too bad for him, Eme felt his generosity deserved to be acknowledged and fully intended on letting Izzy know he was behind it. She made her way to the door and knocked.

"Hello, Emelise. What brings you by?"

Emelise smiled warmly at her, "Hey, Izzy. Well, two things, really. First, I wanted to invite you to a cookout. It's in the bayou, at the community compound my fiancé calls home." At the look Izzy gave her, she laughed. "It's not that kind of compound. It's not a cult. You know that shifter's exist, right?" At her nod she continued. "That's why their community is out in the bayou. They, we, are shifters." She waited for the other woman to freak out.

"Oh. That makes sense. Man, the look on your face. It's priceless. One of my closest friends when I was growing up was a shifter. I know they're no more dangerous than humans. There are good people and there are bad people; species has nothing to do with it."

"Well. All righty, then. So, anyway, the cookout is this Saturday. You don't have to bring anything but you and Lexi. She'll have kids around her own age to play with."

"It sounds like fun. How, exactly, will we get out there, though?"

"I'll give you directions to the private boat dock where we'll have someone waiting to bring people out to the compound. My best friend, Lily, and several others will be there, too."

"Okay. Thank you for the invitation, Emelise."

"Well, I'd like to think we're friends, or becoming friends, at least."

"I'd like that too. I don't have a huge social circle." She paused a moment before she continued. "What was the other reason you stopped by?"

"Well…I'll probably get in trouble for this…. Well not really trouble but he'll probably growl at me but whatever. He'll get over it. Sorry, rambling. Have you wondered who was behind all the sudden repairs?"

Izzy frowned a little. "Yes, actually."

"After I met you, I was talking with my fiancé and I mentioned how rundown the place looked. He took it upon himself to hire people to come take care of it, but he's the kind of man who doesn't need a lot of attention and he didn't want you to feel obligated to him in some way, so he wanted it to remain anonymous. I, however, think his generosity deserves some recognition."

"That was really sweet of him to do that. I'm…a little overwhelmed by his generosity, if I'm going to be completely honest. Some of the things they fixed were things that…put Lexi at risk because they were fire hazards. I am really grateful to him. Would he really get mad at you if I thanked him for doing it?"

"No, not really. Like I said, he'll just growl at me as if he's bothered by it. He's a teddy bear. Well, figuratively speaking since he's a leopard shifter." They both laughed at that. "I should get out of here. I've got some things to take care of. I'm really looking forward to having you over on Saturday. I think you'll hit it off with Lily and I know Lexi will have a blast with the other kids."

"She doesn't really have any playmates around here so I know she's going to love it." Izzy walked her to the door. "See you Saturday."

"See you Saturday." Eme made her way to her car and waved one last time before she climbed in and headed to the club. Sometimes, juggling her business and her home life got a little crazy, and she could only imagine how much worse it was going to get when she and Caine started having kids. Maybe she needed to hire a second manager. She'd have to give it some serious thought.

Saturday morning found Emelise in a flurry of activity. Everyone who'd been invited to the cookout was coming. There was so much to do to get everything ready. She was feeling a little off-kilter for some odd reason—a little queasy if she was completely honest with herself—but she chalked it up to nerves. She wanted the day to be perfect. Hailey was going to meet her new family and she wanted the little girl to feel welcomed and loved. She already had Emelise and

Caine wrapped around her little finger, and there was no doubt in Eme's mind that, by the end of the day, she'd have the rest of the family wrapped around it too.

"You're lookin' a little green dis mornin'." Mia had come to help with the food and was eyeing her cousin closely.

"I'm not sure what's going on. I feel a little...off. I'm queasy and I've never felt like that before."

Mia turned and really looked at her. "Hey, Eme, when was da last time you had a period?"

Emelise frowned at her. "Why are you asking me that?"

"Just answer da question."

Eme stopped what she was doing and thought back. Her cycle was always on time. It was like clockwork. Her eyes widened and her face paled. "Oh, shit. The clock's broken."

Mia arched a brow. "Come wit' me. When I thought I was pregnant I got a couple pregnancy tests. I have an unopened one you can use."

Emelise followed her on autopilot. This was so not part of her plan. She and Caine were always careful. Weren't they? Was there a time they'd made love without protection? Gods, she couldn't remember.

Once they were in her home, Mia led Emelise down the hall to the bathroom. "Da test is in da cabinet over da sink. I'll wait out here for you."

Ten minutes later Emelise sat there on the floor of the bathroom, staring at the little plastic test strip in her hand. Two lines. Well, fuck. Things just got a whole lot more complicated. It also explained why she'd been feeling unusually emotional.

"Eme? You okay in dere?"

Emelise closed her eyes at her cousin's question. Having a baby right now wasn't in her plans. She and Caine had only just gotten engaged. They hadn't even discussed marriage beyond his proposal. How was she going to tell him about the pregnancy? "Honestly? I don't know." Her voice shook a little and she winced.

Mia opened the door and peeked in. "I know gettin' pregnant before you're ready can be a little...scary, but you know Caine loves you, right?"

"Yeah, I know that. He wouldn't have asked me to marry him if he didn't. This just wasn't part of my plans. Not yet anyway. Fuck. I don't even know how it happened. I mean, I thought we were careful but there must have been a night when we weren't."

"Not necessarily. Sometimes condoms have holes in dem, even if dey're brand new. It can happen. Dat might be da case here."

Emelise got up from where she'd been sitting and groaned. "I guess it doesn't really matter how it happened. Fact is, I'm pregnant. Ready or not, there's no changing things now."

"Dat's da spirit." Mia flashed her a smile. "Come on, we've got a cookout to finish settin' up. You can tink about how you're gonna tell Caine he's gonna be a Papa again while we get it done."

Emelise laughed a little at that. "True. My little life crisis doesn't change the fact, in just a couple of hours, we're going to have a lot of hungry shifters looking for food." Pushing the pregnancy to the back of her mind, she followed Mia back outside and focused on the task at hand. Later. She would deal with the news of her pregnancy later.

Caine

Their guests were beginning to arrive for the cookout but Caine couldn't focus on them. Something was bothering his mate. He could see it in the tension in her shoulders, the way she kept pulling her bottom lip between her teeth, and the way her hands shook every now and then. He couldn't take it anymore. He needed to know what was wrong and fix it. He headed to where she was finishing setting up the long table they'd brought out for the food to sit on. Once he was at her side, he gently gripped her arm. "We need to talk."

Emelise let him lead her away from the table and their guests. "What's wrong?"

"You tell me, cher. You're tense, your hands keep shakin', and if you chew on your lip anymore, you're gonna make it bleed."

Emelise stared at him for several minutes before she sighed. "Let's go inside. Mia's keeping an eye on Hailey and...I'd rather not have an audience for this."

Caine frowned but he ushered her into their home. The second he closed the door behind them, he pulled her into his arms. "Whatever it is, Angel, you can tell me."

"Do you remember a few nights ago, when Hailey was whimpering in her sleep and I brought her into our room with us so she felt safe? Do you remember our conversation?"

Caine thought back to the night earlier in the week that she was referring to. "We said quite a few tings," he started. One particular piece of their conversation stood out and he stared at her. His hand went to her still-flat stomach and he cocked a brow. "Are you sayin' what I tink you are?"

"If what you're thinking is that I'm telling you, in a roundabout way, that I'm pregnant, then…yeah."

A smile lit up his face as he picked her up and spun her around. "You just made me da happiest man alive, Angel."

All her worry seemed to fade away at the sheer joy on his face. "So you're happy about it? I mean, we're not even married yet, Hailey just came to live with us…there's so much going on in our lives right now."

Caine set her on her feet and took her face in his hands. "I am beyond happy, Angel. I'm over da moon wit' joy. Da woman I love is carryin' my child; how could I not be happy about dat?"

"I'm scared, Caine. What if you change your mind? What if this, what we have, doesn't work out? I don't want to raise our child alone. I don't want to end up alone like my mama."

"Dat is never goin' to happen, Angel. You're mine and dere isn't a force on dis earth dat would make me let you go. I'd walk through da fires of hell for you."

"Promise?" There was a quaver in her voice.

"Promise." He kissed her tenderly and wrapped her up in his arms. "I'll let you decide when you want to share da news. As much as I want to roar it to da heavens, I want you to be comfortable wit' our family, our Pard, knowin' about da baby."

Emelise gave him a warm smile. "Thank you."

"Your happiness is all dat matters to me, Angel. You, dat little girl out dere, and da son or daughter you're carryin' are my entire world." He'd give up the Pard if it was asked of him, as long as he had her by his side.

"How do you always know just what to say to put my mind at ease?"

He flashed her a wicked grin. "Because I know you, Angel." After another kiss he escorted her back outside where the cookout was just getting underway.

Beau

Beau Lafluer watched his younger sister with her mate and once again he felt a pang of envy. That pang increased when he looked to his Alpha and cousin. Against all odds, they'd found each other and, although he was happy for them, a little part of him still envied their connection. He'd been seriously considering petitioning another Pard for permission to meet some of their unmated females to see if he could find his mate. The downside to that would be having to leave his family, and home, for good to join whatever Pard his mate happened to be part of.

As the cookout got underway he pushed the troubling thoughts from his mind. Today was about family and friends coming together for some fun. There would be time enough for him to come to a decision later. As Lily and Declan arrived, along with the rest of their Pack, his gaze was drawn to the unfamiliar woman with them. She was holding the hand of a dark-haired little girl that was no doubt her daughter. His gaze raked over her. Whoever she was, she was beautiful.

"Izzy! You made it!"

Emelise's voice reached his ears and he arched a brow. So the woman's name was Izzy. Hmmh, was it short for Isabel, Isabella, or Isadora? Only one way to find out. He made a beeline for his cousin and the woman she was greeting. "Are you gonna introduce your friend to da rest of us, cher?"

Eme turned to him and gave him a funny look. "Hey, Beau. Oh, yeah, sorry. Izzy, this is my cousin, Beau. Beau, Izzy Catalini and her adorable daughter, Lexi."

As he closed the distance between them and reached for her hand, he caught a hint of her scent. It hit him like a ton of bricks. He was suddenly hard as a rock and his cat was growling for release. To say he was stunned by his reaction to her was putting it mildly. She was human, as far as he could tell, and yet his leopard was acting as if she was their mate. What. The. Fuck? "Charmed, cher," he murmured and lifted her hand to his lips.

Izzy

The moment he took her hand in his, Izzy felt a jolt of electricity that left her flustered. Looking into his eyes she felt as though she could get lost there. It took her several seconds to realize he'd spoken. Her cheeks flushed with heat and she gave him an embarrassed smile. "Um, it's nice to meet you, too." Her voice came out in a breathless whisper.

"What's Izzy short for, cher?"

"Isabella." She replied without hesitation, something she never did. What was wrong with her?

"Beautiful name for a beautiful woman. Dere will be music later; I hope you'll save me a dance." He winked at her before he let go of her hand.

Izzy swallowed at the sense of loss she felt when he stopped touching her. "Of course." Eme looked between them before she spoke again. "Let me introduce you to everyone else," she said and steered Izzy away from Beau.

By the time they'd gotten to Caine, Izzy was feeling more like herself and less like a wanton hussy. That was the way she'd felt while Beau was holding her hand. "It's nice to meet you." She had an internal debate with herself over thanking him for his generosity before her upbringing won out. "Please don't be upset with Emelise but, she told me about what you did and I wanted to thank you for your generosity."

Caine mock-glared at his mate. "Dere's no need to thank me, cher. You and dat little angel of yours have had a hard time of tings. Her papa should be da one takin' care of dem, but some men, dey just aren't cut out to be papas. You just focus on takin' care of yourself and dat little girl."

Izzy looked over to where her daughter was already playing with some of the other children. "She's my world."

"Dat's as it should be. If you need anyting, you be sure to let us know. We've been blessed, and we take care of dose who are important to us, be dey family or friend."

Izzy felt herself blushing at his words. "I'll try to remember that. Thank you."

Emelise looped arms with her. "Come on, let me show you around." Once they were away from Caine, she tipped her head. "Okay, dish. I saw the way you and Beau were looking at each other. What was that all about?"

Izzy swallowed. "To tell you the truth, I'm not sure. I swear I felt a jolt of electricity when he touched my hand. It was…okay, don't think me weird but, it was kind of…hot."

Eme stopped and studied her. "Let me ask you a question, Izzy. Is there any chance you might have some shifter blood in you?"

Izzy gave her a puzzled look. "Not…that I know of. I mean, I don't really know that much about my parents. They died when I was a baby and I was raised by a guardian. Why?"

"Because, girl, what you're describing is the way a shifter feels when he or she meets their mate."

Izzy stared at her. "Really? That's crazy, isn't it? I mean, can a shifter's mate be human?"

Emelise shrugged. "If there isn't any shifter in your blood, then it looks like it can be. Don't worry too much about it. Today, just have fun, okay?"

"Sure." Her mind was already puzzling over it though. She was going to have to dig into her family's past, something she'd been reluctant to do, in order to find out more about her parents and her ancestors.

Emelise

Emelise made her way back to Caine's side once she'd introduced Izzy to everyone. Music was playing, people were laughing, and the kids were running around chasing each other. She was almost knocked off her feet when Hailey ran into her and wrapped her arms around her legs. "Hailey? Pumpkin?" She could hear the little girl's sniffling. She scooped her up and was instantly worried when Hailey buried her face in her shoulder.

"I miss my mama," she whispered.

"Oh, sweet pea. I know you do." Her arms tightened around her gently.

Caine happened to look up at that exact moment and frowned. "What is it?" He, too, heard his daughter's soft cries and growled. "What happened?"

"Don't be growling at me. Hailey's missing her mama." Before Caine could respond, the mother of one of the boys Hailey was playing with, approached them.

"Alpha, Emelise." She inclined her head at them. "Jared has something he'd like to say."

The little boy looked up at his Alpha and swallowed. "I'm sorry. I didn't mean to make her cry." He looked on the verge of tears himself.

Emelise turned to Caine. "Why don't you take Miss Hailey inside, get her a popsicle while she calms down."

Caine took his daughter into his arms, gave his mate a look, and went into their home.

Emelise knelt so she was eye level with the boy. "Why don't you tell me what happened?"

"We was all talkin' and playin' and...I asked her where her mama was. Cuz we know da Alpha is her papa. I didn't know it would make her cry, honest!"

"It's okay. I know you didn't." She stood back up and raised her voice. "I need all of the kids gathered up and brought over here for a moment. There's something I need to say and I don't want to have to chase them all down one at a time." It took several minutes before they were all standing in front of Emelise. "I know y'all are probably wondering the same thing Jared is. Where is Hailey's mama? Well, you see, her mama got really sick and recently passed away. Caine didn't know about Hailey until just this week or she would have spent time here before now. The reason she started crying was because she's sad. I know you didn't mean to upset her, Jared. It's okay. When she comes back out you can tell her how sorry you are that you made her cry. I just want all of you to understand—she's a very sad little girl right now so if she starts to get upset about something, I want y'all to promise me you will try to make her feel better. Can you do that?"

"Her mama died?" Jared's face scrunched up. "Dat's so sad. I don't tink I'd ever stop cryin' if my mama died." Several other kids echoed his words. "I promise, Miss Eme, I won't do no'ting to make her cry again and I'll make sure no one else does, either."

Emelise ruffled his hair. "Thank you, Jared. You're a good boy. Your mama should be real proud of you."

He beamed at her praise. "Thank you!"

By the time Caine brought a much calmer Hailey back outsidem the kids were back to playing tag. As soon as he saw them, Jared ran over to stand in front of his Alpha. "I'm real sorry, Hailey. I didn't mean to make you cry. Do you wanna play tag wit' us?"

Hailey gave him a shy smile. Her earlier upset was all but forgotten. "Can I?" she asked, looking up at Caine.

"A'course you can. Y'all stay inside da fence. No goin' out to pester da gators, you hear."

A chorus of "Yes, Alpha," echoed through the compound.

"He's a good boy." Eme slipped her arm around Caine's waist. "He didn't know Hailey lost her mama and he asked where she was. I made sure they all knew her mama passed away and that makes her a very sad little girl. I don't think they'll be saying something to upset her again."

Caine kissed her temple. "I should have known you'd take care of dat. It hurts seein' her so upset."

"I know. We'll help her heal, though. It's just going to take time. I have a question for you, babe." When he cocked a brow at her, she continued. "What's the likelihood that a shifter could find their mate in a human?"

"Not very. Why?"

"I think Izzy and Beau may be mates but if it's not likely for a human to be a shifter's mate, then somewhere in her family's past, someone hooked up with a shifter but the baby didn't have outward signs."

"Interestin'. Did you ask her about it?"

"Yeah, she says, as far as she knows, no one was, but her parents died when she was a baby and she really doesn't know much about them."

"Could have been kept quiet dependin' on when it was. Dere was a time when da world didn't even know we existed. Food's ready; let's get someting to eat."

"Gods, yes. I'm starving."

Caine chuckled at that. As the food was laid out, all the kids were brought in from the game of tag, plates were filled, and everyone took a seat at one of the many tables. Looking over the gathering, he couldn't help but smile.

Emelise spotted his smile and arched a brow. "What's that smile for?"

"Dis gathering. Dere was a time, not so long ago, when this wouldn't have been possible. Not wit' Zachary as Alpha. Dere wouldn't have been enough food to go around, and some of our guests never would have been allowed here."

"Have I told you lately how glad I am that bastard is dead?"

"Dat makes two of us, Angel," Caine said before he helped her get a plate of food and found a spot for them to sit.

Emelise waited until everyone was sitting with plates in front of them before she stood up. "I need everyone's attention for just a minute. Then you can get to stuffing your faces with all this delicious food." Laughter and chuckles greeted her comment. "Caine and I have something to share. Well, actually, two things." She smiled warmly at him before she continued. "First, a few days ago, Caine proposed and I said yes. I know some of you already know because certain people were present during the proposal, but I wanted to let all of our family and friends know at once." She waited until their cheers died down before she shared the rest of their news. "Also, I just discovered, earlier today, that I am pregnant. We're going to have a baby."

More cheers and shouts of 'Congratulations!' echoed across the bayou. There were even a few roars from some of the Pard. Their Alpha and his mate were expecting. This truly was a day of celebration.

Later that night, after everyone had gone home, after the leftovers were dispersed between the guests, everything was cleaned up, and Hailey was sound asleep in her bed, Emelise lay curled in Caine's arms. Her hand rested on her stomach. "I still can't believe we're going to have a baby. I just wish my mama was here to meet her first grandchild."

Caine's arms tightened around her. "I know, Angel. She's watchin' over you, though. Wherever she's at, she's watchin' and she's happy for you."

"I'd like to think so. She didn't want me coming to New Orleans, but I'd like to think she'd be happy for me if she was here right now." She yawned and smiled sheepishly. "I love you."

"I love you too, Angel. Get some sleep. You've had a long day." He nuzzled her and caressed her side.

"Mmmh, so have you." Her eyes were heavy and after a moment she stopped fighting and let sleep drag her under.

Chapter Twenty-One

Emelise

How does one go about getting an ultrasound done when they're a shifter? Normally, it wasn't easy. Emelise was stunned to find out that, had Mia not gone into labor when she did, she would have given birth in the small clinic Sabine had in New Orleans. She saw both human and shifters in her little clinic and it was there Emelise went to make sure her baby was healthy and to try to get a good idea of exactly how far along she was.

Eme lay back on the bed and stared at the screen. She had no clue what the gray images were—it just looked like a blob to her—but judging by the look on Sabine's face, she saw something that had her struggling to keep a straight face.

Caine sat at her side with her hand held gently in his. He kept glancing between her and the screen before he noticed Emelise was looking at Sabine. He looked to her and cocked a brow. "What are you seeing?"

Sabine turned to them and gave them a smile. "You two are blessed. You're havin' twins."

Eme blinked. "Wait. Did you just say twins?"

"I did. Congratulations."

Emelise turned her attention to Caine. "Oh. My. Gods. Twins." Her voice came out a stunned whisper.

Caine grinned from ear to ear. "You are amazin', Angel. You're goin' to be such an amazin' mama." He dipped his head and kissed her. If they were at the compound he would have roared his joy to the sky.

"And you're going to be an amazing papa."

Sabine cleared her throat. "Judgin' by da ultrasound, I'd say you're two months along. You've got a long way to go but I'll get you through it."

"Thank you, Sabine. I'd be lying if I said I wasn't a little scared about bringing two babies into the world at one time. Maybe I should talk with Eliza, see how she handled it. She did it twice."

Caine chuckled. "Dat, she did." He turned to Sabine. "Is dere anytin' she shouldn't do or should avoid?"

"Just don't overwork yourself, Emelise. You'll find yourself gettin' tired more easily, so if you do, take a nap. Don't be stubborn. And you'll need to make sure you eat right, and eat often. Dem babies will take a lot of nutrients from your body."

"I'll make sure she follows your orders to da letter." Caine winked at his mate.

Emelise gave him a dark look. "I don't overdo it anyway."

Caine snorted. "Yes, you do. But dat's one of da many tings I love about you." He leaned down and kissed her gently.

Eme melted at the kiss. "Fine. I'll admit I sometimes get wrapped up in too many things." She only admitted it begrudgingly.

As soon as the gel was wiped off her stomach, Emelise pulled her shirt back down and slid off the bed. She had a moment of sorrow as she thought of her mother and wished she was there for her to share the news with. Then she pushed the sorrow away. Dwelling on it wouldn't change anything. "You realize this means we have less than seven months to get the nursery ready, right?" She was suddenly excited by the thought of having twins. Scared, sure, but also excited.

Caine chuckled. "We'll get it done, Angel. We've got plenty of time. You just tell me what you want and I'll make sure you have it."

Emelise leaned up and kissed his cheek. "I know you will." She was quiet on the ride home. She'd finally gotten all of her stuff moved out of the apartment and ended the lease with the landlord. It had come at a steep price but it was worth it to be in Caine's arms every night.

Caine

Caine had stood at his mate's side while they'd waited for Sabine to give them the news. When she'd finally spoken, he'd felt like he'd been hit in the stomach with a sledgehammer. Twins. They were having twins. He'd waited for Emelise's reaction to the news before he'd grinned. This woman was amazing. She blew him away at every turn, even when she wasn't trying. Like now.

"When we get back to da house, I want you to start lookin' online at furniture. I'll get some of da Pard to help clear out da room next to Hailey's." They'd already put her in the room closest to them. "Unless you want to move her to dat room and put da babies in da room closest to us."

"No, I don't want to move her to a different room when she's just getting settled. Plus, it might make her feel like we love the babies more and that isn't true. We both have excellent hearing, and they make baby monitors for a reason. They'll be fine in the next room."

"Dat's what I thought you'd say but I wanted to leave dat up to you."

Emelise leaned over and kissed his cheek. "That's because you're a smart man. You don't want to risk pissing off the pregnant lady." She winked at him and they both laughed.

By the time they got back to the house, they'd more or less processed the news. Emelise couldn't wait to tell their family and friends. "Oh my gods, we have so many people to tell. It'll take forever to call everyone."

"Well, we can tell da Pard all at once. Dat just leaves your papa and Lily, because I know you want to tell her, and Malcolm."

"And Izzy. Don't forget her. I really like her and, honestly, seeing the way Beau was around her and her daughter during the cookout, I hope they get together."

Caine chuckled. "He did seem taken wit' her. It was good to see him finally findin' someone he felt connected to."

"You just want everyone to find their mate because you have." There was a teasing note in her voice.

"Maybe, Angel, maybe."

Caine and Emelise were headed to Mia and Gage's home to pick up Hailey when Mia met them in the yard. "Thank God you're back."

They both startled at Mia's words. "What's wrong?" They asked in unison.

"Hailey is really upset. She has dis irrational idea dat you're not comin' back, and no'ting I said could calm her down."

They rushed inside and the instant they saw Hailey, Caine's heart felt like it was breaking. She'd been crying and she looked almost as lost as she had the day they'd walked into the hotel and met her. He went to her and scooped her up. "Shh, it's all right, cher. I'm here. We're both here. We're not leavin' you alone."

Emelise reached up and rubbed her back gently. "Your papa's right. We're not going anywhere, pumpkin. We will always come back."

Hailey clung to Caine's shirt and whimpered. "Promise?"

"I promise."

"But…you're havin' a baby and I'm not yours; won't you love it more?" Her pale blue eyes were filled with tears when she looked at Emelise.

"Oh, no, sweetie. I might not have been the one to bring you into this world, but I am your mama now and I love you just as much as the babies growing inside me."

"Babies?" Hailey looked puzzled.

"Mm-hmm. We're having two babies. As a big sister to two babies, you're going to have to really keep an eye on them when you're older," Eme said and gently tickled her side.

Hailey giggled. "Two babies? Wow." She gave Emelise a wide-eyed stare. "I can do that. I'm a big girl." She nodded as she said it.

"I know you are, pumpkin. Why don't we go get some lunch and then we can all cuddle up and watch a movie."

Caine's heart swelled with love for the woman at his side. She was doing everything she could to help Hailey heal and adjust to all the changes happening in her life. What did he do to deserve such an amazing woman?

Later that night, after finally getting Hailey to bed, Emelise lay curled up in Caine's arms. Her head rested on his chest and her fingers drew idle designs on his skin. "Let's get married."

"I tink dat was da idea when I proposed and you said yes." Caine smirked at her.

"No, I mean let's get married now. Well, not right now, because it's late but, soon. Look at how quickly we were able to get everyone together for a cookout? They'd come just as quickly for a wedding. I don't need a big, drawn out, fancy thing. I just want to be Mrs. Emelise Bordeaux and I don't want to wait months for it to happen."

Caine growled at that. "Woman, I like da way you tink." He rolled them over until she was pinned beneath him. He locked eyes with her and smirked when her eyes darkened to the green of her leopard. His mouth lowered and he claimed her lips in a heated kiss. His hands slid beneath the camisole top she wore until he cupped her breast. His thumb caressed her nipple into a pert little nub before he trailed kisses down her throat. He dipped his head and took her nipple between his teeth, teasing it through the thin cotton.

Emelise arched when his teeth gently gripped her nipple. They were already getting sensitive and the sensation had her panting in no time. "We have too many damn clothes on."

Caine chuckled. "Patience, Angel. I want to tease every inch of your luscious body until you're soaked and begging for release." Ever so slowly he slid her top up and off, then took one nipple in his mouth while his fingers teased and tugged the other until she was whimpering. God, he loved the sounds she made.

Trailing kisses down her body, Caine slid her pajama shorts down her legs and off before he continued his path. He dipped his tongue into her belly button, kissed and nipped at her hips, then kissed his way down one leg and up the other. He nipped her inner thighs, making her cry out, before the lure of her scent was too strong to resist. With a growl he buried his mouth between her welcoming thighs. He tasted her, teased her, tormented her. He moved his lips to her clit and suckled the sensitive nub while he slipped two fingers inside her, curling them just right to hit her G-spot with every thrust of his fingers.

Emelise

She was dying. Of pleasure. Of need. She was burning up and any moment now she was going to spontaneously combust. Caine was like a man possessed. He teased and tormented her body until she lost count of the number of orgasms he wrung from her. Several times she had to muffle her cries with a pillow out of fear of waking Hailey. She didn't know what was driving him but she wasn't about to complain. "Oh gods...Caine...please...please, please, please..."

"Please what, Angel?" he growled against her before he flicked her clit with his tongue.

Her body shuddered with need. "Please, just fuck me. I need to feel you inside me."

Caine kissed a path up her body and claimed her lips, letting her taste herself. "Dat's what I wanted to hear." He slid into her with a groan. "Always so fuckin' tight." They decided to forgo the condom so he got to feel her wrapped around him with nothing between their bodies. With her already pregnant, there was no need to use a condom.

She gripped his shoulders and arched to take him as deep as possible. "I love the way you feel inside me."

"I love da way you feel wrapped around me," he growled and began to move in slow, deep thrusts.

Her eyes about rolled into the back of her head when he began to move. Her hips arched to meet each thrust and her nails raked his back. She was already rushing toward the precipice of release again and this time she wanted him to follow her over the edge. With that in mind she dipped her head and bit his shoulder before she growled, "Harder."

The bite, combined with her request, seemed to drive him to madness. His thrusts grew erratic as he did what she asked, what she needed. Harder. Faster. Deeper.

When her orgasm crashed over her, Emelise muffled her screams against his shoulder. Her nails raked his back and her inner walls clenched him so tightly, she wondered if it was painful for him.

She felt the strain in his muscles. She knew he hovered on the edge of release, fighting it with everything he had in him, because he wanted her to fall first. That was how it always was between them. Caine always wanted her to find release before he let himself follow her. She knew her walls spasming so tightly around him was his undoing. With a roar he muffled against the pillow beside her head, he spilled himself deep inside her. He half collapsed atop her before he rolled, taking her with him.

Emelise lay sprawled over him, one leg entwined with both of his, while her breathing slowly returned to normal. "I don't know where that came from but damn. You can do that to me anytime, baby."

Caine chuckled and nuzzled her. "I plan to, Angel, I plan to." He caressed her side a moment. "Let me get you a cloth to clean up."

Emelise shook her head. "No. I want to fall asleep with your cum inside me."

A soft growl rumbled through his chest. "What my woman wants, my woman gets."

Eme laughed softly at that. "Mm, careful with that. I just might take you at your word and then you'll be in all sorts of trouble."

"As long as it makes you happy, Angel, I wouldn't mind. When are you gonna realize your happiness is what matters to me?"

"I think it's beginning to sink in."

"Good." He kissed her tenderly. "Sleep, Angel. We can discuss weddin' plans tomorrow."

"Mmmh. Okay," she replied, already half-asleep. The last thing she heard before she drifted off was his soft chuckle.

Chapter Twenty-Two

Emelise

Lily stared at her best friend. "You and Caine are getting married in two weeks? Wow. What's the rush? Is it because of the pregnancy?"

"I'd like to know the answer to that myself." Malcolm was sitting with his feet stretched out in front of him. They'd gathered at Lily's apartment because Emelise had a surprise for both of them. Surprise was one word for it.

"No, it's not because of the pregnancy. I just don't want to drag it out. We don't have to wait for people to be free to fly in for the wedding, since everyone we want to invite already lives here. I already have my dress picked out; I did that the morning after he proposed. I don't want or need a big, fancy wedding. I thought about doing it at the compound but I've decided to do it at the club. I'll close it for the day, pay everyone extra for working the reception…. This is what I want. I thought you, of all people, would be thrilled I'm not putting it off indefinitely," she said to Lily. Lily knew how hard it was for her to let go of the shield she'd used to protect her heart all these years.

Lily scooted closer to her on the sofa and hugged her. "Oh, sweetie, I *am* happy for you. I just wanted to be sure you weren't rushing it out of some silly idea that you had to be married before your baby gets here."

Eme realized that, in all the excitement, she hadn't shared her other news with them. "Babies, actually."

Malcolm got it before Lily did. "Did you say 'babies'? As in, more than one?"

Eme nodded. "We're having twins."

"Holy shit! That's fantastic! I get to be 'Uncle Mal' to two babies at once."

Emelise laughed. "Yes, you do. So you'll have three to spoil instead of two."

"How is that sweet little angel adjusting?"

Before she could answer, Lily cut in. "Oh my gods, Eme, this is…wow. I can't believe you're having twins. I can't believe you're having a baby before me. I always figured I'd end up the one popping out a baby first, and here you are with two."

Emelise blushed even as she laughed. "Yeah, well, get in line, girl, because I can't believe it either. I kept saying we were so careful, we never had a condom break, and then last night, while Caine and I were talking, it hit me. The first time we had sex, we didn't use a condom. You know the saying, all it takes is one time? Yeah, it's fucking true." She bit her lip. "If I'm completely honest, I'm a little scared. It's not like I'm exactly big in the hips area; what if I can't carry them?"

"Oh, Eme, you'll be fine, even if you end up like, on bed rest or something." Lily hugged her again. "Don't borrow trouble."

"What are your plans for the club, Eme? You're going to need to hire a manager, especially once the babies are here. They're going to take up a lot of your time." Malcolm watched her closely.

"I know. I've been thinking about that. I guess I need to put some feelers out. Unless…you want to do it? The two of you, I mean. Lil, I know you like working at Gathering Grounds, but you've also complained about how, so often, you have to manage things but you're not getting paid for it. You aren't getting credit for it either."

"You mean Lily and I split running it? That could work. I'd still be able to be Venus from time to time."

Lily bit her lip. "You're right, I do love my job, but I hate that I don't get the recognition. Emile is a good boss, for the most part, but if I put in a notice and train someone to take over for me, I don't see a problem with it."

"So you'll do it?" Eme gave her a hopeful look.

Lily laughed. "How can I say no to that look? Yeah, I'll do it."

Emelise grinned. "I knew you couldn't pass up the sad little kitty look."

"Sad little kitty? I thought it was the puppy-dog look?"

Eme rolled her eyes at Lily. "Hello, leopard here. I don't do puppy-dog looks," she said and faked an indignant tone.

Malcolm snickered. "I love seeing this playful side of you. You've been so serious lately."

Eme sighed. "I know. Life's been a little crazy. So, back to the topic at hand. My wedding. I want you both to be in it. Please? Lil, you're my best friend and I want you to be my maid of honor. Mal, will you be a bridesmaid. No, you don't have to dress as Venus for it. And…maybe sing something at the reception?"

Malcolm gave her a look. "As if I'd say no to either of those things, darling? I'd be honored to be part of your wedding."

"Eme, do you really have to ask? Of course I'll be your maid of honor!"

"Thanks, you two. I want the people who mean the most to me to be part of my special day. I just wish my mama could be here for it, too."

"She will be, in spirit, Eme. As long as she's in your heart, she'll be there."

Emelise thought about what Lily said. "I suppose you're right. I won't be wearing the traditional white wedding dress. My dress is red and black because the color scheme for the wedding is red, black, and silver. I know, it's not the traditional colors and its a bit goth; those are my favorite colors. You two will be in silver. Or gray, in Mal's case since men's suits don't come in silver."

"Oh, I like that color scheme. Gray suit with black shirt and red tie, I think, since I'm sure your man will be wearing a red shirt with silver tie."

"Yes he will. He just doesn't know it yet." Eme grinned. "I hadn't gotten to that with him. We're getting everything in order but I'll be talking to him about that tonight. I should get out of here. I have a few things to do before the club opens tonight. I'm so glad you two will be in the wedding. Let me know when you can start as manager, Lil, and we'll go through everything you'll need to know."

"Sure thing. I'll let Emile know today that in the next few months I'll be quitting to take over management of the club for you. That will give him plenty of time to find someone to replace me."

"Thanks, girl." Emelise felt relieved.

"You're welcome," Lily replied and walked Emelise to the door.

"I'm going to get out of here too. I do have a show to get ready for." Mal kissed both their cheeks before he and Emelise left, heading their separate ways.

The next two weeks were a flurry of activity. There was a lot to get done in a short time, but Emelise wasn't deterred in the least. The day of the wedding, half the Pard went into the city to Scarlet Flux to get it ready for the wedding. Long-stem, dark red roses were placed in vases, with baby's breath, and set on every table. More roses adorned the edge of the bar and were entwined in the satin streamers that ran up the length of the stairs. Candlelight cast a soft glow throughout the building and soft music seeped through the speakers.

After spending hours getting pampered, Emelise was now in the VIP section of the club, putting the finishing touches on her wedding attire. She hadn't seen Caine since the night before; she kept to that tradition even if she didn't wear the traditional wedding dress. Her dress hugged her frame until just below her butt and then it flared out in tiered layers of red lace in a floral pattern and black tulle. The bodice was backless from the middle of her back. The inner layer was black satin and felt delicious against her skin. The outer layer was the same red floral lace as the skirt, and the thin straps that graced her shoulders were made from black floral lace with red and silver embellishments. The black lace also wrapped around the bodice, just below her butt, tying the ensemble together. In her ears were red and black earrings.

"God, Eme, that dress is absolutely gorgeous." There was admiration in Lily's voice as she took in her best friend's gown.

"Thank you. I knew it was perfect the moment I saw it."

"We don't have a lot of time before da ceremony starts so let's get dis done." Mia stepped forward. "In true weddin' tradition, you need someting old, someting new, someting borrowed, and someting blue." She held up a garter that was made of dark blue and black satin. "I got da someting blue."

Eme laughed, took it from her, and managed to get it up her leg with all the layers of skirt in her way. "Thanks, Mia."

"Emelise, if your mama was here, she'd be so proud of you right now. Dis was supposed to be hers, on her weddin' day, but now it's yours." Eulalie held out a silver locket for her. "Dis was my mama's and her mama's before her," she added and helped Emelise to put it on.

"It's beautiful, Mamere," Eme murmured. She had to wipe a stray tear from her eye.

Malcolm stepped forward and kissed Emelise's cheek. "For something borrowed, what better thing for a queen to wear than a tiara?" He winked at her and carefully placed one of the tiaras he wore, when in drag, on Emelise's hair. The way the light caught on the gems suggested they were real.

Emelise laughed. "You always have such pretty things."

"You know it, honey," he said with aanother wink.

Finally, Lily stepped forward. "Eme, we've been friends for years and I have never seen you happier than you are right now. This last item is a gift Caine asked me to give you, so you could have it when you go speak your vows." She opened a small box to reveal a 'Mother's ring'. It had Hailey's name and birthstone in it and the other spots had diamonds until the twins were born.

Emelise felt herself tear up. "That man, he always knows just how to get to me," she said softly. She put the ring on and again had to wipe away some tears.

"No crying, it'll mess up your makeup," Lily teased just as music filled the air. "Looks like it's time. You ready?"

"I've been ready since the night he proposed."

Hailey, Sophie, and Ava went down the steps first, a basket of flower petals draped over one arm, and every step they took, they picked out a handful of petals and let them fall to the ground. They were followed by Lily, Malcolm, and Mia, who took their places once they reached the stage where the officiator waited.

"You look beautiful, sweetheart." Derrick offered his arm to his daughter. When she'd asked him to give her away he'd been beyond touched. They'd only known each other a short while but already they were close.

"Thank you. Dad." It was the first time she'd called him that.

Derrick blinked. "When I'm old and gray, and look back on my life at some of my happiest moments, this, right here, will be one of them." He kissed her cheek and guided her down the stairs and then toward the stage where Caine waited for her. Her gaze locked with his and her heart swelled with love for him.

Caine

Caine Bordeaux was many things. Stupid wasn't one of them. When his mate decided she wanted to get married quickly instead of having a drawn out engagement, he'd readily agreed. When she told him she wanted a red, black, and silver color scheme for their wedding, again he'd agreed. When she'd said she wanted to hold the ceremony and reception at Scarlet Flux, he'd agreed. Seeing her come down those stairs in that dress, he was glad he'd agreed to everything she'd wanted. She took his breath away.

When she reached his side, he held out his hand and waited for her father to place her hand in his. He nodded at Derrick before he turned his attention to his mate. "You're beautiful."

"Friends, family, we gather today to watch as two lives become one. Marriage is a sacred pact between two hearts. If there is any here who feels these two should not be wed, speak now or forever hold your peace."

Neither of them was worried. They knew all of their friends and family supported them. After a moment, the officiator spoke again. "Caine and Emelise have chosen to recite their own vows. Emelise will go first."

"I grew up believing that you couldn't depend on a man to be there when things got tough. You couldn't depend on them to always have your back. When we first met, I fought what was between us because of the fear that, if I gave you my heart, one day I would wake up to find myself alone. As much as I held onto my walls, you chipped away at them a little at a time. You made me realize that what I'd always believed was wrong. Your love, your steadfast nature, your determination to show me, that if I just let you in, I would never be alone again, brought down my walls and brought me more happiness than I have ever felt in my life. You opened my eyes to a new world; one filled with love, passion, and family. I know that when I need a shoulder to cry on, or a hand to hold, you'll be right there at my side. I love you, with all that I am, Caine, and I will spend the rest of our lives together showing you that every day."

Caine's heart swelled at her words of love. When a tear slipped from the corner of one eye, he lifted his thumb and wiped it away. "Angel, I always thought I knew what I wanted in life. I became Alpha of da Pard to make dere lives happier and healthier. I took care of da needs of everyone else while ignoring my own. I told myself I didn't need anyting else to be happy. My people were being taken care of, dat was enough. Den you came into my life and you turned my world upside down. I love ever'ting about you, Angel. I love dat you're strong, independent, and determined to make your own way in da world. I also love dat you don't let me get away wit' anyting. I love dat you're soft when you need to be, you have so much compassion in your heart dat you have to reach out to others when you see dem hurtin'. You're an amazin' woman, Angel, and I am da luckiest man in da world because I get to hold you in my arms every night for da rest of my life. I love you wit' all dat I am today, tomorrow, and always."

"Do you have the rings?"

Dempsey approached with them on a red satin pillow. Emelise had wanted to include members of her family in this special occasion, and Dempsey had practically begged to be the ring bearer.

"Caine, place the ring on Emelise's left hand and repeat after me. With this ring, I thee wed."

Caine slid the wedding band on his mate's hand before he growled the words just loudly enough for everyone to hear them. His voice was gruff with emotion.

"Emelise, place the ring on Caine's hand and repeat after me. With this ring, I thee wed."

Emelise lifted her gaze to Caine and gave him a beautiful smile. "With pleasure," she whispered before she slid his wedding band on and recited the words.

"Not everyone is as blessed in this life to find the other half of their souls. Caine and Emelise have found that in one another. Let their love be a testament to the rest of us and let no man put asunder what love has brought together. By the power vested in me by the state of Louisiana, I now pronounce you husband and wife. You may kiss your bride."

"About damn time," Caine growled and pulled her into his arms. He didn't give her a peck on the lips. No, he kissed her so thoroughly she was panting when he ended it.

"Wow," she breathed against his lips.

Roars, howls, and cheers erupted and echoed in the club. One by one their guests came to them to congratulate them before moving on to find something to eat or get a drink.

Emelise

"Eme, I have never seen you so happy." Lily hugged her and kissed her cheek. "You're positively glowing and I don't think it's just the pregnancy. You're truly happy."

"I am. I'm happier than I ever thought I could be." She touched her wedding band. "I never believed I'd get married. I always thought, well, you know what I thought. I'm so glad I came here. Yeah, I wish my mama was here with me, but you know how they say there's a reason for everything even if we can't see it? I think this is the reason why Mama was taken from me. So I could find the other half of my soul. It still hurts but it helps, just a little, to think that maybe this is why the fates decided it was time to cut her thread."

"I understand what you mean. It makes the loss a little easier to bear when you think of it in those terms."

"Exactly. I knew you'd get what I meant."

Malcolm moved to the stage and tapped on the microphone that was set up. "Hello, all you lovely people. Today we come together to celebrate Caine and Emelise. Eme asked me if I would sing something for their wedding and then Caine asked me the same thing. Are those two perfect for each other or what?" He waited for the cheers to die down before he continued. "When Emelise told me the song she wanted to dedicate to Caine, I knew it was perfect." The music began and after a moment Malcolm began singing Bon Jovi's *Thank you for Loving Me*. When he got to the words, *You pick me up when I fall down, You ring the bell before they count me out, If I was drowning you would part the sea, And risk your own life to rescue me,* Emelise leaned into Caine and whispered the words in his ear.

Caine's arms tightened around her. "Always, Angel. I will always pick you up when you fall down," he growled.

After the final notes faded, Malcolm spoke again. "Now, the song Caine chose to dedicate to his mate—at first I wanted to roll my eyes because it seemed like such an obvious and cheesy one to go with. Then I realized that maybe it's not so cheesy after all. It's sweet, and romantic, and I can't think of a better song to dedicate to one's other half." Again, the music began and after a moment, Malcolm began to sing Aerosmith's *I don't want to miss a* thing. "*I could stay awake, just to hear you breathing. Watch you smile while you're sleeping, while you're far away dreaming…"*

Eme tipped her head up to look at her mate. "You're perfect, you know that?"

Caine dipped his head and kissed her. "Mmmh, I could get used to hearin' dat from you." He pulled her closer and trailed kisses along her jaw. When Emelise moaned quietly, he nipped at her skin. A wicked gleam lit up his eyes as he took her hand in his and headed toward her office.

"Where are we going?"

"Your office." Before she could argue with him, he had her in the office with the door closed behind them. He flipped the lock, then pulled her in for a passionate kiss.

"Caine." Her voice was a mere whisper against his lips. "We have guests."

"Dey can make do wit'out us for a bit."

Emelise knew she should have argued with him. It was their wedding reception. The club was filled with their family and friends, all wanting to celebrate their special day with them, but in that moment the only thing that mattered was the man in front of her. She slid her hands beneath his shirt, leaned up for a kiss, and whispered against his lips. "Okay." He drove her crazy and she was looking forward to feeling that way for the rest of her life.

Caine

Caine deepened the kiss, even as his fingers moved to the zipper, all but hidden within the lace that graced the back of her wedding dress, just above her waist. The back of the dress dipped low, exposing the smooth skin of her back, and his fingers had itched to caress her ever since he'd laid eyes on her in it. The bodice fit smoothly over her ass, otherwise he might have just pushed the skirt up to get to her. As soon as he had it unzipped, he slid his hands up to her shoulders and eased the straps down. When her breasts were revealed to him, he dipped his head to take a nipple in his mouth.

"Caine."

Her needy whisper made him growl against her skin. "You are so beautiful, cher," he murmured before he helped her to step out of her dress. She stood there in just a lacy, red thong and he felt himself harden even more.

"I need you, Angel; I need to taste you." He dropped to his knees, grabbed one of her legs to hook it over his shoulder, and buried his mouth against her.

"Oh fuck." Emelise's fingers slid into his hair as her hips bucked into his mouth.

"That's it, Angel." Caine slid a finger into her and closely followed it with a second. He curled them to stroke her G-spot while he teased her clit with his tongue. Within minutes, Emelise was muffling her cries with one hand while her inner walls clenched in orgasm.

Caine stood and quickly rid himself of his clothes. Then he picked

Emelise up so she could wrap her legs around his waist. He set her down on the edge of her desk, positioned himself at her entrance, and buried himself in one hard thrust. He dipped his head to kiss her while he moved.

"I love you, Angel," he growled against her lips. He was glad Mia had offered to keep an eye on Hailey so they could have this moment together.

"I love you, too. More than I ever thought possible," Emelise replied. Her hands slid down his back as they moved together.

Caine felt her nails graze his skin and his pace increased. He could feel the tension building in her, and he slipped a hand down between them to caress her sensitive clit. It was exactly what was needed to send her crashing over the edge again. A few thrusts later and Caine followed her in release.

They stayed like that for several minutes while their breathing slowly returned to normal. Then Caine helped Emelise get her dress back on, got dressed himself, and offered his arm to her. "Let's go join da party, Angel," he said with a wink.

Emelise laughed. "You do realize just about everyone out there is going to know what we did in here, right?"

"I am, yes, but dey won't say a word. Dey know better."

She rolled her eyes. "I am never going to live this down but I wouldn't have it any other way. I love you."

"I love you, too." He opened the door and escorted her out to the front of the club where their friends and family were waiting to help them celebrate the beginning of their lives together. Glancing at his mate, Caine made a silent vow that their future was going to be filled with nothing but laughter and love.

Acknowledgments

I'd like to take this time to thank the people who have helped to make this book possible. First, my cover artist, Najla Qamber of **Najla Qamber Designs**. Her work is amazing and I absolutely love the cover. Also, a big thank you to my editor, Kathy Bosman the Indie Editing Chick. Her advice helped to clean up some problem areas I had when I started out on this endeavor.

To the beta readers I had on this book, Kathy Wright and Jacinta Russell, thank you, for taking the time to read the relatively raw document and provide such valuable feedback. There are a few scenes within these pages that wouldn't have been so well written without your input! You ladies rock!

To my ARC Team, thank you for offering your time to read this book before it went live and giving me your honest feedback on it! I appreciate it so very much!

To my readers, thank you so much for giving my books a chance! There are so many new authors out there and I am honored to have your support. Without each and every one of you, we authors would not be able to do the jobs we love; bringing our characters to life so others can enjoy them as much as we do. You are our reason for sitting down every day and putting pen to paper or fingers to the keyboard. Again, thank you, so very much.

I hope you enjoyed meeting Caine and Emelise and the rest of the cast and crew of the NOLA Shifters Series. There are more books in the works for this series so keep an eye out for them!

About the Author

Angel Nyx is an author of paranormal, contemporary, and historical romances (eventually!). She is also a mom, a reader, an avid gamer chick, and a cook in a nursing home. When she's not working, writing, reading, or gaming, she is usually relaxing to music or spending time with family. She has a long time love affair with the city of New Orleans and has future plans to move there, hopefully in the next couple of years.

If you'd like to be kept informed of upcoming releases you can join my newsletter, and read my blog, at https://angelnyx.com .You can also follow me on Facebook at https://www.facebook.com/AngelNyxAuthor/ , twitter https://twitter.com/AngelNyx , and Goodreads at: http://bit.ly/AngelNyxGR. I also have a reader/fan group on Facebook, Nyx's Goddesses, and can be found at: http://bit.ly/NyxsGoddesses

Other books in the NOLA Shifters Series

Trailing Moon Flowers: A NOLA Shifters Prequel

Wild Lilies: Book One of the NOLA Shifters Series

Made in United States
North Haven, CT
18 February 2023